Leaving Lovestiff Annie

Natalie,

Thanks so much
for everything!

Books by Chris F. Needham

An Inverted Sort of Prayer
Falling from Heights
Leaving Lovestiff Annie

Leaving Lovestiff Annie

A NOVEL

CHRIS F NEEDHAM

| N₁ | O₂ | N₁ |

CANADA

Library and Archives Canada Cataloguing in Publication

Needham, Chris F.
Leaving lovestiff Annie : a novel / Chris F. Needham.

ISBN 978-0-9739558-2-8

I. Title.

PS8627.E43L43 2009   C813'.6   C2008-907403-3

Printed and Bound in Canada on 100% ancient forest-free paper.

Now Or Never Publishing
11268 Dawson Place
Delta, British Columbia
Canada V4C 3S7

nonpublishing.com
Fighting Words.

This book is for Lori.
Because I am a son of a bitch.

With thinking we may be beside ourselves in a sane sense. By a conscious effort of the mind we can stand aloof from actions and their consequences; and all things, good and bad, go by us like a torrent. . . . I only know myself as a human entity; the scene, so to speak, of thoughts and affections; and am sensible of a certain doubleness by which I can stand as remote from myself as from another. However intense my experience, I am conscious of the presence and criticism of a part of me, which, as it were, is not a part of me, but spectator, sharing no experience, but taking note of it; and that is no more I than it is you. When the play, it may be the tragedy, of life is over, the spectator goes his way. It was a kind of fiction, a work of the imagination only, so far as he was concerned. This doubleness may easily make us poor neighbors and friends sometimes.

—*Henry David Thoreau, Walden (Solitude)*

And in the autumn of the previous year we moved back into the house on the hill looking out across the ocean at the islands and the mountains. And at the base of the hill stood the pier, wet and grey and wooden, and when the tide was in the water was dark and grey and rippled around the pilings, and when the tide was out the sand was dark and grey and rippled too. And as the cars went by and down the road, or else up the road and past the pier, the mud they raised and washed to the sides of the road splashed onto the patios and the bases of the empty tables. And the legs of the chairs too were muddy and the umbrellas, placed together in the corners of the patios and furled tightly around their poles, were, for me, the flags of some inevitable surrender in the face of some overwhelming defeat somewhere.

And the winter rains stayed late that year. And sitting on the bench and waiting for the sun that would not come, I saw the people passing along the promenade before me, and I saw the pigeons alighting along the promenade before me, and afterwards I saw nothing except for their guano. And sometimes, at night, sitting alone on the bench in the dark, I would hear the people passing along the road behind me, and I would hear the cars passing along the road behind me, where there would be much traffic despite the weather of that year. And the cars and the trucks, both those with passengers and those without, moved slowly along the road where there were larger supply trucks too, their progress impeded by their brakes and their gears and the slower moving foot traffic of that year. And to the east I could see the high flat top of the mountain, white and barren in the wet grey afternoons, and beside that mountain I could see all the other mountains and of course that other country too. And the pilgrimage, if you could call it a pilgrimage, came from that place—an appalling migration as incessant as the season and often as indifferent too.

And in the spring of that year as it continued to rain and still the leaves abstained from the trees, the people came down the promenade and past the bench or else went straight on to the pier. And as the mud from the cars continued to rise and cover the bases of the empty tables and the legs of the chairs on the patios, the produce, what little there was delivered by the trucks, was as limp and off-coloured as the whale would be in the ongoing weather of that year. And there were mists over the ocean, and clouds around the mountains, and the cars, impeded by the rain, splashed the mud to the sides of the road and onto the feet of those people who, wet in their jackets and stubborn under their umbrellas, refused to take refuge out along the promenade where I sat waiting for the weather to break against my will. And in the end, when the damage from the flood had finally been tallied, more than an entire month's revenue had been lost that year.

Leaving

*B*etween the bare branches, through their belated flower absences, I can
see them. Going towards him one after another, first the one boy
whipping and then the next boy whipping. Then the rest of the boys go
ahead and whip him together a while. I go on whispering at Annie. Annie
goes on ignoring me. Then she goes down along the line of bushes to where
across the street a man is raking—she calls out to the man but he does
not hear. Meanwhile I go on whispering and watching the boys whipping
between the bare branches, through their belated flower absences,
he can see her. Going towards the patio with a red tray in her
hand. He goes on sitting at Annie. Po goes on ignoring Stephan.
Then, abruptly, he stands up from Annie as she takes her tray and
places it on the table, then wipes the chair down with her beach
bag. Next, from the corner of the patio, she takes an umbrella and
places the pole in the hole in the centre of the table, and then she
sits, so he sits. He goes on sitting at Annie. Po goes on ignoring
Stephan. Eventually he sees her remove the umbrella from the
table and, furling it up, place it back in the corner of the patio.
Then she sits, so he sits, and the next time he looks between the
bare branches and through their belated flower absences he sees
her drop her hot dog in the puddle at her feet.

He waits for all the cars to pass before making his way across the
street.

You can't sit here, he says, and she rotates to him with one eye
squeezed shut against the rain, the other eye blinking erratically.
Then, with both hands, she gathers up the enormous hot dog and
places it carefully on the attendant tray.

You can't sit here, he repeats. Not with that hot dog. The Dairy
Queen patio is right over there. Over where? Over there. But
you're not even open, she says, smiling with thoughtful regard,
revealing the fact that at least one of her teeth is dead. The tooth

looks slightly dark and hollow inside. No, he says, but he will be soon. And he has to set a precedent now doesn't he.

Chuckling whimsically, she extracts a big blue book from her cream-coloured beach bag. Do you want to see my whale book? she asks, brushing bits of beach from her wet red hair. Meanwhile the rainfall intensifies, beading from his chin, nose and brows, running in searching rivulets down the nape of his neck and fanning out across his shoulders. There's whales in there, he's told.

Taking a chair from the stack, he flops down to flip through the big blue book's many impressive pictures of whales while the woman, preparatory to consuming a good large chunk, takes to wringing out her ridiculously long hot dog in a fittingly ridiculous and ultimately futile attempt to rid it of excessive moisture.

He places the aptly named *Big Blue Book of Whales* on the table and says, Listen—

Now do you by chance live on the reserve? she interrupts, holding up, seemingly as case in point, the soggy, wrinkled, to some extent twisted hot dog. Because you just seem so, you know, *reserved*. He tells her he prefers the term stoic. Okay, she says, stoic. Reminds me of my sister Edna. Now Edna never spoke a word. Not a word? he says. Not a *word*, she says, and shuffles her chair up closer to his. So you know what our mother did? Took Edna to the hospital. Yessir, right to the hospital, and you know what they found? A tumour the size of a fist behind her heart. Yeah, a fist. Behind her heart. Daddy always claimed that by the time they got around to telling Edna, she'd already told herself.

She smiles contentedly as he picks up the book again and politely flips through, feeling, if nothing else, obligated to be enthused. In the meantime, across the street, in amongst the beach clutter of wave-tumbled timber and stone, a child complains bitterly to his father about this ongoing insult of salt-stinging rain, this constant west coast Canadian downpour. The child continues to complain, and it continues to rain, as a pair of bright yellow taxis, their hoods dimpled and glistening in the rain, glide past to hover in front of the Ocean Beach Hotel, discharging two flocks of boisterous young men therein.

Watching through the pall of falling rain the last of the young men enter the hotel bar, she says she had to ask. It's just that it's getting so bad right now. In fact it's getting so she can't stand *any* of those people anymore.

At the words "those people" he closes the book and taps the cover meditatively, sweating profusely from the forehead and underarms despite the inclement weather. At length he says there are a lot of whales in here though.

Looking both absorbed and delighted with this acknowledgment, she smiles provocatively at the book, so he too smiles at the book, and eventually looks up to see her staring out at the ocean, her expression a similarly dark and unfathomable sheet of shale.

Look, she says, don't get me wrong, I like the few I know. It's just that I can't stand the pigeonholing anymore. The pigeonholing? he says. That's right, she says, the pigeonholing. I can't stand the pigeonholing anymore.

She gazes out over the sea at the last of the daylight—what scant light the day managed to scrape up—now draining into the islands fringing the horizon far beyond the confines of the bay. Look am I boring you? she says, and he says, No, not at all. Well I thought maybe I was boring you, she says, and he says, Oh on the contrary.

Forming two fists, and stacking one upon the other, she rests her considerable chin atop the resultant tower. Then she removes her chin from her fists in order to rest it more comfortably, if improbably, on the rain-wet surface of the table. She surveys him from this position a while, then pivots steadily in the direction of the sea, raising the bluntness of her chin against the cold wet wind now tumbling in over the bay.

So anyway, she says, this one time Eddie's on the train, and there's this little green jawbreaker rolling around all over.

She glances over, tentatively, and seeing that she's taken sufficient hold of his attention, continues on with the story.

So there it was, she says, this little green jawbreaker, just rolling around all over the floor. Train pulled forward and it rolled to the back; then the train came to a stop and it rolled on back.

And as providence would have it, she explains, there were actually these three children present, toddlers really, all boys, each
one helplessly intent on the little green jawbreaker himself,
when suddenly the train came to a stop and this big fat Indian
got on and sat down. Beside my Eddie, she says. And I do mean
right beside my Eddie—like *there*—and so of course Eddie started to get a little uncomfortable. And itchy. It seems odd, he
thinks, but this Eddie of hers is getting awfully agitated around
overweight aboriginals evidently. Eddie just *loves* his smoked
salmon, she sighs reminiscently, becoming increasingly animated
with the story. It's time for him to say something now, he knows,
about Native Indians, or maybe it's East Indians, or both, but
instead he remains silent, becoming gradually more engrossed
not so much with what she is saying, but with that one hollow
tooth she has and the way it reveals itself to him in her less self-
conscious moments.

So anyway, she says, this Indian, what did he do? Why he picked
up this little green jawbreaker and tried to give it to one of the
children. Like *right* to the children. She suggests they were Indians
too incidentally, though of what type she has no idea—you never
really do—and the children's mother, well she said absolutely not
of course, and so the Indian simply shrugged and sat back down
beside Eddie—again like right beside Eddie, like *there*—rubbing
up against him she supposed *some*what accidentally, this due to the
fact that he, not Eddie but the Indian, was wearing somewhere in
the vicinity of a dozen layers of clothing, each article just reeking
of salmon, that fact alone seemingly enough to sanction a hefty
measure of bigotry. And then this Indian, what did he do? Why he
just popped that little green jawbreaker right in his mouth—
Pop!—and started chewing. *And* chewing. *And* chewing.
Naturally out loud and everything too.

A strange, almost doglike growl rises in her throat as she casually removes her hand from his and endeavours to sit up straight.
And finally, overcome with laughter, she leans towards him with
mouth ajar, revealing a ready mix of bun, meat and mustard-laced
saliva cartwheeling around a thick pink tongue.

That's a nice bracelet by the way.

She's wearing a white cotton dress, the skirt of which rides up a little, and she's spent some time under house arrest lately, the evidence of which proves impossible to miss in that dress unfortunately.

Ex*cuse* me? she says, turning abruptly his way, then away, and he says, Well it is. A nice bracelet, he means. Do you really think so though? she says, assembling herself in a position better suited to receiving compliments, modelling for him her smooth, white, black bracelet-ed ankle and wiggling her long, widely spaced toes affectionately. And he says, Oh yes. Very nice. She must be cold though, he adds, indicating the high-riding dress and then the open-toed sandals below, and she says she manages. Well we all *manage*, she's told. But then just *managing* is hardly the point somehow.

She smiles just once, but with all available alacrity, and then averts her eyes and casts about sullenly. She would, if she could, just like to nurse again if possible though. She would? Sure she would. Unfortunately though she's of that age, having accumulated that set amount of experience, whereby she seems to slip all too easily into the manager's role. She does? Well sure she does. But then her employers always seem to see her as far too experienced and therefore overqualified to waste simply as an RN anymore. Look, she says as, across the way, pigeons begin to alight out along the rain-slick, pink-bricked promenade. First the one alights and then the next one alights. Then the rest of them alight together of course.

She asks if he sees them. Well sure he sees them. Well you see what I mean then, don't you? she says, and he says, Oh you mean the jawbreaker story? I guess so, sure. In a way.

From her beach bag she extracts a small compact, makes a few minor upgrades to her face, and then returns the compact to the bag, just as a brisk salt wind lashes down on top of his head and blows up under his arms, corkscrewing him out of his chair an uncertain moment before gradually giving up and moving on down the Drive.

Oh God, what time is it? she asks, having dropped one thick, altogether masculine hand to his knee and glancing anxiously about. Oh it's not time yet, she's told. Oh good, she says, offering his knee one more experimental squeeze, a test really. Now where was she? Oh yes, she has to manage. It's her cross to bear, she supposes. She has to be this silly little manager, with this silly little accountability, who puts together silly little schedules and watches silly little labour costs, all the while hiring silly little women she thinks might be able to rotate the occasional silly little bed and— Oh yes!—she has to work a silly little strike every once in a while as well. And that's it. That's a manager, in her eyes anyway. A moot point really, but nevertheless interesting, in a way.

Calvins are on sale, she says, holding up a flyer produced from her beach bag. Calvin Klein jeans. They're on sale. At Sears.

And as she grips his knee, then lets his knee free, he studies the resulting dimples in the denim.

Wednesday, 7:03 pm

Thomas bounds on by in the rain. Thomas looks like he wants to stop and talk, but then his eyes widen at sight of the woman and he bounds on by for now.

Who's that? she asks, and he tells her that's Thomas. Used to be Tom, he says, but now it's Thomas—with an h. Tends bar part-thime down at the Ocean Beach Hotel. That's where she recognizes him from, the OB, she says, smiling the only way it's possible to smile while wearing a white cotton dress in the rain.

Tell me, though, what's he like, she says, and he says, Thomas? Oh, you know, the usual: Pina Coladas and getting caught in the rain. I do recognize him though, she says, hardly listening, intensely interested in a rapidly receding Thomas instead. He does triathlons too, he says, if you're into that sort of thing. Triathlons, huh, she says. Well he's very attractive. I mean I find him very attractive. He's in fantastic shape, I'm guessing. Thomas? he says. Oh yes, fantastic shape. He's selling Amway apparently.

Sheltering the pages from the wind and rain, about to offer the *Big Blue Book of Whales* what he hopes will be one last exploration before returning it, finally, to its rightful owner again, he suddenly feels a deeper chill drift across his face and neck, bringing with it dredged-up memories of ferocious winds, of flooding rains, of the terrible stagnation that followed and, finally, of death.

Flipping through the book, he pulls up his coat collar limp and embalmed with rain. He can't believe how many whales there are in here, he says. He didn't know there were that many species of whale even *out* there. Thirty-three, she assures him proudly, smiling her hollow-toothed smile, brushing rain-flattened red hair back across a shoulder. Suddenly she chokes, coughs, and spits up hot dog into an already awaiting napkin, then casually secrets the entire expelled bolus away beneath the table somewhere.

Now where was she, she says, bringing the still formidable remains of hot dog perilously close to her lips, only to abandon the exercise at the last possible instant. Instead she pulls a stack of photographs from her beach bag and eagerly passes them over, seemingly intent on explaining them at once, individually and, as luck would have it, at great length as well. He sees she has them organized according to subject matter—people, pets, places—while continuing to flip indifferently through the whale book some more.

That's her sister, Edna, he's told. The dead one. And that one there's her second husband, Ernie. He's dead now too. . . . Anyway, she says, the first time I talked to Ernie, he calls me Wendy Wilson—Wendy *Wilson*, mind you—he calls me this and I don't even recognize him and I think, "Any man I don't recognize calling me by my maiden name, well that's trouble." She snorts spiritedly, leaning in close to admit that ol' Wilson maybe used to run around a little.

Struggling to sustain interest, he returns the stack of much-handled photographs to the table, at which point she glances over, a small furrow emerging between her eyebrows, and so he reaches over to rub it for her.

And this one here's the fish farm where I first found Eddie, she says, allowing the impromptu massage to continue. And on their first date back in town, she explains, in keeping with the theme, she and Eddie went out for salmon at the since-destroyed Just for the Halibut Seafood Palace, where of course they had to ask about the specials. Because, in Wendy's experience, waitresses never really know the specials. It's sort of a little game we have, she rather wanly smiles, lending the tale a slightly conspiratorial air. She closes her eyes as he works his thumb down the channel between her brows and the rain taps a meditative tattoo against the exposed, suddenly fish-grey planks of the patio.

So the waitress started telling them about the Neapolitan salmon special. "One pink, one white," the waitress said, "in a Portobello mushroom pomegranate sauce." No kidding, Wendy says, a Portobello mushroom pomegranate sauce. So she asked the waitress why it's white. "What?" Why's the one salmon white? "Cause it's wild," the waitress said. Wild? How the heck could she be so sure it's wild? "Cause it eats shrimp," the waitress said. Can you beat that? "Cause it eats *shrimp*," this waitress said. Well we thought *that* was weird, Wendy laughs, talking on and on in that vein until, as he loses himself in the rhythm of the rubbing, her voice slips down, out and away from consciousness, and all but disappears *like this Malcolm, I say, and she says, Malcolm? What does Malcolm have to do with it? And why the hell are you so threatened by this? Oh I don't know, Annie. Maybe because I don't feel the need to air our dirty laundry to some fucking therapist. What's wrong now, I say as suddenly she starts to feel it coming—there it is, here it comes, there it goes, out the rolled-down window and down the passenger-side door again. And afterwards, as she wipes the remnants of vomit from her face, we sit side by side staring straight ahead at the rain-swept parking lot where two young boys elevate their find for closer inspection. It hangs there like that, its wing agonizingly elongated, its carcass covered in grease, appearing much larger than it ought to, more terrestrial maybe, though less real, and I wonder aloud if it's not some other breed of bird perhaps. No, it's definitely a seagull, she tells me* with that wonderful smile of hers, managing, in the face of enormous odds, to bring him reeling back to the conversation which consists, ostensibly, of an account of why she and Eddie felt they ought to be treating the waitress this way—that is, asking her such silly questions really.

What's wrong? she asks, again fitting her hand to his knee, its present perch of choice evidently. Nothing's wrong, he tells her, finishing up the massage and offering the wet and well-worn pages of the *Big Blue Book of Whales* one last reverent tour for good measure. I'm sorry, she says, refocusing on something, it would seem, just beyond his right shoulder. Typically I don't talk this much. Typically I'm much more . . . Stoic? he says. That's it—stoic, she says, astonished at his insight. Typically I'm much more stoic, I'd say.

Across the way, looking more than a little ridiculous in their matching orange raincoats, a family of five piles forth from their bright new cyan minivan and together gaze out the length of the pier.

Down that way, he says. Pardon? the mother says. The whale, he says, it's down that way. And despite himself, nods the lot of them off in that direction.

Did you see that look that woman gave you? says Wendy. She's angry. Sure she is. But then so's this entire town apparently. You see it in peoples' faces when they first come out in the rain, in that first fraction of a glance—that first flicker of rage—and then it's gone: you're not one of them. You're not one of those Indians that killed that girl. And yet you've still be pigeonholed by comparison, she somewhat sagely maintains.

The family recedes west along the beach, their matching orange raincoats bunching awkwardly above their matching rubber boots.

Smiling that smile, Wendy asks what time is it now. Oh it's time, she's told. Well she'd better get going then, she says, as they want her home by nine now.

She continues to flip through her whale book as they make their way to her ten-speed parked outside the public restrooms a short walk down the Drive. She invites him to ride, but he explains how that's not such a good idea just now. So then she begs him to ride, until finally he capitulates, but only on the strict condition that she ride the handlebars the vast majority of the way.

In the dark and the rain, then, aiming deliberately for potholes and puddles all the way, they ride east along the beach and past the naked brown woods of the Semiahmoo reserve, then out towards the highway and the American border where, just prior to customs and subsequent to the driving range, she finally falls off, managing to stick the landing impressively however despite such suspect high-heeled footwear. After a time she tells him to take a right down a meagre potholed side street, then park in the garage of an old piss-yellow clapboard rancher. Children's toys lie scattered throughout the yard, along with what appears to be an old rusted-out Corolla. Wendy assures him that neither Eddie nor the children are home, and more importantly, in hers eyes anyway, that neither the toys nor the Toyota belong to her.

She unlocks the door and follows him inside. The interior walls are finished with a faux wood paneling scratched here and there by countless anonymous claws, while all shape and size of empty cardboard box clutter the thick green-carpeted hall.

He asks if she is moving, but she assures him she is not. Got a dog or something? he says, tracing along the wall an almost parallel series of four deep scratch marks. Oh Eddie's a dog all right, she laughs good-naturedly, and at Eddie's expense apparently, as having moved into the kitchen he spots a clematis expiring on the windowsill.

It's dying. What's dying? Your plant, he says, wiping dust from the chipped-paint windowsill, losing himself in the rhythm of the wiping as Wendy's voice ebbs to a mere murmur before disappearing below the waterline altogether *then? he asks, and I tell him that it drowned, poor thing. So too much love again? he says, and I say, Yup, too much love again. And not enough sunlight got in.*

We watch her approach from across the lawn, her face looking grey and drawn. What are you two losers conspiring about? she asks while dabbing at her eyes with a tissue, first the one and then the other, careful not to dab away any of those precious few lashes remaining. I was just explaining your particular brand of horticulture to Stephan here, I say. Why are you crying though? Oh it's nothing, she says, knitting her imperfectly pencilled-in brows together. Just the girls. What about the girls, I say, massaging her forehead with a thumb, losing my mark a moment and regrettably smudging her would-be brows together as one. Oh just this baby bird they've got cornered by the fence, I'm told as, across the yard, dressed absurdly in what appears to be Lisa's lingerie, the children shriek out loud as once again they manage to corner their frightened and ailing prey.

Christ, Annie, they're just kids, I say, and she says, I know, but still. What the hell are they doing in that get-up though, Stephan wants to know, currently sporting as a shoe an empty bread bowl, formerly a vessel for spinach and artichoke dip, much to our collective enjoyment of course. And she says, Oh I don't know, Steph. Playing fairies, I suppose.

And in the twilight, thinking she's still very beautiful standing there, I place my arm around and under her arm, only to find that she's uncomfortable this way. So then I place my arm up around her neck, finding this too to be uncomfortable as my arm catches on her wig, causing it to shift slightly, and off she runs to the bathroom to fix her beach bag, spilling its entire contents to the floor. Sobbing, she crouches to gather up her photographs now fallen out of order as, moving cautiously amid the assortment of cardboard boxes into the adjoining living room, her guest finds himself all but overwhelmed by the distinct but mingling odours of rotting garbage, damp animal and wet wool. He removes his wet clothes and, dropping each article to the floor, manoeuvres naked through the maze of boxes in the direction of the bedroom at the very far end of the hall. All at once he smells his own rank body odour, and finding on the dresser a bottle of *Glow by J. Lo*, proceeds to douse both himself and the bed with it. Finally Wendy arrives, stack of photographs in hand, each damp and discoloured from washing now, naked herself except for ratty leopard print underwear, furry leopard print slippers, and of course that large black bracelet weighing equally on both his conscience and her ankle.

Wednesday, 11:41 pm

Hey, Wendy? Yes, Chris? Eddie *is* a dog isn't he, he says, and she pauses a moment, seeming exhausted and thoughtful, then says of *course* Eddie's a dog. Why? Just confirming, that's all, he says. He may have, what, misjudged her a little, he admits.

And later, lying prone in bed, having set his face firmly to the claw-marked wall in protest, he, Chris, not the real Chris but a false Chris, a faux wood-paneled Chris, listens carefully as she continues to flip through the *Big Blue Book of Whales* behind him. He has this terrific headache now, no doubt another symptom of what is becoming, despite all best efforts to the contrary, an ongoing and even mounting crisis of conscience somehow.

Oh and Wendy? Yes Chris? I've got this terrific headache now, he says, and no sooner has he said it than her feet are swinging to the floor, launching her out of bed and into the adjoining bathroom where drawers open and close, crash and bang with theatrical offstage commotion until eventually she returns with a tall vial of pills and a taller glass of water.

What are these then, he says. Tylenol Threes, she says, offering him a couple along with the glass of water. He pops the Tylenol in his mouth and swallows them down with grim determination, then returns his attention to the wall. Eventually she wiggles up behind him, gently kissing his shoulder.

You're so surreal, she says. Well I'm so glad you think so, he says, drawing his shoulder abruptly away. What's wrong? Nothing's wrong. Well you seem, you know, upset, she says, and he says if he does—and he's not saying he is—the only thing that would make him that way would be her calling him *surreal* for Christ's sake. Not yet, he says, pushing her roving hand away.

Feeling her rise up behind him, he suddenly feels as though he might be sinking into the mattress beneath him. Vertigo, he's thinking, when suddenly she descends upon him.

Tell me about her, she whispers, her large black bracelet wearing a deep painful trail into his ankle. Who? he says, and she says his wife. His *wife*? How the hell'd Wendy know he had a wife? Platinum? she says, reaching over to twist his wedding ring around his finger. Silver, he says, drawing his hand away. Purchased for the princely sum of twenty pesos in Los Cabos, Mexico—on a beach. Yeah exactly, Wendy. A beach. We were married on a goddamned beach. How romantic, she says. Not really, he says, reluctantly returning his hand to hers. You can get very sick down there, hey. Very sick. Of course she's not very well now either. I'm sorry, Wendy says, and so he tells her not to be. After all, it's not her fault. Not entirely anyway.

He pulls his shoulder clear of her probing lips and studies, in the slowly obliging darkness, the patterns of scratches on the faux wood-paneled walls. That sinking feeling is still there, although not quite so overwhelmingly as it was before, and studying the patterns of absent Eddie's scratches makes him feel, by comparison, that much more stable and even buoyant somehow.

What's she like then, this wife of his, and he says Stephanie? Like the, what, the little man behind the curtain, he'd say.

Wendy laughs wildly and out of all proportion to this remark, then foot-pushes the only remaining sheet clear of the bed. Now, stretched naked and spread-eagled across the mattress, she flips over onto her stomach and laughs all too wildly once again. Tell me about her *honestly*, she says, so he says well, to be honest, it's getting difficult to tell where his wife ends and he begins anymore.

He slides his feet together, one against the other, and hugs his knees against the cold. In truth, this is one of my devices, this sliding together of the feet for warmth, one he feels particularly guilty deploying here with this particular companionship of course.

What's she *really* like though, says Wendy, wanting more, so he says stiff. Stiff? Yeah, stiff, he says. As a board. Something's happened so that he and Stephanie can't be romantic anymore. That's sad, she says, and he says it is sad. What's worse, though, is this . . . Yes? she says. This terrible and somewhat debilitating feeling of trying to leave someone who's become, despite all your best intentions, completely dependent on you, he says.

She hesitates. You must still love her then, she says, and he says Stephanie? Well of course he still loves her—he's her *husband*. She's his *wife*. They were married on a *beach* for crying out loud. Jesus Christ.

He returns to the wall as she props herself up in bed behind him, flipping quickly through her photographs of Eddie, Edna, Ernie, et cetera some more.

So you'd never, you know, leave her? says Wendy, and he says he doesn't think so, no, he doesn't think he can. Well if she knew about this she'd kill you, I bet, Wendy says, and he says, Believe me, Wendy, if I thought she knew about this I'd kill himself.

He slides his feet together, one against the other, and listens to the beleaguered drainpipe outside the window. After a while a car rattles by and up the road, casting angled amber lights briefly across the bedroom wall.

I'm sorry, she says, so he says, Forget it. Don't worry about it. Though I do appreciate your apology of course. More than you realize, she sighs. Excuse me? Sorry? What's that supposed to mean? he says, flipping over to face her, and she says she doesn't understand. That statement, "More than you realize," Wendy, what's that mean exactly? She says she still doesn't understand. I'm simply asking for a definition of "More than you realize," he says. Like in lieu of something more, some act of physical violence or something, I'm *lucky* you're only apologizing? Is that it? Like I'm getting off *easy* perhaps? Or is it that you're simply apologizing *more* than I realize. Is that it. That must be it. But then that couldn't be it. After all, that wouldn't make any sense, he surmises. At least not in this particular context. After all, I didn't say I appreciate the fact you're sorry, or that I appreciate how sorry you are—because I don't—I said *I appreciate your apology*. I'm afraid I still don't understand, she says, so apprehensively in fact that the furrow between her eyebrows emerges like never before, and it's all he can do to resist the impulse to abandon his protest and massage it into submission for her.

Well Christ, Wendy, what's not to understand? After all, you're the one who said it. "More than you realize"—that's what you said. Well I'd just like to know what that means. In fact, I'd like to know *exactly* what that means. Because, hey, if that's some sort of threat or something, well then I'd really like to know. So that I might, you know, prepare a proper defence. I'd at least like the opportunity to prepare a proper defence here, Wendy. I think I have that right, he says.

She pulls away to lie stiffly in the bed, breasts pancaking unattractively into her armpits, appearing oddly white and inorganic in this lack of light, mummified with resentment. Soon enough she is fast asleep. And some time later, long after midnight perhaps, he will move around to her side of the bed to where the Tylenol Threes are kept. He will open the container and choke down its entire contents, making sure not to miss so much as one pill, in the end taking in something like ninety, he thinks. Then, moving out to the kitchen, he will happen upon a large bottle of Pinesol, stored where else but under the sink, and for a moment he will consider choking this down as well, but then think better of it, as Pinesol would of course be impossible to keep down *the bed with her already in it, having raced in ahead to lie there naked, curled up against the cold. And so I take the sheet and spread it over her eager squirming body, making certain it's square to the bed—Is it square? she says, and I say, It's square, Annie.—followed by the blanket and then of course the duvet as well. And as I fold the sheet over and down, she giggles and moans with satisfaction, twisting her hands up under her chin in a manner somehow reminiscent of a bird's wings, asking me to kiss her eyelids, and I do kiss her eyelids, softly, first the one and then the other, before turning off the light and whispering softly, Goodnight, you godless little whore.*

Thursday, 5:17 am

He awakes sometime before dawn, that much he knows, but for the longest time with no idea where, let alone what for. Slowly, though, recollection returns, triggered by the scratched faux wood-paneled walls, the green shag carpet, and the vast array of empty cardboard boxes piled between his awkward position here in the bedroom and the relative freedom of the front door.

How is he? wonders Wendy. Broke, she's told. What does he mean by *broke*, she says, and he says bankrupt. He's morally, emotionally and monetarily bankrupt. Oddly enough, though, he's feeling just fine at the moment.

He feels pensively about the bed in search of vomit, but there's simply no vomit there to be found. What's he looking for, she wants to know, and he says, Nothing, now go back to sleep. Fake it if you have to. Please.

He lopes out to the living room amid the boxes in the hall and, once dressed, over towards the front door and the dazzling array of beach bag contents spilled there the night before. Every object, every line and curve, stands out so sharply against the others that it proves almost painful to the eyes. In fact, he's seeing things more clearly now than he's ever seen things in his life. Two items in particular capture his interest, and in a brief moment of something that feels remarkably like atonement, he reaches down to take two crumpled twenty dollar bills from the pile before moving on out the door.

Outside it's grey, misty, still dark for the most part but not raining, with a trace of light leaking into the night just out over the crowded mountains to the east. Cars rumble by and up the road. He ponders borrowing her ten-speed, but then that might feel too much like stealing, *Annie. It's not stealing, it's borrowing, she tells me, then goes on chewing her half of the Twix stolen just a few moments before. She chews, I choose, and finally, at the appropriate time, stuff the torque wrench down the left pant leg of my jeans. Unfortunately, with these Levi's being as tight as they are, and a torque wrench being as long as it is, the head tends to hang down well past my knee, effecting an impressive limp, consequently catching the attention of the cashier absentmindedly grooming his moustache over near the exit.*

Hurry! she tells me, standing there at the bottom of the stairs. And I do hurry, managing to make it all of halfway down before losing my footing and tumbling the remainder of the way to the ground. At this point I'm grabbed roughly by the elbow and escorted back into the store, noting at once in this the cashier's other hand the very torque wrench so coveted before, the one I don't even want anymore. And I tell him as much, but he doesn't seem to care, as he drags me into the storeroom to administer a beating the likes of which neither of us has ever experienced before the street, and left towards the highway, coming up alongside the driving range where thousands of golf balls lie scattered across the grass. There must be a hole in this fence somewhere, mustn't there? Sure there must. But no, there's no hole anywhere, at least none that he can find. And so, leaning there against the netting, twisting his fingers in amongst the ropes, he decides to climb up and over the wobbly barrier, managing to get all of halfway up before growing thoroughly bored with the entire ridiculous endeavour *evolves. No longer are we content to stay amongst the head-high grass, but instead venture out onto the course itself, stealing down into the various moats and bunkers, intent on finding something lost by someone else.*

Suddenly a voice bellows out from behind. Turning, I see a large fat man limping hard across the fairway towards us, a rifle clutched awkwardly across his chest, his makeshift mask bouncing loose, his cloud-white breath billowing out in protest. Together we scramble up the embankment, she up ahead and me in behind, and twice more the man bellows out, but we do not look for fear of falling.

After the embankment, we hop the fence and head into the head-high grass where I lurch, trip and stumble flat on my face, spilling my entire cache to the ground. I think we should stop, I say, and she says she thinks we should go. But he'll catch us, Annie. He can't catch us, she says. Now come on, you big cry-baby.

And through the swaying grass ahead I see the lines of the road and of the roadblock across it, and beyond that, though no one at home likes to talk about it, the line of low flat armoured vehicles in which to put them, having but two pockets to spare, and so he returns to ground, turning a cold shoulder to the driving range and bending forward instead to the task at hand.

Across the highway and past the reserve the air is chilly, though not quite so chilly as it was before, and gradually, almost imperceptibly, the sky begins to brighten, leaving the morning mist to dissolve completely and the wind to rise off the ocean once more. The overcast sky continues to brighten, the wind continues to rise, and soon it's nothing more than an early morning wind coming off a clean grey ocean and walking further along an empty road. He takes a deep breath—the feeling of the previous night's rain is gone—replaced instead with cool morning air, more dry road and ever-whitening clouds, and instead of staying along Marine Drive he cuts right and north and heads up the hill for home.

A little later, with the clean fresh smell of ocean morning clinging to his nostrils, and the wide flat bay rippled with breeze below, he steps off Columbia Street and down the embankment into the neglected little yard of his mother's rental property. Cojimar is there and cocks an ear. The obligatory seagulls hover about as well. Currently engaged in the industrious plunder of what appear to be two raw chickens recently discarded on the driveway out back, their beaks poke in and out of the raw pink flesh, tearing off each quivering morsel, heaving them skyward and away somewhere.

As Cojimar follows along obediently, he reaches down to offer her a quick scratch behind the ear, an affectionate exercise she accepts in kind until lashing out quite suddenly with a paw, demonstrating yet again her quick sympathy for fisticuffs and the more fashionable turns of violent behaviour.

She cackles all the way up the grey and creaking wooden stairs, and back along the deck towards the door. He urges her to remain quiet—this despite all the squawking of the seagulls and the squeaking of the floorboards—but she doesn't fare too well: although she can evidently suppress many instinctive urges, she can't suppress all those. He unlocks the door and steps inside, while Cojimar, of course, remains outdoors. Here she licks herself fastidiously before capsizing backward onto the top stair, recovering quickly to glance about in shock, seemingly no worse for wear for the mishap barring perhaps a vaguely unsettling awareness that she was, until very recently, exactly one station higher in life.

He refills her bowl in the kitchen and places it back outside the door, but not before finding a single black ant scurrying across the counter and pounding it to death with a well-worn copy of *A New Earth* by Eckhart Tolle. Then, tiptoeing softly down the hall, he opens the bedroom door to see me lying asleep in the bed. He sees the shadow of my face on the pillow and the shape of my widespread legs beneath the duvet. He reaches across the bed to give my foot a playful squeeze, but unable to locate it amongst the great heaps of bedding, listens closely for my breathing instead. He hears it, just barely albeit, way down deep and nearly out of range altogether. It seems a little difficult. Slightly laboured even. And so he opens the window to relieve some of the stuffiness, perceiving, at that exact moment, the distinct sound of scratching somewhere.

On a whim, he retreats swiftly from the bedroom, crossing the living room in four great strides to rip open the front door, effectively busting two large crows up to the railing in the process— off they hop to the neighbour's roof next door. Down the far end of the deck stands Cojimar, contentedly cleaning a paw. He curses her once and calls her back, reminding her once again how Cat Chow is for cats, not crows.

Using the toilet and afterwards, lighting a match, he wanders out to the living room windows to look out across the ocean at the islands and the mountains. He can't actually see the islands or the mountains. He only knows that they are there. Instead he sees a single massive thundercloud creeping left to right, east to west across the horizon, all but obscuring that horizon from view for now. From time to time lightning fractures the face of the cloud, followed by the inevitable thunder rolling in to rattle grumpily against the panes of glass. And while directly outside the windows it's not raining, at least not yet, it's clear that something is in the works from the escalating sway of his neighbour's firs and the now frosty crests of the nearest slate-coloured waves.

At the bottom of the hill stands the pier. When the tide is in, the water is dark and grey and rippled around the pilings, and when the tide is out, as it is now, the sand is dark and grey and rippled too. Around the piled-granite, arrowhead-shaped breakwater protecting the small armada of boats anchored there at the end of the pier, tiny white flecks of seagull slide hard against an invisible wall of wind, sliding down, out and away somewhere. And off to the southeast, amid its own orbiting escort of gulls, a solitary fishing boat pilots out and away from the Semiahmoo reserve. He watches the boat, accompanied by its escort, bump its way out through an endless succession of white-crested waves in the direction of the peninsula on the opposite side of the border. He doesn't bother with the west end of the beach. He doesn't even bother to go there. There will be plenty of time to go to the west end of the beach when things get back to normal down there.

Outside the door, the crows continue to hover about restlessly, and since there is food in the cat's bowl, and the cat is gone, he places the bowl back inside for now. Then he moves down the grey and creaking wooden stairs and out onto the driveway out back, feeling the first faint raindrops begin to fall in the bleak indeterminate light. The seagulls are gone and so is the meat. He glances up at the highest sad and sagging deck, but apparently Jeff is still in retreat.

Down the driveway, he goes, and out onto the lane in the rain, cutting across to the cracked, grey, concrete steps on the opposite side where small green shoots have recently appeared on the slowly encroaching vines and, on the adjoining trees, small green leaves. Along the mud-sullied cracks of the steps, legions of black ants pursue a frantic activity. He stops in the rain to observe the progress of the ants, and observing, gnaws a little too aggressively at the thick white calluses of his palms. With each scrape he gains a little more skin, and a little more skin, until, finally, having rolled it all together with his tongue, employing his saliva as mortar, he deposits the entire knotted mass into one of the cracks at his feet. Soon enough two ants discover the knot, one from either side, and after searching it over vigilantly, each retreats down along the crack to inform the others of this his magnificent discovery. And to gather reinforcements, Chris supposes. And sure enough, two ants gradually return, one from either side and with reinforcements in tow, each band tugging and pulling at the knot until they decide to act jointly—that is, hoisting it onto their collective shoulders. And so he follows the clumsy but impressive journey of the saliva-soaked knot of skin along the concrete crack until eventually it disappears into that underworld below.

The heavy wet wind continues to rise as, out along the horizon, the thundercloud continues its slow but steady western campaign. He stops every few steps to watch for the lightning, and noting the lightning, waits a moment more for the ensuing thunder to begin. One stairwell leads to the next, eventually emerging atop the bluff that, for a distance of maybe two hundred meters, separates Drive from beach, train tracks and promenade. Across the street, in the rain, stands the eastbound bus stop where that woman was crushed to death by a car a couple of months back. Presently only a single makeshift cross remains, leaning monumentally against the curb just so, most of the other mementos and flowers having long since washed away, or else been stolen by someone once more. Down the bluff, past the tracks and promenade, the tide remains a fair distance out. Though the wind and rain continue to blow in, far out over the bay the thundercloud continues steadily on its course.

Down Marine Drive and past the Trap & Gill in the rain, he goes, not bothering to look inside, then past the Dairy Queen, the juice bar, the Ocean Beach Hotel, the other juice bar, and the assorted gift, card and clothing shops all joined together in a line,

if only by their storefronts much of the time, before finally making Monk's coffee shop at the very far end of the line. Beside
Monk's, below the Why Suffer in Vein™ laser clinic and alongside
the Opa! Greek Taverna, stands a weak wall of embryonic tulips,
all that remains of the once popular Just for the Halibut Seafood
Palace, all but swept away in that freak flood of a month ago.

Darcy stands behind the counter at Monk's biting what little is
left of her thumbnail and, with what passes for the index finger of
her left hand, coiling an impressive and intricate rope of straight
blonde hair. She smiles, yawns and says hello as he wipes excessive moisture from his coat, head and hair.

So, uh, how you been? she yawns again, catching herself ajar,
managing to morph this perceived impropriety into an oddly
effective and even sympathetic smile. All right, he tells her. Well I
was getting kind of worried, she says. I mean I haven't seen you
in a while. Well I'm kind of under new management, he explains.

Asking what that means, she screws up her eyes in a feigned air
of suspicion, no doubt trying to alleviate the suddenly sombre
mood he's just dragged in. Nothing, he says, nothing at all. She
thought she detected a hint of sarcasm, she says, so he says she did-
n't, so there.

Darcy shrugs and picks up the same big blue whale book Wendy
forced on him as a fleet of cute ceramic seals keep wide-eyed
watch from the counter. A sign beneath the adjacent baked goods
display, accompanied by a photocopied reproduction of the read-
er, advertises "Tea Leaf Readings by Dawn." One gets a steady
diet of that sort of thing here at Monk's. It's just that kind of coffee shop. And White Rock is just that kind of town.

Flipping over the *Big Blue Book of Whales* for show, balancing it
on her prosthetic arm that begins, he well knows, at the elbow,
Darcy tells him how the blue whale, on account of being the
largest creature on earth, happens to comes equipped with the
largest penis as well. Up to sixteen feet long it says here, she says,
and he says, Sixteen feet, huh. That's a heck of a lot of penis, isn't
it. It sure is, she agrees. Well did you know the blue whale also has
the loudest voice on earth, Darcy? Yup, loudest voice in the world,
they say, but you and I can't hear it at all. Why not? she says, and

he says because it's out of their range of hearing apparently. Subversive bastards, she scowls.

Sliding over to the espresso machine, she asks if he wants something to eat. No, just coffee, he tells her, extracting a single white napkin from the pile and wrapping it around the index and middle fingers of his left hand. In the meantime, releasing a few errant strands of hair from her cheek, Darcy splashes milk from a jug into a tin and begins the all too earsplitting task of steaming it.

So I suppose you've been wondering when it is you're going to get your money, he says, and she says the thought has crossed her mind. Especially as she hasn't seen him now in so long, she adds after a time.

He twists off the napkin roll at fingers' end, and then continues twisting tightly down the roll towards the end.

No pressure or anything, but when do you think that might happen? she asks, forced to elevate her voice over the piercing scream of steaming milk. Well as soon as I get the Trap & Gill back up and running and make a few bucks, he tells her as she lowers the metal tin from the steamer, wipes the wand clean with a cloth, finishes up the latté, and passes it over the bar with a frown.

I'm serious, Darcy. You're going to get your money. All of it. It's just that—

No it's not that, she says. She was just thinking about his restaurant. What about his restaurant? Well she was thinking that maybe he'd want to hire some new staff, she explains. He needs some new staff. His staff have absolutely no personality. Plus, they're ugly. What he needs in there is some eye candy, Darcy goes on with this sudden air of shrewd business savvy. You know, big racks, short skirts, prosthetic limbs—like her, in other words.

Halfway down the stem, he folds up one corner of the napkin as a leaf, and then continues twisting down the roll towards the end. Not that he has any choice in the matter, he supposes, and she smiles and says she supposes not, no. Well he could offer her, say, minimum wage, not to mention very few bonuses, if at all. Unless of course she counts physically inactive, entirely unsatisfactory affairs with an unhappy married man, but she says she doesn't, no. Then she smiles again, sad rather than sly this time, at which point he offers the paper rose a few finishing touches, sprucing up the flower petals. Eventually he hands her the completed project, which she receives with surprisingly welling eyes.

Aw isn't that sweet, says Stephan from behind.

Thursday, 6:22 am

The rain has stopped, or for the moment at least it has, and so he cuts across the street to the promenade and up towards the pier, coffee cup in hand. Their calluses recently removed, his palms remain somewhat tender, and so, in order to avoid any sort of discomfort here, he holds his cup with fingers curled down around the bottom and thumb wrapped up around the lid like so.

Far off over the islands to the southwest the last remnants of the thundercloud disappear. Despite the rains, the usual morning crew is out on the promenade in abundance, and so he stops to greet as many as necessary, or, in reality, as few, managing to avoid a great many by simply deploying his now familiar stricken expression en route. A few joggers, some early morning strollers, too many whale-watchers and the requisite pairs of elderly women clutter up the mud-puddled path, the latter moving arm in arm, an all too obvious anxiety stiffening their stride, watching carefully the placement of their steps along the bricks, checking and rechecking any irregularities that might seek to trip up what is in all probability the last remaining, vaguely romantic ritual of their lives.

Out on the pier, he walks the fifteen hundred and fifty-nine feet to the end before turning abruptly, ready to walk the same fifteen hundred and fifty-nine feet back again. Stopping for a moment, though, he allows his eyes to continue on up ahead. From this perspective the town begins to take shape anew: Marine Drive, with its string of brightly painted storefronts and neon signs, retreats deep into the hillside at the base of the pier, the cedar and spruce trees of the hillside dominate the Drive, and the crowded terraces of California-style beach houses dominate the trees. In amongst the dark green trees and pastel-painted houses stretches of dark grey road appear. He can see the Trap & Gill from here. And he can see the four hundred and eighty-six ton white rock too. He can see across the face of the rock that someone has scrawled in enormous black spray-painted letters, under a crude swastika, LEAVE WHITE ROCK WHITE, and he can see, scattered along the beach, the heaps of driftwood and various other unintended ironies proven all but immovable over the years.

He walks up alongside Po and Stephan Soon, the latter having just now returned from Monk's, and together they stand sipping at their coffees and staring down into the bucket at their feet.

That one's pretty small, Chris says, and Stephan says, Which one? That one? He's right, Po, it is pretty small. So? says Po. So put it back, Chris tells him, extracting from the bucket the crab in question and tossing it over the side of the pier.

Eventually Stephan goes about emptying and stacking the last of the traps, while his father packs away the fishing gear. And in keeping with custom, Chris carts the lot of it back along the pier, at the conclusion of which he and Stephan take a seat at Annie and wipe off the pigeons' most recent contributions. From here they watch Po stow the gear, placing each piece carefully in the bed of the old Nissan pickup truck as he does twice a day every day the vast majority of the year.

Christ, look at this mess, Chris says. I swear to God, if I could just *once* get my hands on one of those dirty bastards. Believe me, I've tried, Stephan says. They're scared, though, that's what they are. Chicken. And they'll walk everywhere those chickens, he adds, gesturing towards Monk's a moment before levelling a look at Chris. Including across the road apparently.

Po packs. Stephan yaks. And eventually Chris asks them how the fishing went this morning.

Not bad, Po says, dragging down the back of his daughter's John Deere baseball cap, and Chris says, Not bad, huh. Well you should go deep-sea fishing, Po. That's where the real action is. No money for boat, Po says. Besides, too tired. Too old. Too *old*? says Stephan. What are you talking about, *too old*.

Ignoring this outburst, in the same efficient way he ignores just about everything, Po casually disjoints a rod. Meanwhile, his message more or less delivered, Stephan retires to another bench between Annie and the parking lot.

Stephan says, He's right though, Po. You're being a bit of a chicken. And the chicken, I do believe, came first, he adds for the benefit of no one in particular, himself conceivably.

Having disjointed the rod, Po slides the entire assembly, reel and all, deep into the bed of the truck. Meanwhile Chris shifts about uncomfortably, his pelvic bone bruised from Wendy's repeatedly bashing up against it all night.

I must say, Po, your gift for conversation is truly awe-inspiring, Stephan says. Really, though, you're a supremely accomplished conversationalist in my opinion. Rather like the blue whale though. Largest creature on earth apparently—biggest organ—and not only that, but blessed with the loudest instrument as well. But you know what? You and I can't hear it. Nope, out of our range of hearing somehow. Too high maybe. No, probably not, probably too low. Either way, loudest voice on earth, they say, but you and I can't hear it at all. Well I wonder what it sounds like. I wonder what they say. "Egg came first," no doubt. Just to spite me, I bet.

Po goes on packing up the gear while even now, at this hour and from this distance, a large crowd can be seen gathering around the carcass of the whale. And in light of this recent beaching, Stephan would like to ask his father a few questions. About suicide for instance. I mean it's the method, Po, the *means* that seems unsound, for the goal itself remains quite clear: one simply wants a say in saying when it's over.

Far out across the sand, its head tilted aggressively to one side, a heron fishes studiously in the shallows of the low tide.

Stephan wonders if maybe the whale drowned though. Like maybe its death wasn't intentional at all. Regardless, he wouldn't want to drown though. No, there's nothing redeeming in drowning, Po. Sinking maybe. Choking certainly. But nothing redeeming as far as I can tell. And that's why the fish have it so good. Fish? says Po. Fish, Po. Stephan thinks it has something to do with air spaces and pressure equalization though. You see, you and me, we have these air spaces that require equalization the deeper we descend into the ocean. If a man—or a whale, say—doesn't equalize his air spaces as he dives, well then they'll implode, causing, as you're no doubt aware, serious physical damage. And interestingly, every atmosphere you descend into the ocean, every ten meters or so, is equivalent to a double martini—a double mar*tini*, Po—but then that's nitrogen narcosis and that's something different altogether. No, pressure equalization has to do with the compressibility of gases, and as we learned in scuba class just yesterday, rapid decompression upon ascension can lead to decompression sickness, or "the bends."

Po slams shut the tailgate of the Nissan and moves around to the driver's door. In the meantime, employing his supine body as measure, his son goes about calculating the length of the bench in carefully calibrated Stephans.

Actually it's the *in*compressibility of *fluids* that gives the fish control, that gives him the ability to dive and not just to drown, or so the story goes. Metaphorically speaking, Stephan says, it's almost as if the fish is one unending material with the water. He's one with the water. One with the—whatever. Now that's deep, no? Isn't it though? But then that's fish, Po. Chicken of the sea, amigo.

Po says nothing as Stephan moves from the bench to the guardrail alongside the tracks, where he watches the heron pace precisely and majestically along the broken shoreline, its prey hidden away in the tide pools below.

No, Stephan thinks that whale there maybe had it right. Now the heron here, its plucky approach to life is certainly worthy of admiration, although for him, right now at least, a touch too daunting a task. No, that whale there definitely had it right. And he gets his inspiration from that whale all right. Along with his motivation. Unfortunately he doesn't quite get the look so much. Now from the heron here he gets the patience as well as the perseverance, but unfortunately he also got this penchant of his for long walks on the beach and such. And from his father here he got, what, the power of the unspoken word, and from his sister he got many more important things, though they're not so easy to put into words.

The heron stops. Its head cocks. Then it high-steps elegantly along the shore as be*fore in this very hotel, I say, and she says, That's*

interesting. Really. Now come on back to bed. Well did you know Trudeau
was the first Western leader to visit after the missile crisis, Annie? He was,
you know. Again, terribly interesting, she says. Now come on back to bed
and let's see if we can't make us a baby.

Out the window, far out over the gathering darkness of the harbour, I
can see along the curved crumbling façade of the Maleçon the lights of the
recently refurbished tenements blinking to life one after another.

I wish the old man in Cojimar had been in today, I say, smelling the
last of the storm on the warm sea air, and she says he was in. He was
sleeping. Yeah, I know, I say. I just wish he'd been up to talking, that's all.
I really would've liked to talk to him, Annie. What about? she says, and
I say I don't know. The Old Man and the Sea, I suppose.

And finishing what little is left of my Mojito, feeling sugary shreds of
mint leaf lodge themselves between my teeth, I take one hesitant step
towards the bed as, down below in the lighted courtyard, unbeknownst to
most, a peacock makes a successful leap into a nearby tree.

Stop, she says as I attempt to gently insert myself. Stop? Yes, stop. For
Christ's sake, stop—fuck, she gasps. What happened, I ask. It hurt like
hell, that's what happened, I'm told, and the next morning at the hospi-
tal in Old Havana an elderly man introduced as the late Che Guevara's
personal physician finds the tear in her vaginal canal tighter than a
tourniquet. "Stephanie, You are Tighter than a Tourniquet," if I
remember the title correctly, and contrary to what he might
remember, that's the first and only poem Chris ever really wrote
for me.

Thursday, 6:46 am

Having declined the ubiquitous *Big Blue Book of Whales* a second
time in as many minutes, he politely offers her a drink. She wavers
momentarily, then reluctantly shakes her head in the negative. She
thinks that maybe she's had a few too many Bacardis already.
Bacardi? Where the hell was she drinking Bacardi? At the hotel,
she says. That was last *night*, Wendy. Yes, but it's only quarter to
seven in the *morning*, she says, shaking her head in wonder, passing him a stack of photographs instead.

A little later, tipping his chin at the patio window, he mentions
that he happens to have some Bacardi right here. So this is his

place? He owns the Trap & Gill? Well no, he says, the Brothers
Beasley do. So he's the manager then, she says. Really. But he
looks too young to be the manager. Believe me, Wendy, people are
always saying that though. And that bothers you, she says, and he
says, Yeah, that bothers me immensely. I mean I'm young, but I'm
not *that* young, you know? Not so young you can pigeonhole me
anyhow. And besides, I'm a paragon of business acumen, I can
assure you.

She asks him why, if he's such a paragon, the Trap & Gill has
been closed for like a month now, and he tells her it's because of
the flood. She doesn't know which flood he's referring to—she's
been away, she says—and so he explains about the waterspout
that, touching down on the bay one morning a month ago, gath-
ered up such a massive amount of water—an amount it proceeded to unload all at once over the immediate hillside—that the
ensuing deluge not only overran the existing drainage and sewage
systems, but flooded to varying degrees most of the establishments
along the Drive.

What's a waterspout? she asks. A sort of water-based tornado,
she's told. Don't worry, though, it was just a freak occurrence, he
assures her when he can see her growing increasingly anxious at
the prospect of another such phenomenon transpiring now. He
stands up and moves towards the door.

Look at all those keys, she says, watching him go. Sorry? he says.
I said look at all those *keys*, she says, indicating the set now dangling from his hand. You have a lot of keys. You wouldn't believe
how many keys I have on my keychain these days though, she
goes on, fishing around in her beach bag to show him oh, about
twelve or so. Wow that's a lot of keys, he tells her, holding open
the door for her to follow. She looks at him. He looks at her. And
finally, but only after much deliberation, she elevates gracefully
from her chair and slowly approaches the open door, clicking past
him in maroon high heels and some sort of matching velvet
tracksuit ensemble.

Now what were we talking about? she says. Keys? he says. That's
right, keys, she says. Well the key to remembering anything is to
leave yourself a note, hey. Good tip, he says. But the thing is, she

goes on, she hates to leave herself notes nowadays. She'll leave other people notes, sure, but when it comes to herself, she just can't be bothered these days. So what she does is, she leaves a box in the hall. A box in the what? A box in the hall, she says. She's got these empty boxes she likes to keep under the bench in the hall, and so what she does is, she mentally *imprints* whatever it is she wants to remember on a box, then leaves that box in the middle of the hall, so that the next time she sees it—or trips over it, more likely—she asks herself, "Now what in God's sweet name is this box doing in the middle of the goddamned hall?" And then, of course, she remembers whatever it is she wants to remember, and it all makes sense somehow.

He leans in behind the bar to deactivate the alarm while Wendy clicks her way across the brand new hardwood floor. Having brought along the tray, the very same Dairy Queen hot dog tray from the night before, she looks for a place to set it down without further disturbing the sanctity of his small sixty-seat chapel.

Must you? he says, and she says what. Must she what. The tray, he says, frowning at the tray and the cold, shrivelled, half-eaten hot dog currently fossilizing upon it. Must she bring the tray. Should I just put it on the floor then? she asks, and without waiting for an answer proceeds to do just that, stepping back to check the overall effect before looking up and smiling with surprised satisfaction.

He grabs the bucket from beneath the bar and steps through to the kitchen where the ice machine is housed, eventually returning behind the bar to find Wendy sitting quietly at the nearest table, wholly absorbed in her whale book once more. Sighing, he studies the photographs on the walls. For purposes of decoration and ambiance, black and white photographs, chiefly of fishermen, adorn most of the stained wood walls. Above the fireplace hangs the largest photograph, and before it, not surprisingly, resides one of the more popular tables. Eventually his attention comes to rest on one particular photograph, small in comparison to the others, of a young girl coiling a length of rope aboard an old barge somewhere. He can tell it's an old barge she's standing on as it says so in the caption there. He always stares at this particular photograph as it's a pretty photograph and therefore pretty tragic, people say.

Hey Chris, did you know that girl? she says, and he says which girl. That Chinese girl that got hit up by the bus stop there, she says, and he says oh *that* girl. Sure, he knew her. And did he know her well? Pretty well, he tells her. But then not for as long as he would've liked to.

Shame what happened, she says. Trouble is, in this town, you're always going to get run down by a carload of Indians eventually. Yes, he sighs, it does seem to be a favourite pastime in these parts. Still, they don't know it was Indians for certain, hey. Well who does he blame then? Oh he blames himself, no question, he says.

He gazes out the window at the early morning pedestrian traffic drifting down the length of the pier, beyond which stretches the slowly undulating ocean in the direction of those few dark and distant islands clinging to the edge of a soaked and sullen world.

This is yours, he says, offering her forty dollars. I don't understand, she says, staring at the two twenties before her. It's your money, Wendy. I stole it. Well then I want nothing to do with it, she says, pushing his hand aside, turning her attention to the glass face of the table and, pinned there beneath, again for decoration and ambiance, the nautical map of some neighboring maritime locale. She continues to study the map a moment more before gradually gravitating back to her book, at which point he leaves the cash on the table and steps in behind the bar, taking a small tumbler from the shelf and filling it with ice, making sure to pack it full. Next, he measures out exactly one ounce of Bacardi rum, dumps it over the ice, tops it up with a burst of Coke and, drink in hand, steps out from behind the bar.

It's terrible about that Chinese girl, she says, indicating the photograph of the girl aboard the barge. I heard she was crying out for like an hour and nobody came. How old was she, twenty-nine? Yes, twenty-nine, he says.

Placing the drink before her, he drags back a chair on the opposite side of the table. Finding a wine ring on the glass, he rubs it off with a thumb, then wipes the glass clean with a cloth where his thumb left a smudge. At length he notices how someone has taken the liberty of inscribing the table's edge with a clearly defined "FU*rrowed suspiciously, standing there behind me, sporting a pair of my briefs as a hat. What are you looking at, I say to her reflection in the television, and she says she's just seeing what ol' Coyote Ugly's up to, that's all. After that display at the bar last night she has no idea what to expect from me anymore.*

And standing there in the bedroom doorway, feet splayed wide apart, she continues to brush her teeth in textbook rotary motion for now. And later, taking a momentary break from brushing to adjust the lay of her tattered grey underwear beret, she asks if I'm getting ready for work soon and I say yeah, pretty soon. Remember now, no more skimming, she warns. No more skimming, I promise the television as it shifts its focus over Shania Twain's shoulder, out over her veranda, and out over the edge of the unnamed Swiss village where the road climbs up through the surrounding hills before dropping down over the long slow shoulder of a deep meandering valley beyond. And in the valley stand what appear to be chestnut trees along both sides of the road, the surface of the road reflecting white and bright in the sun, and further along the valley the road becomes a series of white stone bridges crossing a wide flat river, beyond which stand another series of bridges, one of which has fallen over what they were. Just really itchy, Wendy. And I mean *really* itchy. So what I did was, I walked on up to the campus pharmacy to purchase the special shampoo. Only problem was, the young woman working behind the counter happened to be awfully damned cute, so of course I had to steal it. And I did too. I just crotched the bottle and paid for a chocolate bar and walked on out the door.

Wendy looks up at him, her glass arrested halfway to her lips.

I crotched the crab shampoo, Wendy. Clearly an ironic move. Oh, *crotched*! she says, blurting out a laugh. She tries the drink, refuses it, then asks if she might try a glass of wine instead. Sure, he says, and steps in behind the bar, eventually returning to the table with a newly corked bottle of Merlot.

Thing is, I think she knew, he says, and she says how so? Well she did charge me eleven dollars for the Ma*rs bar from the inner folds of his robes. Mars? he says, and I say, No thanks. Mars, Annie? How about you, Stephan? You probably want some of Chung Huk's chocolate*

bar, I tell him via the rear-view mirror. No, no Mars, they answer togeth-
er, labouring through some new tune on their recently purchased harmon-
icas. And when no one takes him up on his offer, the monk shrugs, tucks
the bar away, and taps another Omar Sharif free of its pack, later begging
me repeatedly to drive as he just can't be bothered to negotiate all this
Seoul traffic.

   Energy Bar, he says, and I say, What's that? It called "Energy Bar"
now, he says through a thick grey cloud of smoke, holding up the Mars as
proof. Meanwhile I manoeuvre our little Suzuki aggressively through the
throng, hell-bent on the mountain there and some sort of separate sereni-
ty somehow he steps away from the table and back towards the bar,
managing to step squarely on the red tray en route, sending his
foot out and away, dropping him bodily to the floor.

   He looks up at her a second. She stares down at him a spell.
Then, slowly regaining his feet, he picks up the tray and hurls it
Frisbee-fashion at the door, sending the hot dog careening off the
window—to her credit, however, Wendy doesn't so much as
flinch at the clamour of the tray against the door. Instead, she
takes the pile of photographs from her beach bag and arranges
them hastily but precisely on the table before her.

   He pours her a glass of Merlot.

   You're not having a drink? she asks, scratching her thumbnail
across the glass. She does this twice, this aggravating scratching of
the glass, two times too many as far as he is concerned. And so,
having registered this objection, he promises himself that if she
does it again, he will politely but firmly ask her not to.

   A drink? he says. Me? Not right now, no. Why not? she wants
to know. Well here's to a month on the wagon, Wendy. And all the
senseless suffering it's caused.

   Wendy hides her face, blows her nose, and eventually excuses
herself to the restroom. And so, with nothing else to do, and not
really wanting to be left alone, he steps in behind the bar and
picks up the telephone. He dials the number, then curses when
the answering service places him on hold. Finally a man comes on
the line and says his name is Tony and thanks for holding and
what can the Tone-man do for him just now? Well Chris would
like to order some flowers—for delivery, he says, feeling his

bottom lip quiver a little in anticipation of a flood of emotion that somehow never quite materializes. And once he's through taking down the delivery address and credit card number, Tony asks Chris what sort of arrangement he's after. Well what's the flower for cancer? Hey Sam, what's the cancer flower, Tony inquires away from the receiver. The zodiac sign? says Sam, a woman, presumably standing there beside him at the counter. Yeah, the zodiac, Tony tells her. Sniffling, Chris says no. No? No, not the zodiac. Tony thought he said cancer though. Yes, but the *disease*, Tony. Cancer the *disease*. Oh right, Tony says. Sorry. Hey Sam, what's the flower for *cancer the disease*. Tulip maybe, Chris hears Sam say. Or orchid maybe. I thought maybe it was the daffodil, Chris says. Hey Sam, how about the daffodil? says Tony. Really? Yeah, Sam thinks it might be the daffodil too, hey. All right then, the daffodil it is, Chris says. To be honest, though, I'm not really sure. Neither am I, says Tony. Neither is Sam. Well then I guess we're all in agreement that we don't know what the fuck the cancer flower is then, Chris says, and Tony pauses. Yes, we are, he says. In full fucking agreement, you might say.

They both fall silent a moment.

Well then just put something cancerish in, says Chris at length. Do your best. Unless you think it's somehow inappropriate for someone one year-clear today. No, Tony doesn't think it's inappropriate. Sam? No, Sam doesn't think it's inappropriate either, especially for someone—what'd Chris say—one year-clear today. How about roses, Tony suggests. Roses? says Chris. I don't know ... What does Sam think? Roses? says Tony. Yeah, Sam thinks roses might be best. Well roses it is then—red ones, make it a dozen—and hey, Chris says, maybe you could find out what the hell the cancer flower is and stick one of those in too, okay?

He replaces the phone in its cradle just as Wendy reappears fresh from the restroom, clicking her way across the Trap & Gill's brand new hardwood floor with strident high-heeled enthusiasm. In the meantime, due perhaps to their similar shape, but more likely their similar colour, he can't help but notice the rather remarkable resemblance her tracksuit-clad torso shares with the bottle of Merlot on the table.

Seeing as Nick has seen him, there is simply no avoiding him now.

Reopening day isn't it? says Nick, cutting him off on the sidewalk. Reopening day it is, Champ, says Chris. And, uh, who was that? Nick asks, pointing up the road to the slowly receding tenspeed and its rider's slowly pumping, velvety-smooth maroon rear-end. Oh just this girl, Chris says, forget it. Nick purses his lips, then smiles suggestively. Right, he says, I get it. Actually, I doubt you do, Nick. In fact I'm pretty sure a fag like you has never gotten it.

Suspended on the breeze, Chris catches the brief scent of engine oil and railway ties. The road too smells good, and the bracing wind feels invigorating on his eyes.

After what he evidently deems an appropriate and conciliatory pause, Nick asks Chris if he's been down to see the whale at all. Not yet, no, he's told. Pretty creepy, nods Nick appreciatively. Actually, I'm heading down right now if you're interested. Thanks, says Chris, but no.

Just then Billy Henry comes lumbering up, absentmindedly petting the stubble of his recently shaved skull. Chris says, Don't tell me you're heading down to see the whale too, Hank. Na, Billy Henry smiles shyly, idly petting his pate. Check this out though, he says, nudging with his toe an empty beer bottle discarded there on the sidewalk. So? So I like these Sleeman bottles, he says. I like the way they don't have a label. I was actually thinking of starting a collection sometime. A collection, huh, says Chris, and Billy Henry says, Yeah, you know, a bottle collection. That's a fantastic idea, Billy. Thanks, Nick. Actually I was being sort of facetious, Billy. Well fuck you, Nick, says Billy Henry. It's a wonder I tell you anything anymore.

Billy Henry turns his considerable mass on Nick, his forehead furrowing anxiously, his lips struggling silently, both sets of muscles working themselves up to the task of denouncing his friend in front of Chris. Finally, though, having thought of nothing cunning or biting to say, he toes the Sleeman bottle along to where it finally falls down over the edge of the sidewalk and onto the street, rolling noisily down the gradient to finally lodge itself up against *it won't start, she says, so I say, Well I can see that. What'd you do to it though? I didn't do anything to it, she says, and so I stroke my lip thoughtfully with a thumb a moment.*

So it just stopped running, and you pulled it over here against the curb, I say, and she says, No, I was parked *here, waiting for you, and when I couldn't find you because you were fucking around with your finger-puppet friends, I went to leave again and it wouldn't go. Wouldn't go or wouldn't start, Annie? Wouldn't start, she says. I already* told *you that.*

And so, getting down on hands and knees, I gaze in under the carriage of her brother's car. These tires are bald, Annie. Christ, the goddamned cords are showing. So? So? Yeah, so what? she says. That didn't stop it from starting. I told you I need it to start. Yes, but the state of one's tires is a fairly accurate gauge of how well one cares for his car, I somewhat pointlessly point out.

Eventually I stand up, brushing my hands clean on my jeans and steeling myself for a scene. Oh well, I guess it's the bus, I say, and she says, You're serious. You want us to take the bus. All the way to the clinic downtown. No, I say, I want you *to take the bus. Oh so you're not coming now? she says, and I say, Annie, let's be serious. I'm not taking a fucking* bus, Nick says, and Chris says, No, you guys go ahead. I have no desire to wake the dead just now.

They both continue to regard him in a sympathetic way until eventually Nick turns to walk away, waiting a moment more for Billy Henry who, if his frown is any indication, appears to be expressing even more concern with Chris. Don't worry about it, Chris says when Billy Henry asks if he's okay. And once both he and Nick are safely out of range, having scampered back to claim the Sleeman bottle for himself, Chris makes his way up to the Trap & Gill to find Pat watching pornography on the big screen. Watching it in his whites of course. Chris walks over the new floor and quietly checks over the rest of the tables, finding them moderately clean, a few freshly wiped, the remainder a little dusty, but in reasonably good condition for the most part. He checks over their bases carefully, checking for damage from the flood. Again, everything seems to be in relatively good condition. Evidently it makes little difference whether he's here to look after things or not. Once upon a time, he imagined that the general condition of the Trap & Gill, from whether or not product was available to the day-to-day functioning of preparation and service, depended to a considerable extent on himself. Evidently though, and the conclusion he reached a month ago, was that it makes little difference whether he's here or not. The whole thing seems to run better while he's away, or at least not taking part, one of those many aspects of management that serve only to undermine any false sense of superiority he somehow musters up.

He takes Wendy's forty dollars from his pocket and steps over to the bar, punches a Bacardi and a glass of Merlot into the computer, then places the two bills in the empty cash drawer for now.

Right back in the saddle, eh Pat? What's that? asks Pat, scratching his beard, continuing to gaze up at the big screen from which he's taken so much inspiration over the previous year. Chris says, You're right back in the saddle, Pat. You're—

You could say that, Pat snaps, determined, it would seem, to preserve his early morning insularity intact. Meanwhile, up on the big screen, a young woman happens upon a penis, towards which, as is the custom, she soon displays a vast and detailed intimacy.

Chris asks how the new prep cook is coming along. All right, he's told. Just all right? he asks, turning to the photograph of the girl aboard the barge. He closes one eye, aligns his open eye with his thumb now held out before him at arm's length, and manages, despite himself, to completely eclipse her face. Yeah, just all right, Pat says. A bit meek, in my opinion. Sikh women, hey, they're always so bloody meek and intimidated. Not to mention the fact you can't understand what the fuck they're saying half the time.

Chris steps over to the kitchen door to see what the new prep cook is up to back there, finding hard at work a short, severe-looking woman decked out in the standard hairnet, chopping vegetables and pre-cooking something-or-other, performing whatever it is the Trap & Gill's prep cooks do in the early morning hours. In the meantime, up on the big screen, only a single young woman remains in the scene, evidently intent on taking her pleasure into her own hands. And wagging his head enthusiastically up and down, Pat grins as though, for him, a supreme, much anticipated moment has finally arrived in life.

I did that once, Chris says, and Pat glances over in surprised indignation at this continued violation of Trap & Gill protocol. Did what, he says, and Chris says, Prep cooked. I was a prep cook once. Back when I was like seventeen years old. I remember it being extremely tiresome, not to mention tiring, so maybe you could try cutting her a little slack, okay?

That said, he steps over to the server station where, astonishingly enough, coffee is already on. He tops up his cup, adds a little sugar, and wanders back to the dining room to see, up on the big screen, a naked man entering the scene well in hand. And so, in exactly the same way as he did with the photograph on the wall, Chris places a thumb over the man's face and proceeds to track him with it, until ultimately losing interest and abandoning the project in place.

You bug me, Pat. You and your pornography-watching ways. Resistance is futile, Pat retorts. You'll all be assimilated shortly. Still, you'd think you'd get a little sore after a while, Chris says, and Pat says hey, he's got to supplement his old lady's rations somehow. And besides, he's been in withdrawal for like a month now. Make no mistake about it, he adds, the road to hell is paved with unwatched porn.

Together they watch the porn a while.

So what's this one then, Pat? This? says Pat. This is *Black Beach Patrol Five*. So then not really a seminal work, Chris decides. What's it about then? Oh, the usual, he's told. The fun-loving gals of the famous Black Beach Patrol discover a lost lifeguard on a remote desolate island, and it turns out he's part of their team "from the old days." Sparks fly as the hot new recruits push both themselves and their long lost friend to physical perfection, Pat states as though reading straight from the satellite guide—which he is of course. In other words, Chris says, a whole bunch of black people fucking the crap out of one another all over the beach somewhere. Exactly, says Pat. Take this gal here, he goes on, indicating the woman presently bobbing up and down onscreen. Well she appears to be performing some bizarre new form of resuscitation on our poor helpless castaway here. Well of course she is, Pat. I mean what else is a lifeguard for.

Chris watches Pat watching porn, then glances restlessly about the restaurant a while. He can smell the new wood and fresh wax, and somewhere below all that, when he searches for it, the faint but telling scent of recently snaked pipes.

New floor looks good, he says. New floor looks *great*, Pat agrees. And they did a helluva nice job in the kitchen too, I might add. It's higher now though hey, Chris says, and Pat says, What's higher. The floor's higher. It is? Sure it is. There's no step down at the door anymore, Chris says, and Pat risks a quick glance towards the front door. Well I'll be damned, he says with clearly mitigated interest, returning at once to the big screen where the castaway, thanks in large part to this large red-clad lifeguard, appears to be coming along rather swimmingly.

Pat asks how high they raised it then. Well to the level of the flood, he's told. One step. They raised it that one step. But rest assured, Pat, the other stuff's still down there. The old floor, or rather, the old foundation, it's all still down there. Well below the watermark, in other words.

Back at *Black Beach Patrol V*, a particularly sallow and lanky candidate, climbing aboard an altogether obliging lifeguard, begins his tour of her shuddering abundance with workmanlike efficiency yet gentlemanly aplomb.

Pat asks if he's been down to see that whale yet. No, Pat. You? Sure, Pat says. That sucker's *huge*, dude. Got a picture too, I bet, Chris says, and Pat says actually he got a few. Got this great one of me and the kids. Tried to get one with the wife too, but the batteries in the remote, hey, they went dead. Too bad, Chris says, and Pat says, Yeah, too bad. So then I guess you got one of the wife and the kids, eh Pat? You know what? says Pat. I totally forgot.

Apparently inexhaustible, yet finished with the first leg of his tour, the lanky castaway succumbs to his lifeguard's seemingly all too abrasive ambition, but not before waving a fraternal hand to an approaching pal. And into this fascinating mix Chris finally introduces his beer bottle.

What's that? says Pat, and Chris says, That, my friend, is a Sleeman bottle. So? So you see that raised emblem of a beaver there? Well *that's* their label. Interesting, says Pat. Yes it is, Pat. It is interesting. What's more though, "Sleeman" is actually a nickname I was given years ago by this guy I worked with at the Unicorn downtown. Guy's name was Hum. At least that's what everybody called him. Now this guy Hum, he was an actor by choice, and a waiter by necessity of course—

Again, very interesting, says Pat, clinging stubbornly to the big screen where events continue to unfold at an incredibly rapid, incredibly un-porn-like pace. One husky young fellow happens upon one young lady, and together they happen upon another young lady, and eventually all three get together with yet another young lady for phoney cocktails and phonier conversation before the rest of the sexual drudgery inevitably takes place.

But the problem with the Unicorn, Pat, was that it was known as a "destination" restaurant. What this means of course is that it wasn't considered in any way convenient to get to. And it wasn't either, to tell you the truth. In fact it was way out in the middle of nowhere. But things being as they were in those days, and being as Hum and I eventually formed the bulk of a very weak management team, it naturally fell to ol' Sleeman here to try to come up with new and intriguing ways to get the customers in.

Their management meeting having hit a lull, they continue to watch the big screen a while.

So how'd it do? How'd what do? This Unicorn place you and this Hum guy worked at, says Pat, taking, it would seem, a slightly more than passing interest. Not very well to be honest, he's told. The place sucked at best. But then not simply because it was a destination restaurant either. Hell, every restaurant's a destination when you think about it; otherwise no one'd go there. A person can get food and drink anywhere, Pat. Hell, he can get it at home for Christ's sake. What he's looking for is ambiance. *Romance.* Much like what they're witnessing here, Chris suggests. By which he means of course the big screen, where two young women who, to this point at least, have been little more than perfunctorily introduced, begin jettisoning each other's bikinis in an orgy of cheerful interest and slightly disturbing self-indulgence.

But then do the people arrive for the dining experience? Or does the dining experience arise out of the arrival of people? One thing's for sure, nothing attracts a crowd like a crowd—yes, it's all chickens and eggs, this deal. What we need then are some more customers to partake of our fine chicken and eggs meals. But then that's the problem isn't it, Pat. As a restaurant, the ol' Crap & Swill here is very much a *non*-destination, as it were.

For a brief but dramatic moment the prep cook appears framed in the kitchen doorway, perhaps to ask a question, perhaps not, before spying the overabundance of sexual activity on the big screen and quietly scurrying off.

Christ, that's impressive though, Pat. It really is. But then an old porn buff like yourself's seen some fairly big hammers in his time, I'm guessing. Speaking of which, my brother was in the navy for the longest time, and boy can *he* tell you some stories, hey.

Take this one time, Chris says. My brother's got this little Seaman under him named Sutcliffe. Well Seaman Sutcliffe was very shy, understand, very reserved, and stayed that way for the longest time—that is, until she finally got promoted to Petty Officer and started hanging out with these other Petty Officers, sick bastards that *they* are, understand. Well then things started to change. And so, to make a long story short, my brother goes down to the infirmary to get some shots. He's quite a high-ranking officer, see, so I take it they're giving him vaccinations all the time.

Anyway, there he is, my brother, about to receive his two shots—God knows what for—one from each Petty Officer (these two bastards, they're black as hell of course), and the one black bastard says, "Would you like a Sutcliffe, Captain?" and my brother says, "A Sutcliffe? What the hell's a Sutcliffe, soldier?" and the other black bastard says, "Why, sir, that's two pricks at once."

Yeah ain't it wonderful? says Pat, gazing up at the big screen where one petite young woman, already occupied with one enormous male specimen, insinuates with a cagey gesture that she would in fact like this other large Speedo-clad buck jogging by to join in on the festivities here.

Now, with only three hours remaining prior to reopening, he contemplates heading up the hill to the gym, but not before asking Pat to please ensure Lisa wipes down all the tables and chairs and places ketchup bottles on all the tables when she comes in. Pat inquires as to whether the patio is to be opened, and glancing out the windows at the light drizzle he says no, he doesn't think so, not yet. Then he heads east on the ocean side of Marine Drive, cutting across the bluff at the makeshift bus stop memorial to mount the concrete stairs three at a time.

Up top of the stairs, moving along the back alley towards the house, he notices, smoking a cigarette on the bedroom deck, a curiously paste-faced reflection of himself.

What's that smeared all over your face, Capt'n? he says, and the face says, Don't call me that. You know I don't like when you call me that. All right, what's that smeared all over your face, Jeff. Why, Preparation H of course, Jeff says. So, Chris sighs, why is it you have Preparation H smeared all over your face, Jeff. Well if you must know, Jeff says, I find said product good for the skin. And as you know, a good clean hide has always been a hallmark of mine.

Together they turn to contemplate the vast, grey, wave-wrinkled bay opening up to the south.

Chris asks about the pigeons. What about the pigeons? Well are there any in, say, the barbeque perhaps? Not anymore, no, he's told. Jeff chased these two bastards out like an hour ago. But you know that chicken was for you, Jeff, not the seagulls. You shouldn't have thrown it out. Yes, says Jeff, but I really like the sound meat makes when it hits the ground.

Jeff stands there, arranging his face in rare geometries, sucking the cigarette down to its filter with a rapid series of hard punishing drags. Then he stabs it out on the lid of the barbeque and crushes the remnants under the toe of his moccasin.

Pull your chin in, Jeff. It is in, Jeff insists. No, it's not, Jeff. Now pull your chin in—that's it. And having retracted his chin from its familiar forward-thrust position, Jeff promptly offers him the finger, his one dilapidated moccasin listing dangerously to the left before stabilizing, more or less, once again.

Chris asks if Penelope's been by yet, and Jeff says no, but Detective Dinallo was. At least that's who he assumes it was. As he recalls, there was Preparation H in his eyes at the time. That said, he prepares to light another cigarette, but not before propelling his glasses back up the paste-glazed bridge of his nose with the same finger still deployed in Chris's direction.

So what'd the good detective have to say, Jeff? Nothing, Jeff says. No thing. Other than the fact that he had absolutely nothing new to say, that is. He was very solemn actually. Almost . . . Christ-like. But then there ain't no big thing being Jesus, brother. We're all just speak. King he. Brew anyhow.

Chris steps around to the east side of the house to take a seat near the top of the stairs. Soon Cojimar comes rolling along, evidently intent on head-butting his shin with whatever force it takes in order to get her point across somehow. And so, taking up the old curved-straw monstrosity of a broom stationed near the door, he provides the bulk of her coat some aggressive and much needed housework, particularly up around the neck and shoulders, leaving her toppled over in a purring docility of sorts. Eventually the flower delivery man arrives, bringing an abrupt end to this absurd chore.

Good morning, says the man. Good morning, that was quick, Chris replies, taking the flowers from the man's outstretched hand. The man smiles, checks his files, and moments later stumbles back along the deck and out into the front yard in the custody of one very large, exceedingly flirtatious, broom-groomed feline tart.

Inside it's quiet, and dark, and not wanting to make too much noise, he takes a moment to experiment with several strategic deployments of the flowers. He takes a rose from the box and places it next to a candle on the coffee table. Then he places another rose next to another candle, and another—but then that just strikes him as utterly contrived. The entire sentiment seems rather stupid, let alone counterfeit in his eyes. And so, noting the absence of any particular cancer flower, he gathers up the roses from around the living room and stuffs them as one tangled mass into the kitchen sink garbage disposal.

He grabs the laundry and scrapes up some detergent, but first makes a note on a small two-by-three inch card—

Ain't no big thing being Jesus, brother. We're all just speaking Hebrew anyhow.

—and places it under one of the lamps. He glances around at the other cards stored here and there in the same shoddy system of organization, then chooses one at random—

Dear Mr Needham,

Thank you for going underwater for us. My favorite part was when you put a starfish on your head and then we said there's a starfish on your head and you said there's no starfish on my head and then you said to Mrs Needham is there a starfish on my head and she said probably and then you said you gies are lieing and then you felt your head and took it off.

Lori, *Grade 3*

—and replaces it under its lamp. Then he takes the quilt from the couch and removes its cover, at which point he notices a few black hairs still attached. Carefully, and with a great deal of ceremony, he gathers up each separate strand, placing them together with the others in the designated vase and then, laundry tub in hand, walks out and around to the west side of the house where, for whatever reason, the laundry room is housed. Jeff is there, having seemingly appeared from nowhere, setting out some dishes for the cat. Cojimar's brunch today appearing to consist of the usual bowl of beer accompanied by some rather stale looking cabbage rolls and sauce.

After starting the laundry he heads uptown to the gym, cutting north up Fir Street then left and west along Buena Vista to find a blind woman teetering towards him on the street. And trying his best to avoid her, he somehow manages to avoid his way right into her, stumbling along and past in a silent lunge *to back up, but I can't back up, as there's no longer any room available behind us.*

Sweet Jesus, she gasps, covering her mouth with her hand, appearing more like her mother at this very moment than she ever has in her life. And he's coming on fairly hard now, his cane beating a rigid path, and

the only thing left to do is sit and wince and await the inevitable impact.
Suddenly she starts to shriek with laughter—lo and behold, she's crying
now—and the cane beats closer, and her laughter rises higher, and in the
*end the blind man smacks square into our right front fend*ing for herself, the somewhat shaken, slightly amused blind woman taps off
towards some distant and indefinite goal.

Finding Katie at the gym, he sneaks up from behind to take a
seat at the bench alongside.

Hello there, Katie.

She has two dumbbells, one in each hand, and presses them up
over her head.

Hello there, he repeats just as she drops both dumbbells to the
black-matted floor, resting a moment between sets to rub and
stretch her surprisingly muscular shoulders. Watching her via the
mirror with something like spectator's interest, he at length
observes that of late he seems to have developed this rather nasty
reputation of always pulling the plug on their plans. In response, she
hoists the dumbbells again, first the one and then the other, lifting
them up over her head in a strong, smooth, exceptionally controlled
motion, managing to snub him completely in just this manner.

And, he says, for the most part at least, I feel this accusation is
somewhat unfounded. Now perhaps I should have shown up at
the theatre last night like I said I would, but then let's not be the
kind of couple that lets our spouses come between us.

Katie dumps the dumbbells onto the rubber-matted floor and
proceeds to stretch her neck. Finally she sits up straight on the end
of the bench and issues a long resonant sigh at her own tired tus-
sled reflection.

Eventually she gathers up the dumbbells again and proceeds to
elevate them over her head. I had my tarot cards read, she says. And?
And—this according to the cards anyway—I've apparently got a lot
of pent-up aggression. Yeah it appears as though I've got a lot of
anger, she says, and apparently I don't always deal with it so well—
I'm confrontational, in a sense. Like lashing out at errant husbands
perhaps, he suggests. Something like that, yeah, she admits.

Katie asks about the bar, so he tells her about the bar, explaining yet again how the Trap & Gill is not a bar at all but a

restaurant, despite the fact they run it like a pub of sorts. She rolls her eyes at that, so he tells her that, all kidding aside, the new floor looks good, and the old tables look good, and that it will be good to get back at it, even though they both know this is a lie.

Performing another quick set of shoulder presses, she tells him she saw him talking to his wife earlier. She did? Where? At his bench, she says. Down at the beach. And what, pray tell, was young Katie doing down at the beach so early, hmm? Thinking of killing myself, she admits. How come? he asks. Because I think it's something I'd like to try, she says. I think I'd be rather good at it. I'm finding the whole idea of non-existence pretty appealing of late.

Anyway, she says, there she was, at the beach, contemplating killing herself, when she saw him talking to his wife. You were talking, she says. To your wife. Yes, well, a husband's known to do that sometimes, he says, and she regards him loathingly a moment before launching into another quick set of spiteful presses, appearing as though she might not mind impressing those weights on him at some point.

Actually, he says, I tried to kill myself last night. Tried? she says. What happened, didn't take? Didn't take, he says, and she nods knowingly. So then here you are, she says, and he says, So here I am. Not training today, Chris? Not today, Katie. No calluses, see? he says, showing her his ruined hands. I see you're still wearing your wedding ring though, she says, and he says yes, he finds it's kind of like a hair shirt. A hair what? Shirt, Katie. It's a religious torture device. Sort of like you, in other words.

She chuckles quietly at that, and so he makes sure to chuckle back, settling in to check over his face in the mirror, or more accurately, the new crop of pimples surfacing in the middle of his forehead here. He holds his breath until his face turns red and in turn the pimples all but disappear.

Thinking of having a little housewarming party this weekend, she says, and he says oh so she found a place? Yeah, that house on Buena Vista she told him about, she says, and he says well that's great, he looks forward to seeing it. Yeah she'll probably be dead by then, she sniffs.

Holding his nose and blowing steadily, he stares at his redden-
ing face in the mirror.

What, may I ask, are you trying to accomplish exactly? says
Katie, and he says, What do you mean? Why are you holding your
nose like that? she asks. Well if you must know, I'm blowing air
into my ears via my Eustachian tubes, he answers. Well of course
you are, she says. But *why*. Why? Well for purposes of equalization
of course, she's told. You know, Katie, you could try acting a little
less indignant all the time. Hey, you're the one who insisted I was
"getting too attached," she retorts.

He holds his nose and blows gently into his ears, verifying his
technique in the mirror. It's important to maintain a steady
rhythm of breathing, Katie. No, never stop breathing, they say.
After all, it's not intended as exercise but as relaxation. Stop me if
I'm garnering too much attention though, he says.

Katie finishes her exercises and takes her leave but, for the
moment anyway, he remains behind, watching an overly aggressive gentleman attempt to toughen up an overly gelatinous
teenaged son. Eventually, though, no longer able to endure such
spectacle, he races outside to request a ride in the Robert Blake.
Katie drags a small hand through her hair and grudgingly agrees,
but only if they stop by her old house first for her pot supply.

And later, sitting in her blue Beretta outside her old house,
when she offers him a quick invitation inside, he says, You know
I would—in a second I would—but I'm just not sure I'm ready
to put my marriage on hold just now. Clearly all people in your
situation have to move on eventually, she says, and so he calls her
a home-wrecker, and not for the first time, I might add.

Oh must you? she says, and he says what? Must he what? This,
she says. Must you do *this*. It's not even funny. No, you know
what? Fucking tragic's what it is. You're right, Katie. It is fucking
tragic. And what's worse, I'm pretty sure I've got AIDS.

Visibly frustrated, Katie shakes her head and looks outside to
where a cloud of low-lying fog comes creeping up the hillside.

No, but listen, Katie. It just so happens I've been hearing an
awful lot about AIDS again of late, non-stop in fact, so that I think
that perhaps something—or some*one*—is trying to send me a

message. If indeed such a thing's possible at all. Oh, she says, it's possible all right.

Listen though, he says. I was reading this book just the other day, and one of the characters had AIDS. At least I think she did, although of course it was rather difficult to tell, the book itself having been written not all that well, and this particular character, into the plot at least, having failed to make any significant headway at all. But then doesn't Magic Johnson still have AIDS? Or HIV? Well doesn't he? And then I hear on the news just last week how Seattle's got something like nine new cases, and then immediately afterwards they just happen to insert it into the storyline on *ER* as well. The reason it hits me now, though, is that I'm suddenly starting to break out with all these festering open sores. Now perhaps I'm just being unduly paranoid here, and to be honest, I really haven't the faintest idea if a sudden rash of forehead acne is even a symptom of AIDS—I rather doubt it actually—but then you never really know do you? Well I never know anyway.

Katie knits her brows together, triggering the corresponding muscles to fashion themselves into a nearly perfect set of pursed lips. Look, he says, I'm trying to protect you from a very deadly STD here. Oh sure you are, she says. Clearly you're almost, what, celibate these days. What's that supposed to mean? he asks, but she only shrugs in answer, higher lips pursing further, a pucker of reproach aimed exclusively at him.

Check it out, he says, directing her attention to a large grey squirrel bounding its way across the street, taking advantage of this distraction and the subsequent break in Katie's usually impenetrable defence to reach over and massage her forehead with a thumb.

Hey, can you drop me off at the blood donor clinic? he asks as she abruptly returns her attention his way, causing him to abandon his thumb's quest for her forehead and reluctantly massage his own instead. Blood donor clinic? she says. Why the *blood* donor clinic? Well on the off chance I don't have AIDS, he says, I might as well donate a pint to those who need it.

Finished with the massage, he holds his nose and blows gently a while. At length he says, Hum, though, he goes for these STD

checks all the time. Don't, she says. He does though, Chris says.
Take the time I set him up with this waitress—

Don't, Chris. Please. Just don't.

—who just happened to be a car thief on the side, he says. Or
at least she had been previous to me. I saved her, see. Yes, I'm a
regular saint these days apparently, he goes on as Katie moans,
slow and tortured, and lowers her face into her hands, defeated.

But then she was quite cute, and blonde, with a pierced nipple
to boot, and she had these great big teeth that worried you till
you knew her, then worried you all the more after that. And yet
they seemed so completely natural and beautiful that he couldn't
help but want to kiss her that night. This despite the fact she'd just
recently returned from Waikiki where she'd managed to burn
herself so severely that he was afraid just kissing her might facilitate the deposit of some rather large chunks of lip in his mouth.

I really don't want to hear this right now, she says, studying the
squirrel, so he says, But listen, it gets better—so out she came
drinking one night. And I could tell she wanted to sleep with
someone—anyone—and since she was sporting these great big
chompers I wasn't about to risk my person in any way, not to
mention the fact I was feeling particularly married that night. And
so what I did was, I pawned her off on my old pal, Hum. All quite
decent of me, if I do say so myself, even if, to be honest, I did have
other, more personal plans in mind. Well maybe you should have
said something, she says, and he says, Well maybe I should have.
But then there we are, the three of us, out at this club and afterwards, walking along, when all of a sudden we arrive at this cross-
roads of sorts, so off I go and jump in this dumpster. This being
my gorgeous exit of course. It was either that or renege my marriage, and understand, I was in no shape to say no at this point.

Anyway, so off I go and jump in this dumpster. You know, just
to see what all the fuss is about. I was forever seeing people div-
ing into dumpsters in those days, and so I got to wondering just
what the attraction was. Turns out it's all just a lot of garbage of
course, but then you never really know until you try it for yourself. Presumption being too much of an intellectual leap at this
point, she says, and he says, Yeah way too much.

So anyway, there I am, literally down in the dumps, while off wanders Hum with the car thief. And the next morning of course he gets all paranoid because he never gloved up, and so off he goes to get his usual bevy of sexually transmitted disease tests done. He did *not*, Katie says, and Chris says, He did *so*. Don't be offended though, because I tell you what, Hum goes for those STD tests all the time. He does? Oh sure he does. But then Hum and I are no longer friends of course. Not that that's any big surprise.

Looking closely at his hands, he slides his thumbs back and forth across the cratered remains of callus as a stout young couple comes lumbering on past and down the hill, moving steadily in the direction of the whale, scaring the returning squirrel back into hiding with their clothes billowing out about them like sails in the suddenly turbulent air.

Now he doesn't want to discuss Hum any further, as he's already made his views on the bastard quite clear, and in truth he'd rather avoid any further pigeonholing here, but he will say that it's got to be awfully damned difficult establishing any sort of concrete reality when one's entire occupation is based solely on the fabri-*ca*tion of reality, and really who *does*n't take their work home with them anymore.

Katie inspects her cuticles carefully. Fuck me, there's a freckle on my finger, she observes idly.

Not that I take issue with his actual roles themselves, he goes on. No, it just seems to me that if you want to portray, say, a washed-up, drugged-up, former child star onscreen, well then why not get an actual washed-up, drugged-up, former child star to play the goddamned scene. Christ, there's enough of them out there, so pick one. Pick any one. Pick that one that looks like Hum for all I care. Hey, the acting itself might not be all that impressive, but then again, Hum's isn't all that impressive either.

God, you sound just like *Sid*, Katie says, dropping her hands to her lap and glancing impatiently about. Hurry up, she tells the large grey squirrel now bounding its way back across the street in triumph. I have to tell you, though, I really *like* squirrels, she says. How about you, Chris? You like squirrels? Man, I just love squir-rels. But then what's the deal with their tails? Seriously, though,

they're like all tail. And hips. Rather like me, she smiles suggestively, although she still doesn't seem entirely willing to forgive
him just yet.

Thursday, 9:11 am

Before leaving the Beretta, Katie wants to kiss him, but he only
wants to kiss her, just once and on the cheek, and so she lets him,
albeit grudgingly, before insisting that he leave.

Inside, at the reception desk, a nurse greets him with a shallow
shop-worn smile, taking his card and blood sample before handing over his hefty file. He steps over to the appropriate cubicle to
review the literature. There is a lot of literature. But still he
reviews it all. And finally he wanders over to the waiting room to
take a seat alongside an elderly woman deeply absorbed with the
television there.

What's this then? he asks. This is "Canada's Hockey Heroes," she
tells him, and a little later a lab-coated nurse cruising through the
area stops alongside the television to ask whether everything's all
right. Are you sure? she says, directing her attention exclusively at
Chris this time, and he says he's fine, why? You look, I don't know,
upset, she says, and he says oh that. He always cries when
Henderson scores.

He asks the nurse if she'd mind getting him some peach
drink, and while she does get him some peach drink, he never
actually gets to drink it, as, in the interim, another nurse comes
cruising along, this one escorting him into a room a little further along, where she runs him through a series of tough, altogether embarrassing questions *in bed in the emergency room listening to some junky lash out against security in the next stall over, and
of course we can't see the television, as there is no television, and so she
sends me running out to the lounge every five minutes or so to check
on the score.*

*What's happening? she asks upon one late third period return, and I
tell her, Not much. They're double-shifting Yzerman and Shanahan
though. They are, huh, she says. Well good for them. I mean hey, given the
chance, I'd double-shift Yzerman and Shanahan myself* had sexual
intercourse with another man since 1977? she says, and he says no.

Have you ever lived in, or were you born in the Congo? she says, and he says he doesn't think so, no. Have you ever had sexual intercourse with any person who has lived in or was born in the Congo? she says, and he says not that he's aware of, no. And so she takes him firmly by the hand and tells him that there's one more form to fill out, a new procedure, she explains, one last precaution to ensure the safety and security of all those involved herein. And just prior to leaving the room she hands him a piece of paper that tells him to:

READ THIS

■ Each unit of blood is tested for the AIDS virus, but the test isn't perfect.

■ If you've done something that could put the AIDS virus into your blood, you could give AIDS to someone else, even if your blood test for AIDS is negative.

■ Read the following sentences. If one of them is true for you, you *must* choose the NO sticker so that you can tell us secretly that we shouldn't use your blood.

■ There's a chance that I have the AIDS virus.

■ I've come to be tested for the AIDS virus.

■ I think I shouldn't give blood but I feel pressured into giving blood.

■ I wonder if I might have AIDS.

He chooses the *Yes, use my blood* sticker at the bottom of the page and attaches it to the accompanying form. And a few seconds later the nurse returns, escorting him out to the brightly lit room at the far end of the hall and into a large reclining chair smelling of someone's outdated cologne and, somewhere below that, a recent application of pine freshener. Beside him reclines a diminutive old man, performing his civic duty with heartbreaking seriousness.

Nice to see, the old man says, and Chris says, What's that, sir? Nice to see a young fellow like you in here, the old man says, gazing in Chris's general direction but by no means directly at him. Well thank you, sir, Chris says as the old man closes his eyes against the oppressive glare of overhead lights. Soon another nurse comes plodding along, and begins preparing Chris's arm with iodine.

A little later, holding his nose and blowing gently out his Eustachian tubes, Chris asks the old man if he's in town to see the whale, and the old man says, No, I live here. And you? You bet! says Chris, to which the old man says *Jesus!* while staggering sideways in his chair, looking to the nurse for some—any—sort of support here. You young fellows got no class in you.

Telling them both to relax, and Chris to form a fist, the nurse says this might sting a little. What do you mean, Chris asks the old man once the nurse has successfully penetrated his vein. She smells almost exclusively of Burt's Bees Hand Salve, a longstanding favourite of mine, and so he leans in closer in order to better breathe her in. I mean get that fucking thing outta here, says the old man, knitting his brows together in what is, for a man his age, a firm and impressive display of ferocity. Listen, boy, I'm a retiree. A *real* retiree. Just get that fucking thing outta here. Decent people shouldn't have to look at a thing like that. Shouldn't *want* to look at a thing like that. That carcass constitutes an albatross around here.

Having taped the metal drain to Chris's arm, the Burt's Bees nurse probes affectionately at her handiwork. Well *I* think it's good, she says, smiling provocatively at the arm, and the old man says, *What*? Absolutely, Carl. It's good for tourism. Oh sure, Carl tells her, turning away from this latest in a long unbroken line of blood clinic betrayals. They might consider dragging one up every year.

His eyes still closed, the corrugation of his brow swelling ever further, the neighbouring muscles of Carl's forehead contract to form a nearly perfect omega symbol. And so naturally Chris stretches across the void in hopes of massaging it a little. Unfortunately the distance proves a little too great, and the symbol gradually disappears.

Once the nurse has finished her preparations, Carl opens his pale blue eyes and states wearily to the ceiling, You young people have no respect for a fellow living creature's dignity is all.

Soon the nurse returns—actually a new nurse this time, smelling of nothing so much as Vaseline and iodine—and inspects her colleague's work. And so Chris takes the opportunity to mention, on the sly, that while this nice old Carl fellow beside him here seems rational enough, at times he appears to be drifting a little. She nods knowingly.

Carl? she says. Eyes shut firmly, Carl tries desperately to ignore her, occasioning the omega symbol to emerge ever so briefly before subsiding all too rapidly once more. Carl? the nurse repeats, shaking his shoulder a little. Jesus, what? barks Carl, omega materializing beautifully, even transcendently, occasioning Chris's thumb to launch out in desperate need of bridging that gap between them, only to fall a few inches short of its goal.

The nurse retracts her chin into the folds of her fleshy throat, and frowns. She just wanted to make sure everything's all right, that's all. Everything's fine, Carl tells her. Christ, why wouldn't it be fine. Just hurry up and get me the hell outta here. Place is a goddamned gong show half the time.

Chris takes the opportunity to inquire of yet another nurse wandering by if only old folks give blood these days. No, not only, he's told. That Carl there, though, he's given blood over three hundred times now. Three *hundred*? he says. Wow, that's a lot. Sure is, she says. Carl's a regular little *dizzy, and so she excuses herself to the washroom and later, when the waitress comes running up to ask if that's my wife passed out in a pool of her own urine in the hallway, I know for sure that it'll be her right away. I mean I know right away that it's going to be Annie I find.*

Pausing, I look out the window and up towards the bus stop. Jesus, I say, is any of this even relevant? It's all relevant, he tells me while pivoting slowly to his right, momentarily immersing himself in the plight of Lisa's two young daughters currently struggling over a single cold French fry. Slowly he pivots back.

So anyway, I say, I squat down to lift her in my arms, and that's when I feel the rear of my pants give way. Yeah, exactly. Just compounding the problem, you might say. And so there we are, her brother and I, lugging her half-conscious through the restaurant to the taxi out front, me with the ass of my pants ripped out and Annie's all full of piss of course. And so, to make a long story short, we eventually wheel her into the emergency room at the hospital where they conduct a long series of tests, the results

of which suggest some sort of spasm of something called the vagus nerve,
and so of course we refer to it as the Las Vagus Incident after that.

I pause again, waiting for him to laugh, and when he doesn't laugh, I
continue on with the story, And yet it could've easily been a symptom of
something worse, as in retrospect it in all likelihood was, I guess a woman
in a wheelchair glides by the window without any legs to speak
of, while far overhead, sagging limply amid the nearly naked
branches of an elm tree, the last remnants of an old bird's nest
finally disintegrate *unlike the Las Vegas Incident, in which we book in*
at the old Sands hotel, the one that doesn't even exist anymore, and not
even the real hotel itself but this low-level shack out back, when without
warning she decides to call up this stripper. You know, as if that were sim-
ply the right thing to do for a young couple on this their first of many trips
abroad together. Now this stripper, I take it she was a prostitute? he says,
and I say well of course she was a prostitute. I mean hey, it's Vegas, right?

Dinallo scribbles something in his notepad, then tells me to go on, so I
tell him how this stripper or prostitute or whatever she was did come up,
all ninety some-odd pounds of her, and proceeded to put on quite a show
while we got drunk on Malibu as, like I said, we were still fairly young
at this point too. What the fuck are they fighting over now, I say to Lisa
as her still quarrelling daughters appear about ready to drink tepid
peach drink and eat stale Oreos.

So you see, lady, I'm sorry. I'm sorry because it's not really the
kind of story that you should be telling. Not to the cop investigat-
ing your wife's case anyway. No, not to a cop and never to be
funny—although I suppose I just wasn't thinking back then. Or
maybe I was thinking, he says. Yeah, thinking it might get me some
more sympathy in some way. You know, like some sort of trophy
or war wound by association. Yeah, a real badge of courage, hey.

Standing leadenly on the opposite side of the table, a slender but
serviceable audience of one, the elderly candy striper fixes her
eyes on his before closing in quickly to urge yet another paper
cup of peach drink into his hand. She says, Now this one here's
from my own private still way up on yonder hill—my own
private stock, mind you, and more, you can drive on this stuff
too—so I'd appreciate it if you'd have at least three, or are you the
type of boy who only likes two? tirelessly repeating this nifty bit

of blood clinic rhetoric for each new arrival, including Carl, that nice old man who nearly overwhelmed him earlier with his dignity, his generosity, and his compassion.

Thursday, 10:24 am

Chris returns to the Trap & Gill to find, on the patio, Wendy standing languidly astride her ten-speed, hovering threateningly about her knees a large loosely-leashed dog of frightening and indeterminate breed.

Who's that in there watching TV, Wendy wants to know, jerking her considerable chin at the window. That's Pat, she's told. Chris's kitchen manager. But what's he *watch*ing though? Chris isn't sure. Probably black people having sex though.

Chris turns to acknowledge Wendy's four-legged friend. So this must be Eddie, he says, reaching down to pat the dog. Unfortunately Eddie growls, forcing him to rethink their relationship a little.

Easy boy, Wendy says in what seems to Chris an altogether lame attempt at pacifying an obviously ill-tempered animal. She shifts forward on her ten-speed to cup hands to face and prop the entire assembly up against the window. Who's the chick? she says, and he says, Lisa. I don't like Lisa. How come? she says, and he says, Oh various reasons, I guess. Including the fact she's the first person I borrowed money from when I first took over this place. As a waitress, he explains, Lisa's been classically trained—meaning, of course, that she has not—but she's learned to compensate for her lack of technical knowledge with years of dedicated service, and he supposes that for most of their clientele that's been more than just enough. Regardless, he says, she's toast. That is, as soon as I concoct some semi-legitimate reason why she ought not to be employed here anymore.

A pigeon probes enterprisingly, if recklessly, within striking distance of Eddie, managing to make it safely out of range by the time its presence is detected in the periphery.

Wow, his eyes are *glued*, Wendy says, watching Pat watching porn. So, been down to see the whale yet? she asks, having finally disengaged from the glass, and he says no, he hasn't. And nice sweater by the way. Indian sweater, Wendy says, pleased with both her sweater and herself evidently. Should've seen ol' Eddie here tear into that whale though, she goes on, reaching down to affectionately scratch Eddie's dark, muscular, shorthaired shoulder. Thought a big ol' seafood smorgasbord just washed right up on shore for ya, didn't ya, boy.

Chris doesn't bother to reply. Whole seconds tick by. And finally: Wendy? Yes, Chris? You know our patio isn't open yet, he says, and she says, It isn't? No it isn't, he says. But we'll be open inside in about thirty minutes if you're interested. Of course you can't bring your bike in. Or your horse here for that matter.

Eddie stands alertly alongside Wendy's ten-speed, blinking occasionally, breathing in a relaxed subdued way, nothing less than a solitary member of his mixed race standing alone in the middle of all the closed patios in the world against managers, this one especially. Chris takes one more measured step back as Eddie leans forward to sniff his crotch—unsuccessfully, it turns out, thanks in large part to this otherwise inadequate looking leash.

So, she says, the Beasleys. What about the Beasleys. Well all the girls they've got working here are white, she says, and he says, Not all, but some, you're right.

Wendy nods, then leans down to scratch the flank of her side-sprawling dog. Krishna working today? she asks, and he says, Actually she's working tonight. Why, do you know her? *Of* her, sure, absolutely, Wendy says. Everybody does.

Eagerly bouncing the front wheel of her ten-speed up and down, Wendy focuses her attention exclusively on Eddie presently spread-eagled across the patio. She heard Krishna was the one who found that Chinese girl up at the bus stop there, she says. She heard Krishna actually held the girl's hand while she died. Well, he says, you heard right.

He gazes out the length of the pier to the small collection of boats bobbing about the breakwater. He turns to leave, but Wendy catches him by the sleeve. Now Krishna, that's like a Hindu name, no? she says, and he says, That's right. Strange that a white girl would have herself a Hindu name, she says, and he says, Yes, well, her parents were hippies no doubt.

Eventually he escapes through the door and back into the office to change into his manager's garb, applying an exorbitant amount of my Lady Speed Stick to compensate for the shower he skipped this morning. A moment later Lisa leans in to inform him that Detective Dinallo stopped by and, more importantly, in her eyes anyway, that Aimee just called in sick for the day as well. But then Laura might be willing to work the lunch, she suggests before his lips can properly formulate the word "bitch." He tells Lisa thanks, and that the entire Trap & Gill management team would be much obliged if she could find it in her heart to give Laura a call for noon.

Are there any garnishes? she asks once he returns out front, frowning at what she evidently perceives to be the sorry state of the service bar. What the hell, Lisa. What the hell. Hey I was just wondering, she says, so he says, Well give me a chance for fuck's sake, I just got here.

Harvesting some lesion-covered lemons and limes from the cooler, he checks the date on a carton of milk, takes a sniff and consequently gags, then tosses the carton into the nearest trash-can—the milk makes a sickeningly thick solid sound when it lands. Next he retrieves the knife and cutting board from beneath the bar and cuts up enough garnishes to get him through the day, the night and, hopefully at least, most of tomorrow as well.

Taking a well-deserved break from the big screen, Pat steps up to the bar for a Coke. Fuck, you must get tired of cutting fruit, he says. Yes, I do, Chris says. I mean if there's one thing that kills me about this business, it's morning prep, Pat says idly and remarkably without the slightest hint of irony. And stocking up the cooler. And wiping down the menus. And—

Ketchup bottles, Lisa suggests. Yeah, ketchup bottles, Pat says, scrutinizing something scratched from his beard. Ketchup bottles have to be the worst. You know I once had to fire a girl because she refused to refill the ketchup bottles? Not that I blamed her of course. There are some things I refuse to do in this business myself—like cleaning up puke for instance. If there's one thing I won't do it's clean up another man's puke. Or his shit. Actually, I can recall at least three jobs I've lost solely on the grounds that I refused to clean up some fucker's—

We get it, Pat, thanks, Chris interrupts, and Pat falls silent a moment, watching closely as he dissects a lime into eight more or less *complaining all the time, I say, and she says she doesn't complain all the time. All she's saying is that lately I've been mailing it in. Mailing it in? Yeah, it's like I service her just so that she'll be obligated to service me. It's not like that, Annie, you know that. It's never been like that. Oh don't Annie me, she says. Having long ago abandoned all sense of the romantic, she insists I now put forth the absolute minimum amount of effort to achieve my own sexual satisf*act, she's tried to dismiss these rare occurrences as just that, as simply rare meaningless moments in life, but then if you aren't careful, as time goes by and these seemingly meaningless moments string themselves together one after another, what begins to evolve is a somewhat meaningless life. And she's dead-set against the meaningless life. Dead-set. In fact she's decided to live an extraordinary life. And she will too, she says, just as soon as she's discovered what it is she's going to be extraordinary at. Here it comes, Lisa says, and together they turn to watch the train come sliding up from the east one car after another, first the one car sliding and then the next car sliding, then the rest of the cars sliding together.

Thursday, 1:49 pm

After a quiet lunch he heads back up the hill for home, pausing a moment at the bottom of the driveway, unable to face the massive effort of confronting Jeff again just now. To his relief, though, Jeff is not around. However, Cojimar is, and so he scratches her chin a while before offering the property a comprehensive pigeon inspection, finding in the base of the barbeque, as per usual, the guano and gathered-stick beginnings of a recently commenced nest. What a mess. And so he sweeps the sticks out with his foot, sending the two pigeons responsible flapping off to the roof next door, at which point he attends to the laundry, which Jeff has already placed in the dryer by now. And so, pile of wrinkled dry laundry in hand, he plods around to the east side of the house, stopping just long enough to pull the cat's tail before bounding up the stairs and inside.

Returning to the bedroom a few minutes later, I notice immediately that the bathroom door is closed. Everything all right in there, I ask, but no one answers. I definitely hear a tap though. Everything all right in there, I ask again, forced to raise my voice for the door, reminiscent of countless conversations undertaken in the last couple of months or so. Need anything, Chris? Nope, he answers eventually, way down deep and nearly out of range altogether.

I ask how it went today. As expected, I'm told. Not too busy. Some of the regulars were in though. Joe? No, no Joe. Joe's barred. Sid popped in for a moment though. Sid, I say, and he says, Sidney. You know, Sidney Shapiro. Citizen Sid. Oh *that* Sid, I say.

I flop down onto the bed alongside the wrinkled dry pile of laundry, causing a single white sock to fall to the floor. Staring down at the sock, I toe it here and there across the hardwood floor.

He's not *that* bad, he says, and I say, No, you're right—he's not that bad—certainly thinks a lot of himself though.

I reach down to pick up the sock and, holding it aloft, push the remainder of the laundry to the floor. When I tell him that detective came by again, he says, Dinallo? And? And he told me to tell you he's going to be away the next few days, I say. Told me he wanted to tell you himself, but that he can't seem to track you down these days.

Still fixated on this one sock suspended small, white and feminine before me, eventually I place it aside to twist my wedding ring around my finger prior to removing it completely. Next, I flick the ring the width of the bed in cautiously modest increments, careful not to let it fall off the far side. Then, having flicked it sufficiently, I place the ring on the affiliated finger of the opposite hand and, in a slow controlled motion, flex that hand till it cramps. The ring seems to fit, but still I'm unhappy with it, and so I remove it again and place it in the toe of this sock I found instead.

And as for Sid, he says, he just thinks a Jewish writer's supposed to behave that way, that's all. I suppose, I say, sitting here on the end of the bed, taking the first garment from the pile at my feet—a shirt—and placing the ring-laden sock inside it, then folding the shirt rapidly and repeatedly into a small solid lump of cloth.

Sid's my friend though, he says. You'd think you'd be coming to grips with that concept by now. I know, I say, it's just . . . What? he says. It's just that he strikes me as that kind of guy who's genuinely sincere for about two minutes of the day, and those two minutes no doubt first thing in the morning, alone, in front of the mirror, when he's deciding exactly how genuinely *in*sincere he'd going to be the rest of the day, I say. I mean the man's entire identity and belief structure are founded on the fact that he does not, nor has he ever, liked to hang out in *malls*. Noble, sure, but still damned depressing in a way.

A quick swishing of water, then nothing. The bathroom seems oddly quiet now.

Hey, I say, are you by chance giving yourself an enema again? Are you? I don't know why, but I just have this sneaking suspicion you're giving yourself an enema again. That's because you're somewhat anally fixated, he says as I unfold the shirt and remove the sock inside, then return the ring to its appropriate finger and study the arrangement a while. Eventually I drop that hand to my lap and pick up the other, turning my considerable attention to the sadly neglected nail beds now.

You're in the tub then, I say. Aw tell me you're not in the tub again. I need to know you're not in the tub again. All this bathing's getting just a little disturbing. I suppose you didn't check the barbeque either, I say over the sudden rush of running water. Chris, did you check the barbeque for pigeons? Gave blood today, he says just as the tap squeaks closed. Yeah, gave blood today, so we're even anyway. Even, I say, and he says, Six for six. We took six pints and now we've given six pints. So we're even.

I pick a few strands of black hair from a shirt and place them under my pillow.

I tell you what, though, he says, we'd better have ourselves a decent summer or else I'm going to be out of a job again. Cut labour, I say, and he says, Believe me, I've already cut it back as far as it can go. The Brothers Beasley won't let me work any more than I already do and besides, the girls make all their own drinks till I'm back at four.

I pull another errant strand of black hair from my pant leg and deposit that too under my pillow.

Thinking of firing Lisa, he tells me over the sound of tub water splashing down onto the bathroom floor. How come, I say. Too bitter, he says. Entirely too bitter. And besides, we need some eye candy in there. Eye candy, huh, I say, and he says, That's right, eye candy. So, I say, who's the potential replacement then? Darcy? The one we owe all the money? You've *got* to be kidding. Aw come on, I think she'll be good, he says, and I say I bet he does. I bet he thinks she'll be real good. She Indian too? Uh, she's blonde, he says, and I say, Yeah, well, so's Katie. *Touché, she says, wandering hands in pockets among the flowerbeds as a tractor rumbles past out of sight on the road beyond the hedge. The bawl of its engine carries on the still morning air. Canadian Geese fly in echelon overhead. And eventually we rejoin the road, itself now black with tar, across which runs a grey wire mesh fence with a sign that reads* NO TRESSPASSING *in bold red letters. Loops of razor wire further the point. Regardless, we step through the unlocked gate and along the road stretching out through the unkempt field ahead.*

Okay, so half of what we make we put towards our debt, she says, shaking her head in utter disbelief. Christ, I'm tired of being broke, she adds as I reach over to massage her forehead with a thumb, as is the custom whenever she gets to feeling this way about our sorry financial state. Come on, Annie, don't you know that complete financial collapse can be a purifying and ennobling opportunity for personal growth? Well it's true, hey. I heard Burt Reynolds say just as much the other day. Great, life advice from Stroker Ace, she says as somewhere ahead several dogs begin to bark in unison. First the one dog barks and then the next dog barks. Then the rest of the dogs bark together.

Thursday, 4:18 pm

She clicks her pierced tongue back and forth across her bright white teeth and gazes up at the grey overcast sky. She really wants a position tending bar, she says, so he tells her how that's impossible at this juncture, but that she could probably get on the floor five days a week if she'd be willing to stretch herself that far.

Lisa's leaving, he explains, so he'll need another hand at that position now. Darcy, though, remains unconvinced, and so he offers her what is really a ludicrous amount of money for a one-armed waitress—twelve dollars an hour—which in the end she accepts, if only to keep a closer eye on her investment now. Chris explains how she'll be training alongside Lisa for the next few days, but that since Lisa doesn't want anyone to know she's leaving just yet, it would be shrewd if Darcy could refrain from raising that point in discussion, at least for the time being anyway.

She shakes his hand and heads off down the sidewalk, leaving him alone on the patio watching people plod down the promenade in the direction of the whale, or else up the promenade and out along the pier, huddling close together against the wind now whistling in across the bay.

Eventually Wendy comes rolling up, bringing an abrupt end to his isolation, hopping off her ten-speed and leaning it precariously against the patio railing. Would she like a drink? She says she wouldn't mind a beer. From Katie, then, he petitions a pint for Wendy and another double Greyhound for himself—his second such drink in a month—advising Katie to have a drink too if she wants to, and of course she wants to very much. In the meantime, waiting for the drinks to arrive, he watches the people trudge west along the promenade, a migration too extraordinary to ignore. Eventually Katie returns with the drinks, including a double gin and tonic for herself. She appears as though she might take a seat, but then taking stock of Wendy appears to think better of the idea, and wrinkling her nose opts instead for a tactical retreat.

Combining work with pleasure again are we, Chris? asks a familiar voice from behind. What, the Brothers Beasley not around? No, they're not back from LA yet, Chris says, and the voice says sure they are. He just saw Todd and Reena down at the hotel.

Wendy pokes Chris gently on the shoulder in an effort to obtain an introduction, and so he provides the introduction, watching these two grinningly shake hands—Wendy, naturally, because she is smitten, and Thomas, obviously, because he is scared as hell. Eventually his own hand swims into the mix, and much to Thomas's relief, the whole entanglement finally breaks down. Thomas pulls up a chair and leans back to admire the cloud-curdled sky, his long lean athletic legs stretching out his socked and sandaled feet, in Chris's mind, just a fraction too far.

He asks Katie if she'd mind getting Thomas a Heineken along with another gin and tonic for herself.

Looks like the weather's going to hold off anyway, Thomas says presently, idly fondling himself. Eventually his concentration comes to rest on Wendy and the photographs arranged in concise columns on the table before her. He watches her in stunned silence a while, until a cuff on the side of the head courtesy of Chris quietly compels him not to.

Hey Tom, do you know—

Thomas, Thomas says. Right, Thomas, Chris says. Well do you happen to know Darcy down there at Monk's at all? Everybody knows Darcy, Thomas says, stealing one more glance at Wendy before downing a good mouthful of beer to further bolster himself.

Well if you owed her money, say, would you be concerned at all, Chris says, and Thomas cocks an eyebrow, then smiles and shakes his head knowingly. Made a deal with the devil have you, he says. Why you stupid ignorant son of a—

Well would he? Would he what? Be concerned, Chris says. What, with Darcy the dealer? says Thomas. Christ, I don't know. Why, how much do you owe her? he asks, and Chris shrugs, Thousand dollars or so. Oh, well, that's not that bad, Thomas says, briefly cutting his eyes to their tablemate. But to be honest, I really don't know. How *concerned* you should be, I mean. Though she is still affiliated with the Angels as far as I know. Hey are you crazy? he finally inquires of Wendy, unable to resist the impulse, but she doesn't seem to have heard. Chris makes ready to interject as Thomas makes ready to ask again, but then Nick comes strolling up chewing on an enormous pepperoni stick, stopping just long enough to pass on a drink.

Got to check in and see how Dad's doing, he explains, knitting his brows at an oblivious Wendy presently consumed with what appears, from Chris's perspective, to be a photographic game of solitaire. A bunch of whale-watchers just came by the restaurant and he's pissed. What, they were hoping to feed the thing? says Chris, incredulous, and Nick shakes his head and says, Hoping to feed themselves, I guess.

Hey Champ, you know Darcy the dealer right? says Thomas, and Nick says yeah, he knows Darcy. What about her? Well if he owed her money, say, would he be concerned at all? Well of course he would. That woman is scary. And she's got some scary fucking friends too, he might add. Why, who owes her money? Oh, no one, Thomas says. Hypothetical question. How are the renos coming along? Another two days or so, Nick says. Say hello to your boyfriend for me, Champ, Thomas says as Nick turns to leave. Will do, Amway, Nick calls back over his shoulder.

Who's that? asks Wendy as Nick saunters off down the sidewalk. That's Nick, Thomas answers. Nick's a fag. Which isn't all that surprising when you realize he's the World Salsa Dance Champion. Really? says Wendy. But he looks almost, what, Turkish or something. He's Grexican, Thomas says, finishing his beer and holding aloft the empty bottle in an ultimately futile attempt to obtain a free successor. Dad's Greek and his Mom's Mexican. Doesn't look all that gay does he, Wendy says, returning to her photographs. Maybe not, but you should see him dance, Thomas tells her.

Pat steps out onto the patio in his street clothes, asking to speak with Chris inside.

You know, we really shouldn't have this on during business hours, Chris says, indicating the two young blondes currently bouncing their way across the big screen in a boat, and Pat says, What, this? This is *Fishing with Shelley and Courtney*. It's real fishing, he insists. And so it is. Chris asks him how it went over lunch. Oh not bad, Pat says. Twenty plates, give or take. Listen, though, this just came in. Fax from Rick. Here's the cost for garnishes the month before the flood. So? So Rick thinks a hundred dollars a month is maybe a little too much to be paying for lemons and limes, Pat says, especially when we're not selling all that many mixed drinks. And this fax here shows the prices of the various different liquors in American. American? Yeah, Rick says he wants you to start buying the liquor in the States, Pat says, and then bring it across the border. You know, because it's cheaper. And that way maybe we can drop the prices and get them drinking more. Get *who* drinking more, Pat? The staff? Christ, you could shoot a cannon through this place on its *best* days and still be in no danger of hitting a soul.

Actually, Pat winces. What now, Chris asks. Well it concerns the staff. What *about* the staff? Well it's about them drinking on shift, Pat answers. Rick thinks the privilege is starting to be abused a little too regularly perhaps. He does, does he, says Chris. And how exactly did you come by this information, Pat? On the inside track with the owners are we? Why you little fucking usurper. I ought to fire your fat conniving ass. No, no, it's not like that, Pat insists. Honestly. Just a little tête-à-tête over drinks. I see, says Chris. Well then you let your little drinking buddy know that if he's got a problem with how I'm running the restaurant, he come talk to me directly. And the next time you're out having your little *tête-à-tête* with those cheap fucking bastards, Pat, maybe you could mention the fact that smuggling booze across the border is illegal, in case they didn't know already.

Pat shrugs sullenly and turns to the television where the fishing, presided over by the blondes, seems to be improving dramatically, while outside the window, despite the lack of sunshine, faint grey shadows have begun to converge on the patio. There are shadows under the table where Thomas and Wendy are sitting, and shadows across the stacks of unused chairs in the corner. Pigeons fly from the edge of the patio to the trees across the road, and the low grey sky lies heavily against the cloud grey water below. And gritting his teeth, Chris reluctantly returns to the photographs on the walls, inevitably coming to rest on the one of that girl that died some time ago.

Thursday, 7:02 pm

Rick Beasley comes sauntering up to take a seat alongside his younger thinner brother at the bar. New floor looks good, he says after a time. Yes, Chris says, they did a good job. They raised it, hey, Todd says. Yes, I noticed, Chris says, looking around purposefully at nothing in particular. He holds his nose and blows softly, feeling the pressure gradually let go.

So you got my faxes then, Rick says, and Chris says yes, he did. Rick waits for him to add something, and receiving nothing, leans forward with hands spread wide against the bar, elbows slightly bent, occasionally lifting one hand or the other to brush his moustache with thumb and index finger. So I want you to figure out a way we can buy our liquor in the States, he says, and Chris says, Yes, that's what Pat said you said.

Rick glances around at the empty tables with his little hard brown eyes, while out along the length of the pier the lights sputter to hazy amber life. He asks how lunch was and Chris says light. How many plates? asks Todd, having recently taken to the term, and Chris says maybe twenty, give or take. Twenty, says Rick. That's not a lot. Not a lot, no, Chris admits.

Brushing his moustache with absentminded pride, Rick looks at Chris, at Todd, and then at the bar, finally producing a silver cigar container from his pocket while beside him his brother produces its identical counterpart.

Cubans, boys? says Chris. Of course, answer both brothers together, removing the cigars from their containers. Snipping off the ends with a gold cutter of Todd's, they wait for Chris to produce a light, as they always do, and of course don't receive one, something they never do. Finally Pat comes up offering up his own lighter, allowing both brothers to puff away with great conviction and superiority, issuing great clouds of smoke into the squall already there.

Moments later, brushing his moustache with thumb and index finger, the same thumb and index finger even now employed with the cigar, Rick says now *that's* what he's talking about: *quality*. I know what you mean, says Todd, contemplating, over the length of his cigar, the three rows of bottles behind the bar. Most of the ones you get in the States are terrible. Absolutely terrible. No quality at all. Not these Cubans though. Boy, these Cubans are quality. Yes, says Rick wistfully, they really are.

Chris rolls his eyes and walks away from this profoundly dull conversation. And a little later, finding Rick hunting curiously about the bar, he takes up the scoop and thrusts it violently into the ice several times over. What's wrong? he asks, offering the ice one last penetrating stab for good measure, and Rick taps the bar with the heel of his palm and says something's missing here. Yeah, the garnishes, he's told. The garnishes? Yeah, the lemons and limes, Rick, I got rid of them. You got *rid of the lemons and limes*, says Rick. *Why*? Well I thought I was supposed to be cutting down on that sort of thing, Rick. That is, according to your fax. Well not com*pletely*, says Rick. No? *No*. Hmm, Chris says, my mistake then.

The Brothers Beasley continue to puff away at their cigars, each propelling his own cloud of smoke up towards the ceiling and out towards the door. Eventually, when Rick's cell phone rings and he bends away to take the call, Todd glances about covertly and then leans in close to whisper that Reena was wondering what time Chris would be coming by tomorrow. Tomorrow? says Chris. How about tonight? Sure, says Todd. That is, if you think you're up to it. Oh, Chris says, I'm up to it all right. Tell Reena I'll be over after I finish locking up.

Finished with his phone call, Rick returns to the bar and a seat alongside his brother, at which point they both ask for a drink. Both brothers drink Chivas Regal these days, and both drink it exactly the same way—on the rocks, water on the side, without benefit of garnish or straw. From time to time they call out for another round, in the meantime gazing about their nearly empty restaurant to state and then accede, alternately and in turn, that business will surely pick up as soon as the weather comes around—managing to pick up this train of thought right where it left off a month ago.

Never seen a spring like it, offers Todd between rounds. Rick agrees wholeheartedly, saying that it's affecting business all over town. Neither brother knows anything about the weather of course, let alone when it might break, and yet they each speak with such great conviction and sobriety on the subject that everyone within earshot listens attentively.

Chris asks how their horses fared down south, then watches as they both shrug sombrely, Rick running his finger and thumb over his moustache before butting out the last half of his cigar in his brother's ashtray. Had to put our one girl down, he says, and Chris says, How so? Ah, well, she was suffering pretty bad, he's told. That track, it can really eat them up. So you just shot her, Chris says, pouring out a pair of rum and Cokes for Katie. Well there's really not much else you can do at that point, Todd explains while making an unabashedly comprehensive inspection of Katie's rear-end. Except maybe not race her in the first place, Chris suggests. Although at a racetrack that sort of humanitarianism's in relatively short supply, I guess. Rick waves him off, saying, If you're not a horseman, you wouldn't understand. Tell me, Rick, do you race them on Lasix? Lasix? says Todd. How the hell would you know anything about Lasix? Chris shrugs and says he wrote an article on it once. Well sometimes you have to, Chris—when they bleed. Well unless I'm mistaken, Rick, all animals bleed if you run them hard enough.

Chris makes it through the next hour in much the same way, pretending to take interest in the Brothers' weary recapitulations of, and feeble protests against, bad weather and worse racetracks, all the while unloading the glass washer and filling the occasional drink order for Krishna or Katie. However, there are so few customers that stocking and washing glassware is of chief concern presently. That is, when not taking an anxious moment in the mirror behind the bar to examine and re-examine his forehead, holding his breath until the pimples disappear in a pool of red, or else charging off to the bathroom to deal with a suddenly uncontrollable digestive tract. This diarrhoea being a relatively new affliction, albeit fairly pressing now, no doubt precipitated by an extremely poor diet of late characterized by a general unwillingness to supplement with anything more than a random sampling of aging Easter candy and, most recently of course, a fistful or two of Tylenol. And finally, bringing a long-awaited end to the monotony, Sidney Shapiro comes in and orders his usual: a vodka-soda with just a press of Coca-Cola.

What's the matter, citizen? he says, sliding up onto a stool. His coat is dry and his eyes are red and it's clear, from his slightly slurred speech and exaggerated gestures, that he's already been dipping into the sauce somewhere. Just tired, that's all, Chris says.

Hissing through his teeth, Sid turns with great determination upon his drink, and seconds later finishes it, sliding the empty glass back and forth across the bar for Chris to replenish as soon as possible. Finally, he gazes deeply into his glass and, for added emphasis, shakes what ice remains.

Would you like another one, Sid? Another what? Drink, says Chris. Wouldn't hurt, says Sid. Borrow your phone, citizen? he asks a little later. Lost my cell. Pay phone's out on the corner, he's told with a chuckle. *What*? says Sid, standing abruptly from his stool, poised and ready to do battle over what he evidently feels is merely the latest in an ongoing series of unendurable insults to his character.

Yeah it's this wonderful new technological advancement they've come up with, Sid. You pay a quarter and call anyone in the world. No batteries to charge. No brain tumours to treat. You should see. Come on, says Sid, shoring up his posture and hitching up his pants, motioning for the house phone to make its way promptly over the bar and into his grasp. I've got someone who wants to talk to you, he adds. What's the matter, Chris asks, and Sid compresses his lips and pauses, then flashes a quick look at Chris's festering forehead and says, Nothing. Just got someone who wants to talk to you, that's all.

He allows the phone to ring several times before reluctantly hanging up. Must be out, he says, passing the phone back over the bar. Who is it? says Chris, and Sid says, Just a friend I'd like you to meet, that's all. A date, Sid? No, not a *date*, says Sid. A meeting. A casual meeting of responsible citizens in accordance with all the rules governing acquaintances. But I don't want to meet anyone, Sid, responsible or not. Come now, citizen, she's nice. And young. Oh so young. Ass like a twelve year-old boy on a bike, you know the kind.

Chris notices Sid's hands working overtime, each thumb touching down tentatively against the tips of its corresponding fingers one after another, repeating the pattern again and again. She ever lived in the Congo? he asks, and Sid says not that he's aware of, why? Thinking of heading out on safari, are we? Thanks, but no, Chris says. What's the matter, citizen? Cojimar got your tongue?

A little dark meat might be just the thing for you. Nothing, Sid. Nothing's the matter. I'm just not up to it right now, that's all. So then the boss *has* cornered the market, Sid smiles shrewdly, the rapid methodical working of his fingers drawing Chris's attention from his repeatedly arching eyebrows.

If you'd speak up a little, maybe they'd be able to hear you better, Chris says, indicating the bosses seated only a few stools down the bar. Sid roars maniacally and leans forward weakly against the bar, for the moment unable to support both himself and the colossal amusement that's placed him here. Finally, though, his laughter having subsided into something much more manageable, he whispers, Want to know something, citizen? I haven't had any for *days*. What's the matter, Sid? Losing your appetite for adultery? Not at all, says Sid, flicking crumbs across the bar. In fact it's just the opposite. I tell you it's strange. When I get to feeling like this—

Lecherous, Chris says, and Sid says, Yes, when I get to feeling lecherous like this, I just want to be left alone with my mother-in-law.

The door opens, admitting a handful of customers, and together with the Brothers Beasley, Sid watches them come in, all three of them, before rotating slowly back to the bar. Speaking of dark meat, he says. Hey, maybe you ought to start working at Kentucky Fried Chicken again. Get back to your old habits of skimming. Damn you were a good skimmer back then though eh citizen? Remember how much of the Colonel's cash you used to walk with on any given shift? What was it, a hundred a day, at least? Man alive, but there was some good money to be made in chicken.

Sid taps out a rapid beat on his lower lip, watching with keen interest as Chris cleans his fingernails with a broken corkscrew bit. I'm serious, citizen, he says. And not simply because you need the money—and I'm sure you *do* need the money—but simply because these goddamned Beasleys here happen to annoy the hell out of me. Keep it down, he's told. Please. Well you know I'm right, says Sid. When you start losing respect for someone you can start taking them for granted, and when you start taking them for granted you can start taking advantage, and once you start taking advantage—in this business at least—you can really start making a killing at it. And since, being a vegetarian, Chris has no real need for burgers and such, Sid would like to see him skimming himself a few dollars here and there. Nothing too flagrant, understand, just enough to let Sid know his friend is screwing over his bosses somewhat consistently here. It's vitally important to screw over your bosses whenever possible, according to Sid. According to Sid, screwing over your bosses allows you to achieve a certain degree of workplace satisfaction that might otherwise elude you entirely.

Sid studies Chris cryptically for several seconds, his brown narrow-set eyes slitting menacingly beneath his head of dark, short-cropped hair. Then, shrugging, he contemplates the further progress of his thumb against his fingers and says, Just a joke of course. A bad joke maybe, but still a joke. But then there's nothing worse than having to listen to a bad joke. As far as I'm concerned—and I'm sure you'll back me up here—jokes that have to be told, those with a punch line and all, ought to have been flat-out *banned* by now. Nothing worse than an unfunny joke, citizen, and listen, almost all of them are. Even if you haven't heard it before—fat chance of that—chances are you're still not going to find it funny for any number of reasons, this I know. Maybe the timing is off. Or maybe the speaker forgets a part. Or maybe he just stutters when he tells the punch line or something—good God, who knows. All *I* know is that somehow, someway, except on those most infrequent of occasions when you're dealing with some sort of professional comedian or some such thing, the joke finds its way to getting fucked up. And then, of course, you have to laugh just so you don't hurt his feelings. Or if by some remote chance it *is* funny, and you *haven't* heard it before, and you really *do* laugh for real, then you suddenly realize that you *are* in fact laughing—just as you're supposed to—and that ruins it all as well. I mean unless it's knee-slappingly funny, citizen—and really, who does *that* anymore—chances are you're still going to have to fake it, at least to some degree, and I hate the thought of faking anything, especially orgasms with my mother-in-law.

Chris pours out a pair of Chivas for the owners who, if their initial salvos are any indication, appear to be concentrating their tactile attentions on Katie this evening. Meanwhile Sid, as if expecting to undergo some sort of similar workplace abuse himself, spins around in a complete circle before finally settling back against the bar in standard drinking position, at which point he sighs, takes a deep breath and, as though they're some-how impeding his pleasure, turns to the photographs on the wall and curses repeatedly, then slits his eyes and glances about mali-ciously. Next, standing up in order to hitch up his pants, he leans in over the bar just as this kid from the juice bar comes in to ask for some matches. Chris passes him some matches. Sid waits until the kid leaves the bar. Then, having settled back onto his stool, he spins around and around until sufficiently nauseous, allowing the stool to glide to a silent stop before leaning down against the bar, looking to regain some of the composure he's lost somewhere.

Perhaps it lacks a certain dignity, citizen, I don't know. I suppose I'm fairly old-fashioned that way. I mean for the most part I enjoy it, I really do, but I just can't perform to the best of my ability when she insists we do it *every goddamned day*.

Thursday, 8:41 pm

For Sid, though, one interesting aspect of adultery has always been how, after a time, nothing exists of the world but more thoughts of adultery somehow.

Now I know what you're thinking, citizen—that one swallow does not a summer make—but it just seems to me like you step through one seemingly insignificant door, whereupon you're led to another seemingly insignificant door, and then another door, and then another and so on and so forth until eventually you awake to the realization that you truly are this two-timing son of a bitch and more, that you can't quite fathom how it is you even got here. See, your entire mind-set's been changing so gradually and so steadily for so long that, even in retrospect, you can't find the single critical point of departure. Because there is no single critical point of departure. But, like I say, a series of finer, less

intrusive, seemingly insignificant points that, when taken together, form a bridge somehow greater than the sum of its parts that
leads you away from your spouse and, in my case anyway, into the
arms of her mother. That is, until that inevitable morning when
you awake to realize you've broken all of your vows—all the ones
worth maintaining anyway—and that, for one brief transitory
moment, you're truly uncertain who it is lying beside you.

Placing the last of the polished wineglasses in the overhead rack,
Chris turns his attention to dusting the liquor bottles along the
back shelf.

Now I realize that it's difficult to get philosophical about such
things, especially without coming across as somewhat cynical,
even jaded and not a little pretentious, and you'd be wise to pay
little or no heed to the self-styled sage, especially the one bellied
up to the bar. But believe me, I know from experience, getting
into bed with the wife of your boss can be a trying occupation
full of many serious pitfalls that at its best proves utterly bizarre,
while at its worst a seemingly endless stint in a very specific hell.
Understand, many try it but few excel at it, and for this reason said
occupation is often little more than a stepping stone to some
other far more dubious field of endeavour, and really, inevitably
so. And that of course is the road you're on, citizen. There's simply no denying that fact anymore.

Sid lifts his empty glass and shakes the ice around. Then, raising
it straight overhead, he slams it down against the bar. The Brothers
Beasley immediately glance over, but Chris assures them both that
nothing is at all out of sorts here, and so they eventually return to
the business of groping the waitresses, one of whom, Krishna, due
perhaps to the fact that she seems to be playing second fiddle to
Katie this evening, appears to be enjoying their attentions even
more than usual.

Calm down, Sid. Sorry, citizen, bad call. You want me to call
your wife? asks Chris, and Sid nods affirmatively, emphatically
and says no, he just wanted Chris to know what's wrong with
his marriage, that's all. Sort of like Lou Gehrig's Gettysburg
Address, he suggests as Chris passes the telephone over the bar.
He takes the phone, then takes a deep breath and says, with a

hand over his heart, Today I consider myself the luckiest man on the face of the earth—

Okay, enough, Chris interrupts. I mean it though, citizen— thanks, Sid says. In fact I'm going to give her a call right now. Give her a piece of my mind, and maybe that divorce she's been carrying on about. Besides, it's considered indecent in this town not to have at least one estranged spou—he manages to slur into—how's Jeff? Still schizophrenic? Still schizophrenic, Chris says. That's a shame, Sid says. Still the mind goes first, they say. Take Hum for instance, and this ridiculous calf machine obses- sion of his. You've heard about the calf machine of course. Oh come now, citizen, tell me you've heard about the calf machine. I have absolutely no idea what you're talking about, Chris tells him. Hum, says Sid. He wants his very own calf machine. You know, so he can "train" his calves at home. Now this really isn't all that displeasing a notion in itself of course, until you realize that's *all* he wants: his very own calf machine installed in his apartment so that he can train whenever the notion hits him, I suppose.

Sid leans away from the bar at full arms' length, awaiting some sort of reaction here. Jesus, Chris obliges while stepping away to prepare, along with a pair of Chivas for the owners courtesy of Krishna, a tall glass of water for Mr. Shapiro.

Tell me, though, why don't you take this girl out? says Chris, sliding the glass of water across the bar. Which girl? says Sid, and Chris says the responsible girl from the telephone earlier. Impossible, says Sid, declining the glass of water. Only likes single guys apparently. Yeah, loves single guys apparently. Can't get enough of this so-called "single scene," this girl. Gets it from her mother of course. Gets everything from her mother. And what I wouldn't give to get something off her.

So you thought I'd do, Chris says, and Sid says, Closest thing I know to one of those. Still, I look at teenaged girls these days and all I see is an entire generation of women in dire need of an eat- ing disorder. Anorexia. Bulimia. Calista—pick one. Go ahead, pick any letter of the alphabet. It's the ABC's of femininity for me, yessir. Well thanks for the thought anyway, Sid. Think nothing of it, says Sid, glancing about uneasily before leaning in close to whisper that Chris ought to get more fat people working in here. That's the cruel irony of it. And the secret too, by the way. Yep, nothing like having a fat chick prepare your meal, he says. They take ownership. They take *pride*. They make it how *they'd* want to eat it, see, so every time I go out to eat now, I always make sure they've got at least one fat chick slaving away back there. You know, watching out for me, taking care of me, sprinkling in a little extra cheese here and there. Trouble is, with the fat ones, I can't figure out whether I want to fuck or fight them half the time. Fuck or fight, fuck or fight, he chants. Still, you get in trouble for that sort of thing, don't you. I'd think so, Chris says, exchanging the glass of water for a draft. Here, have one on the house, he says, and Sid says no, he couldn't, not *draft*. Go ahead, take it, he's told. It's pouring like piss anyway. Ah, you're a good man, citizen. Much dignity. What you up to later?

Before Chris can answer, however, a dancer from the hotel steps up to the bar and orders a rye and ginger. He makes her a double but only charges her for a single and as a result she happily stuffs the difference down into his jar.

Stepping back down the bar, Chris asks Sid if he knows Darcy the dealer, and Sid says, Why, what about her? Thinking of going into business together? Working off some of that bad debt you owe her? No, but it looks like she'll be working here though, Chris says. *Ah*, Sid nods. Keeping your friends close but your enemies closer. Something like that, yeah, Chris admits with a chuckle.

Sid dismisses all thought of personal injury at the hand of Darcy the drug-dealing barista with a quick perfunctory wave. Fear not, citizen, he says. That Darcy, she's all right. As a matter of fact she made me laugh out loud just the other night. And I mean *right* out loud. Rare, that. Too rare, some say. Besides yourself, no one makes me laugh out loud anymore. No one cares. No one takes the time. No one gives a rat's ass these days.

Chris pours out a half litre of Cabernet for Krishna and two rum and Cokes for Katie, then wanders his way back down the bar to hear Sid say, Last time we went out she caused quite a row though. Yeah, down at the OB. Wanted to smoke of course, and of course they wouldn't let her. So what'd she do, you ask? Well— and picture this now—there she is standing at the open door with her drink in the one hand *in*side the door, and her cigarette in the fake hand *out*side the door, and, well, you can guess what management thought of that. Management didn't like that? No, management didn't like that at all. Neither did the dancers for that matter, Sid goes on. Said it caused quite a draught up near the back door. Well shit, I told them, any place is going to have a draught when you're lap-dancing half-naked or spinning around a god-damned pole.

Anyway, we fought the good fight, citizen. And quite the mutiny too: fucking vaudeville team through and through. Darcy played the bruiser and I played it light—real good cop, bad cop thing we had going, see—routine was tight, tight, tight. Sid takes a swig of beer, then adds, That Darcy, she's all right. Now don't get me wrong, I wouldn't want to owe her any money. But then again, why would I.

Outside, the rain continues to pour down, collecting on the patio in puddles where over the years the weight of constant bodies has managed to wear the wood down.

So, been down to see the whale yet? says Chris, and Sid says, Sure I have. Thinking of moving in actually, in hopes of alleviating this chronic housing shortage. Be like Pinnochio: learn moral lessons through high adventure. Good God, he says, finishing his beer in one long Adams apple-bobbing tilt, I see enough humiliation and degradation without having to go combing about on the beach for it. I knew I could count on my old buddy Sid for a little sanity in this world, Chris says, and Sid says, Don't. As far as I'm concerned the Indians can have it. Or better yet, the Japanese. Yeah, let the Japanese have it. Besides they claim they only want it for research.

Sid turns towards the darkened window a moment, wipes his mouth with his sleeve, and studies his reflection in the glass. It's an odd thing when a whale beaches itself, citizen, he says at last. Polluted waters maybe. Naval sonar probably. Sign of the apocalypse undoubtedly. Just too damned exhausted to continue, I suppose. Runs like a hooked fish until the drag of his suffering sufficiently exhausts him, and then the lure of the beach reels him in after that.

Sid observes Chris blankly, then shakes his head sadly and says, Actually, now that I think about it, I am worried about you. How so, Chris says. Well that manager at the hotel, says Sid, I just saw him sporting a brand new cast from his ankle to his asshole.

Thursday, 10:26 pm

A savage clamour of voices erupts from the far rear corner of the Trap & Gill.

They always like this? says Wendy, taking baleful aim at the lot of them from the narrowed corner of her eye. She pulls out her stack of photographs, as well as her whale book, and proceeds to arrange them meticulously on the bar before her. Like what, Chris says, and she says, So, you know, wannabe *black* like this. Unfortunately yes, he says, holding his nose and blowing steadily. Hey, aren't you supposed to be home by nine or something? So I broke curfew, she says.

Together they watch them a while, the males seemingly all large and muscular, the females smaller and more demure, all of them aggressive and full of attitude however in that would-be black man's manner.

Which ones do you think did it then? she says, and he says, Did what? Ran over that woman, she says, indicating the photograph on the wall. Oh, come now, Wendy. Please. Well I heard it was Indians that did it, she says, and he says still, like he told her before, he doubts it was actually any of *these*.

He casts a pleading eye at Krishna, hoping she might come save him here, just as the front door opens admitting even more, prompting from Todd Beasley what amounts to an oddly embarrassed smile.

Krishna says, Got any Tylenol? and Chris says, Headache? No, he's told, hangover. There's some in the drawer there, Chris tells her. Don't know how much good it'll do though. I mean I took a whole bottle this morning and didn't get anything for the investment whatsoever.

Krishna slips in behind him in search of the Tylenol, making sure to brush her breasts across his back. They stand there like that, Krishna gently breast-brushing his back, until someone calls out for service from one of the tables in the back. Grudgingly she makes her way over to the table as Chris wanders back down the length of the bar, clenching and re-clenching his buttocks against this ongoing threat of diarrhoea he seems to be cursed with now.

Darcy comes strolling in and, lighting a cigarette, takes a seat halfway down the bar. Thanks for coming in, Chris tells her. I want to ask you something. So ask, he's told. He glances down the bar to the Brothers Beasley who, as luck would have it and for whatever reason, seem to be refraining from eavesdropping just now. Then he pours Darcy a Kahlua and soda and places an ash-tray on the bar.

So? says Darcy, raising her drink to her lips, so Chris tells her how he needs another thousand dollars, and that he needs it as soon as possible. I haven't got another thousand, she says, setting her untouched drink back on the bar. Not for you anyway. Listen, Darcy, I only ask because I thought you might know someone who does, that's all. Who told you that? she asks, and he tells her no one in particular. Don't be coy, she says, taking a long drag off her cigarette and expelling the smoke in two great plumes from her nostrils.

So what do you need another thousand dollars for? she says, and he says he can't say. Not just yet anyway. And that's a thousand dollars American by the way. Darcy eyes him shrewdly, then says she can have it for him first thing in the morning. How first thing? he says. As early he wants, he's told. But I tell you what, Darcy adds, extracting from her cigarette one last series of drags, These people I'd be getting it from, they don't like to be fucked with. They're not like me. They're not into missed payments and whatnot. They have absolutely zero tolerance for that sort of thing. Hey I'm not looking to screw anybody over here, Darcy. Other than myself, that is.

Chris retreats to the restroom to deal with another sudden attack of diarrhoea, then washes his hands, checks his glands, and returns behind the bar and calls home. After four rings the answering service finally picks up, replaying my recently recorded outgoing message. And so he listens to my voice several times over before returning to whatever it was he was doing before.

Wendy catches his attention from down the end of the bar, the entire vicinity of which she's managed to all but colonize with her sprawling photographic collage. How's Krishna? she says, and he says Krishna's fine. A little hung-over maybe, but fine. Isn't she though? says Wendy. Fine, I mean? There's just something about her, I don't know. Yeah it's called cleavage, Wendy. No, there's something else, something—oh what's the word, she says, taking a photograph from one column and adding it to another, as though this might help her reach some sort of conclusion somehow. A mother? says Chris. Oh, don't say that, Chris. Please. She's a mother, Wendy. Sorry to be the bearer of bad news but it's true. She is, really? says Wendy, and Chris says, Really. And get this: the father—her husband—he's a bit of a motherfucker too. Gave him up for adoption though. The kid, I mean. Well I'll be damned, she says as together they watch Krishna work the room. Of course she's right, Krishna's something all right, and you miss none of whatever it is in that tank-top of hers.

Friday, 1:06 am

And way down deep, nearly out of range altogether, I can hear them. First the one crying and then the next one crying. Then the rest of them crying *between the bare branches, through their belated flower absences, I can see them. Going towards him one after another, first the one boy whipping and then the next boy whipping. Then the rest of the boys go ahead and whip him together a while. I go on whispering at Annie. Annie goes on ignoring me. Then she goes down along the line of bushes to where across the street a man is raking—she calls out to the man but he does not hear. Meanwhile I go on whispering and watching the boys whipping as one* is coming now—there it is, here it comes, there it goes, sliding past his seat at Annie here in a black blast of grinding steel and slashing rain. And as the train slides past, he feels its passing mass shudder up through the bench, up through his legs and torso and down his arms and into his hands again. He waits for all the cars to pass before moving down the lawn to hop the railing.

The tide is out. He can tell the tide is out by the absence of any water lapping against the boulders below. He listens closely for the crying, but doesn't think he hears it anymore. So then he holds his nose and blows gently, but it doesn't go so well. And so he cuts back across the tracks, over the blue guardrail and up the slight slope of lawn to take a seat at Annie once again. As far as benches go she's a good one, not unlike any of the others lined up along the promenade below albeit slightly higher in space, consisting of four pressure-treated two-by-fours for the seat and another trio supporting the back, the highest of which features the embossed plaque, all seven bolting onto two steel rails curving up and around and back.

He heads east along the beach amid the maze of logs and boulders, feeling beneath his boots the crush and slide of shattered shells tumbled smooth by weather and wave. Not until reaching the longitude of the bus stop memorial, however, does he realize that his instincts have taken him in the wrong direction again. And so, wheeling abruptly in the rain, he moves back along the tracks and past the wide, vacant, dimly-lit pier, walking the rails as far west as possible without having to get too near the whale. He walks stepping on all the ties so as to avoid the sharp rocks and tar in between, heeling the first tie and toeing the next, taking two steps for every three. And passing the museum and the tourist office, he hops the blue guardrail at the public toilets and negotiates the remainder of the way along the street.

Near the west end of the Drive, silent now with the absence of traffic, he cuts up the steep and sloping hill, choosing instead of street or stairwell one of the vague, little-used paths—descendants of what were once Indian trails running here and there amid the terraced houses and cordoned-off yards of sea-swept grass. Knotted roots of cedar and spruce knuckle up along the path, but knowing the way well he manages not to falter—that is, until coming within sight of the mansion itself. Brightly lit from within as well as without, it appears somehow wrong and even unnatural in comparison to its neighbours, themselves presently dark and silent and thankfully oblivious to the more sordid intentions of this particular alien's inhabitants. And standing there at the edge of the street, watching the mansion's wide-eyed windows for any sign of life, Chris feels the branches of the nearest trees tugging gently at his sleeves and listens to the sound of the falling rain against the thick black canopy of conifers above. Presently he catches in his nostrils the distinct and familiar smell of pine, and plucking some needles from the nearest limbs, minces them between his fingers an uncertain moment before leaving them, and the shelter of the trail, behind. He moves cautiously up the road to the circular driveway at its crest, rings the doorbell and awaits an answer, receives an answer, then opens the door and steps inside. Todd Beasley appears in the foyer, smiling his embarrassed smile. It's the same sort of smile he uses whenever people of his own kind come into the Trap & Gill, as though the fact their clientele being predominantly brown in a predominantly white town is somehow wrong and therefore something to be a little embarrassed about. Todd's hair is combed and he's wearing cologne and he promptly offers some wine. Chris accepts the wine and surrenders his coat, then steps away to use the washroom a while.

In the washroom he inspects his pimpled forehead in the mirror, noting what appear to be the crimson beginnings of a brand new sty brewing in the outer corner of his left eye here. Inside his lip a canker sore festers. His gums appear to be receding as well. Then, more or less satisfied with the examination, though not at all with the results, he draws some soap from the sink-side dispenser and thoroughly washes his face and hands. And finally, wine glass in hand, he moves out to the excessively decorated living room and the elaborate flagstone fireplace there.

Where's Reena? asks Chris. Not bothering to answer, but directing him silently to the couch instead, Todd takes a seat in a large comfortable chair somewhat decrepit in appearance, but in concept and cost something of a quiet masterpiece. Holding his nose and blowing gently, Chris asks again where Reena is. She'll be right out, he's told. And the boys? At their grandmother's? Yes, at their grandmother's, Todd says, smiling that smile. They're all going down to see the whale tomorrow.

He looks as though he wants to say something more, but pre-adultery etiquette prevents him from proceeding just now.

Chris takes a sip of wine. Nice wine? asks Todd, and Chris says, Very nice. Where's it from? From the Napa Valley, he's told. Todd got it from the Napa Valley—on a tour. Good tour? Very good. Nice winery? Very nice. Though they must have thought we were someone else, Todd adds, not bothering to explain himself.

Chris holds his nose and blows harder, focusing hard now on the various rough-cut stones of the fireplace. You look wet, Todd says, wringing his hands, and Chris says, Yes, well, it's raining outside. Nice night? Pretty nice. Raining though, Chris adds. Right, Todd says, you said that.

This is, admittedly, less than poignant talk, but there remains for Todd the more practical matter of getting his guest pissed drunk. With this in mind, Chris takes another longer sip of wine, smelling the night's rain on his skin for a time.

Todd asks if he wants some more. More what? Wine, says Todd, smiling with embarrassment at the bottle. Did you want some more wine. Oh, sure, yes—please, Chris says. That is, if you don't mind.

Todd hops up from the couch and, in a suspicious excess of employer-employee charity, takes the bottle from the bar and refills his glass almost to the rim. Chris takes a good long drink, feeling the wine translate into heat within.

You're not drinking, Todd? Pardon? says Todd, frowning as Chris's glass makes its way directly onto the tabletop. You're not having any wine? Not tonight, no, Todd answers. I'm on antibiotics, he explains, and together they nod deeply at the word for a time.

Indicating the appropriate coaster to be employed in separating glass from tabletop, Todd asks how the night finished up. Not too bad, Chris tells him. Most of the regulars were in. Actually it's almost like we haven't missed a beat. Not too busy then, Todd nods knowingly, and Chris glances briefly at the fireplace and says, Not too busy, no. It'll pick up, Todd says, as soon as this weather comes round. It has to come around eventually, Chris says, admonishing himself immediately for actually having partaken in such a mundane conversation out loud.

Taking another long sip of wine, Chris asks again where Reena is. Telephone, says Todd, implying with the upward tilt of his considerable nose some deep distant room of the house. Chris sips prudently at his wine a moment, and then downs the remainder at once before accepting an immediate refill from his host.

She's had some, what, rather unfortunate news, Todd says quietly, approaching the subject warily, leaning forward from the waist with wine bottle fully extended. Her father, you see, he's just been diagnosed with cancer. Prostate? Lymph. Hodgkin's? Non-Hodgkin's. *Ah* yes, regular fucking epidemic these days, Chris says. My wife, she test-drove several before finally settling on a rare version of the lymph herself. Beat it though, hey. That's what's important. She'd be, what, exactly one year clear yesterday, I believe.

Chris retrieves the glass from its coaster as his host sits silently, smiling his embarrassed smile. When Chris tells him he has a beautiful home, Todd dismisses with one wide sweeping arc of his hand any and all accumulations of material wealth, although of course any sort of admission of envy regarding his possessions has always met with his highest concrete endorsement.

So LA was good then, Chris finally says after counting ten solid seconds of silence. What's that, Todd asks. Los Angeles, it was good? Oh yeah, Los Angeles was *great*, Todd says, shuffling forward in his chair. We stayed at that Pretty Woman hotel. What do you mean, Chris says, and Todd says, Well the hotel they filmed *Pretty Woman* at, I even sat in the very same chair. What chair? Well I don't really know, Todd says, but apparently the very same chair Julia Roberts sat in. Man, but I love that Julia Roberts. Can't get enough of that Julia Roberts. What I wouldn't give to get into *that*, if you know what I mean.

They both nod at the image of a ravaged Julia Roberts hovering there in the fireplace before them.

Thing is, Reena probably wouldn't appreciate it, Chris says, and Todd laughs feebly. Probably not, no, he admits. But then, as yet unwilling to surrender the subject, he says man, he'd sure like to get into that Julia Roberts. He can't get enough of that Julia Roberts. What I wouldn't give to get into *that*, if you know what I mean.

Agreeing, finally, that his host has made an interesting point about Julia Roberts, one well worth exploring in fact, Chris stares at the fireplace and sips intermittently at his Cabernet, unable to help but think how much cosier it would be if the fire itself were actually alight.

Todd reaches across to slap his guest's knee. That's it then, he says, you and me have *got* to get to Vegas some time. You'll see: rooms? Comp. Women? Comp. I'm telling you, brother, you won't know what hit you down there.

Chris sits quietly, staring at the empty fireplace, holding his nose and blowing steadily all the while. So Reena, he says, she's taking it pretty hard then? Excuse me? says Todd, adopting a policy of severe and sudden self-restraint. Her father, Chris says. She's taking her father's health situation pretty hard, I take it. Yes, Todd says, his restraint ripening quickly into a long deep sigh trembling just on the verge of compassion. She's been meaning to talk to you about it actually. She has? Yes, she has. She thought you might be able to shed some light on the situation, Todd adds. Well if she wants to, we could talk about it now, Chris says, and his host draws a deep breath, gathers himself, and breathes out again and shakes his head in the negative. Another time, he says. You don't want to burden those already suffering any more than you have to.

Well of course he doesn't. They never really do. And yet still Chris remains a veritable lightning rod for all such similar stories, but then really, who can blame them. I mean he must have some sort of insider's information or something—some sort of revelation by association perhaps—but I'm willing to wager he's just as fucked up as anyone as to why these things happen. Probably more so, to tell you the truth. And yet as much as he states that, as openly and as clearly, he tends to have to field these questions, and on a regular basis too. Because evidently he's seen as some sort of wise but far too young sufferer somehow. Well so be it. If you want a saint he'll be it. Still, I have to think that every once in a while it'd be nice to get a clean break from it.

Eventually Reena steps reluctantly into the living room, and it's immediately obvious that she has been crying. Chris offers her a seat beside him on the couch, deferring immediately to Todd to ensure that no obscure boundaries are being crossed at this point. Everything all right, Reena? he says. Oh everything's just *wonderful*, she sobs.

She sits beside him in her thick green bathrobe with reddish highlights in her hair, and with the way her robe falls open at the throat and her hair drifts down across her face he can't help but feel a familiar sort of stirring somewhere. She sobs a little and Todd, for his part, tries his best to console her. And Chris holds his nose and blows diligently, this despite the fact it really doesn't seem to be getting him anywhere.

He offers them the one joint he has in his pocket, and together Todd and Reena readily accept. They spark it up and smoke it down, and after a quick refill of Cabernet, feeling altogether hazy, he allows his successfully stoned hosts to guide him along in the direction of one of the boy's rooms at the far end of the hall.

He's never really understood why it's always one of the boy's rooms they do it in, or even which boy's room they do it in, and to be honest he's never really cared to know. After all, it's all fairly disgusting when you think about it, and really it hardly matters how one location compares to another when in reality it's all just a matter of principle. And anyway, the room is clean. It's important to Chris that the room be clean. And when he mentions something to this effect, both hosts inform him that the maids have in fact just been in. A skylight in the center of the ceiling reports the muffled downpour persisting outside, while inside, posters of unabashedly implanted white women with names like Bobbi Rae and Toni pass sneering judgment from the otherwise nondescript walls. Some of the women lean coyly over soap-soaked automobiles, while others stand defiantly with fists on hips, one hip, predictably, thrust out just a fraction too far. In the one corner of the room, opposite the bunk beds, stand the unfortunately familiar and suddenly unbearable video camera. Reena, sensing a new level of discomfort, discusses with Chris some of the plans they have concerning the restaurant and later, feeling better, he nods deeply and appreciatively and with critical interest as Todd discusses some new angles of penetration he's been wanting to try. And holding his nose and blowing rigorously, he manages to breathe almost regularly throughout the entire ordeal.

Todd tells him to get undressed. He gets undressed. Oh dear, says Reena at length. What is it now? asks Todd impatiently as his wife reaches over to raise Chris's chin with a finger. Oh honey, she says, I think your nose is bleeding. Aw Jesus, says Chris, and here I thought it was this goddamned rash. Rash? they say. What *rash*. This rash, says Chris, showing them both his forehead, and together they relax back into character. No, your nose is definitely bleeding, Todd says as Reena scurries off to the bathroom for tissue. Todd regards him evenly. Then, laughing aloud and smacking his shoulder, he says, You crazy-ass son of a bitch, you and me have *def*initely got to get to Vegas some time.

Finally Reena returns with some Kleenex, and once she's finished wiping his face, and the bleeding has more or less subsided, they return Chris to the living room to deal with what all remains of the Cabernet and what little is left of his clothing. They remove each article slowly and meticulously until the wine bottle is empty, and then return him to the bedroom for the balance of the affair. Todd helps him struggle up onto the top bunk, while Reena slips silently under the covers of the bunk below. Impatient to get it over with now, he asks if they're ready and Todd says not quite, not yet, he doesn't think so. And so, lying quietly and staring at the skylight, he holds his nose and blows steadily but gently, trying hard to keep this sudden urge to vomit under control.

And finally, on Todd's signal, and following protocol, he manoeuvres out onto the ladder at the end of the bed and makes his way down to Reena's bunk below. And all the while he's on the ladder he's looking over his shoulder at his reflection in the window, beyond which has begun to fall a beautiful and most unseasonable snow.

Lovestiff

In the cold night air I feel the heavy, wet, cumbersome flakes form over my upturned face a heavy, wet, cumbersome veil. I swear I can feel each flake separately as it lodges itself in amongst my lashes and melts gradually, almost grudgingly, into the creeks and crevices below. Slowly the troughs of eyes and mouth fill in, in my mind growing smoothly level with the crests of brows, cheeks and chin, and I amuse myself with the notion that if I were to somehow remain this way too long I might actually drown in a way. And finally, when I can no longer stand the cold, I shake the thin veil of snow away.

I knock on the locked front door of the Opa! Greek Taverna until Billy Henry eventually opens up, drinking coffee, smiling kindly, and diligently offering me a cup. I decline the coffee but take a seat at the bar, rubbing my tender belly until individual curiosity ultimately overwhelms their collective ennui.

Well that's unfortunate, says Billy Henry upon hearing the whole sordid story, and Nick says, Unfortunate? Fucking tragic's what it is. Lay off him, Nick, I mean it, says Billy Henry. But man, in the kid's *bed*room? he adds, turning to me. Yes, in his bunk bed no less, I say, inhaling deeply the smells of electric lights, new drywall and fresh paint. And your boss, he let you get *away* with this? says Nick, incredulous, and I say, Hey, it was entirely his idea. It's always been his idea. Like I said, he's the one been filming it. Well I doubt they'll be keeping any of that footage for posterity, chuckles Billy Henry, his teeth, stained yellow as a result of a long steady diet of coffee, suddenly appearing bright white in the brighter overhead light, a trick of the light he'd no doubt appreciate were I to inform him of it, which I will not naturally.

But man, you *shit* on her? says Nick, to which I respond with deliberate slowness that I simply vomited on Reena, which in turn triggered the unfortunate blow-out against the window behind me. This being your boss's wife, he says. Because you were supposed to be fucking her. *For* your boss. Who was busy operating the camera, he goes on, walking himself through it in stunned disbelief. Yes, I say, but do we have to go on about it? Christ, I feel guilty enough as it is. So is that what this is all about then? says Billy Henry, shaking his large shaved head back and forth. Some sort of displaced guilt? Maybe, I shrug. Who knows. Actually, says Nick, now that I think about it, there have been some rather intriguing rumours going around. Yeah, well, what can I say, Nick. You and Billy here are about the worst kept secret in town.

They both study me a moment as Sid's voice erupts from somewhere back in the kitchen. What'd Sid say? I said the truth's not for everyone, citizen. But that neither's Mensa, so what the hell.

In time a toilet flushes, and Sid's disembodied voice continues to address us from beyond the wall.

Yeah, Mind Maze Challenge, it's called. Only some two percent of the population can do it apparently, and apparently my parents mistakenly consider me one of those.

A tap squeaks open and water splashes down, followed by a measure of paper towel being ripped from a roll.

Well Good God, I told them—my parents, I mean—as if I need *that* kind of pressure right now. I mean *no* one needs to open a book just to realize how utterly ninety-eight percent they are, let alone someone in my perpetually fragile state of mind. But then I guess I shouldn't complain. They did send the very same copy to my sister down in Mexico, the very notion of which will probably stifle her for a decade. Citizen! he says, appearing suddenly and quite stridently from the kitchen, making immediately for the opposite side of the horseshoe-shaped bar. Have you signed your organ donor card? Have you? Eight out of ten people die because they can't gain access to freshly harvested organs, I'll have you know. Nick wants to know what the hell Sid's sister's still doing in Mexico though, and Sid says, Oh didn't I tell you, Champ? Sister Sarah just got accepted into Mexican medical school. Yeah, exactly. Mexican medical school. She just wouldn't be a Shapiro if she weren't a punch-line to a joke now would she.

Stretching out lengthwise over as many barstools as possible, Sid says, Still it's still better than where she was, I suppose. I mean outside of Israel the entire Middle East is safe for no one of Jewish pedigree anymore, let *alone* a girl. Hey'd you know they don't allow their women to work, go to school, or even read books over there? Well it's true, hey. They're not allowed to do a damned thing, women. So now that I think about it, he reflects, that ought to've been the ideal situation for her.

The others immediately fill him in on my night. And upon hearing the gist of the tale, he gradually levers himself upright. And here we have yet another example of those in dire need of having their organs harvested, he says, and there's simply no one willing to do the deed anymore. Our entire generation has failed to harvest its share of organs, boys, he goes on, levelling a stern finger at each of us. Then he adds, Well bring on the organs, I say. Let the floodgates open, I say. Where are all the blessed donors to be found. Down at the beach with that whale no doubt. Getting their pictures taken and generally just hanging around.

Sid assumes a sitting position slumped down against the bar, laying his forehead comfortably against the wood and rolling it slowly from side to side. You've got to get clear of that couple as soon as possible, citizen, he says, and I say, Believe me, you're preaching to the choir here, pal. Well for the love of God, he says, and I say, Hey, at least I offered to clean it up. You mean you *didn't*? says Nick in disgust. No Nick, I didn't. Todd was Windexing undigested Tylenol off the window when I left, the poor bastard. Nice of you to let the husband finally get involved though, says Billy Henry, and I say, Wasn't it though? To be honest, though, I think they wanted me out of there as quickly as possible. Can't blame them really. Rather weird scene altogether. No fucking kidding— Jesus Christ, says Nick, at which point Billy Henry reminds him to lay off.

Sitting there at the table, bent low over his mug, Billy Henry stirs sugar into his coffee with an enormous utensil of some ornate, vaguely Mediterranean design. Every so often he looks up at me in a peculiar way, as though unsure whether to laugh or not, and then slowly lowers his head again. So what happens now? he says, and I say, Well, for whatever reason, we've decided never to speak of it again. Yup, mum's the word on this cautionary tale. And that goes for this chorus of goodwill here as well. Should be interesting for you at work tomorrow though, Sid says, and I say, Hilarious, no doubt.

Nick returns to his painting, and Sid returns to his business at the bar. What, Champ, no tequila? he says. Don't you have anything besides *ouzo* in this godforsaken little dump you call a restaurant? All the liquor's locked up in the cooler, Nick tells him. Help yourself to whatever's there though.

Quietly, compassionately, finally given the opportunity to address me individually, Billy Henry says I have to stop sabotaging myself. I *have* to. I'm trying to, I tell him, and he says well I should try harder. Listen, Billy, receiving sympathy from the likes of you isn't really a burden I can handle just now. Yes, leave the citizen alone, says Sid, spinning steadily on his stool. And besides, too many Métis in his life, that's his only problem right now. Of course what he really needs to do more than anything is sign his organ donor card as soon as possible. Have I mentioned that eight out of ten worthy recipients die waiting for transplants? Have I? Well good, someone's got to shed light on this predicament. Predicament nothing, he says, regular fucking tragedy's what it is.

Billy Henry's mouth tightens into a thin hard line. Blame it on the Indian, he says. How'd I know it would come to that. William Henry, you're right! says Sid. You're absolutely right! Good God, you're an inspiration. It never ceases to amaze me this ability of yours to slice to the very heart of the matter—to dissect it really; to boil it all down—Great Scot, you inspire me. You really do. In your simple, straightforward, surreptitiously homosexual yet strangely skin-headed way, you've cut to the proverbial chase yet again. Now I see what all those early settlers were trading for when they gave up all that invaluable whiskey.

Fuck you, Sid, says Billy Henry, and Sid says, Now take it easy, Henry. Your secret's safe with me. Hell, you and the Champ could gear down and go at it right here on the floor and you wouldn't hear a single peep from me. Other than a few words of encouragement and maybe the occasional cheer, I mean. And listen, I've got nothing against you full-blooded Injuns. Really. You're at least somewhat dignified—a little thin-skinned perhaps, but at least *some*what dignified—even if you do seem to consider a fucking *bottle* collection a productive use of one's time. No, it's this bloody half-breed, organ-hoarding half-sister of yours who chafes me.

Billy Henry turns to me. If he keeps this up I might start to take offence, he tells me, and Sid waves him off, turns to the bar, and flexes his nostrils in the vicinity of the Ouzo bottle. Then he pours himself a shot. How about you, citizen? Want one? he asks. Help celebrate the sausage-fest we've got going here tonight? No thanks, I say, sliding my feet together, one against the other, seeking the means to a moment of clarity. I actually just smoked some cancer weed of Stephanie's. So why tell us? asks Billy Henry, his head retracting into his shoulders quite involuntarily. Well you're some sort of cop aren't you? says Sid, licking Ouzo from the back of his hand. So obviously the citizen here thought you ought to know. Now as for me, I'm not entirely sure where I stand on the drug issue anymore. All I know is that I've got to get this car-stealing sister of yours signing her organ donor card as soon as possible. Well have you signed yours? asks Nick. Have I not, he's told by Sid. But then really, who's going to want them—my kidneys are shot and my liver's shrunken up to the size of a raisin. But as for the citizen here, I bet he's still got a couple of decent beans in there. How about it, citizen? If I got some shirts made up would you wear one? PLEASE SIGN YOUR ORGAN DONOR CARD, I'm thinking. Straight to the point. No messing around. You've got to understand, boys, it's my mission.

Sid knocks back the shot, then asks if any of us know where he can get hold of a decent whore. What, like a prostitute? says Billy Henry, and Sid says, *Yes, like a prostitute*. Good God, Henry, is there another kind? Nick wants to know what Sid needs a whore for though, and Sid says why the hell does he think? To whore around with of course. Make him forget all the time wasted amongst champion salsa dancers and their Native Indian life partners over the previous month or so.

Sid pours himself another shot. Then, knocking that one back, he pours himself a backup. Actually I wanted one for the citizen

here, he says, and I say, Whore nothing, what I need's a boat. And
when Billy Henry asks what for, Sid says, Why, for the mission of
course. One that requires a great deal of skill, strategy and stealth,
Henry, thereby disqualifying an avowed lawman like you on principle. Only guy I know with a boat's your actor buddy, Nick puts
in at this point. Say'd you ever give him our screenplay, Sid? Why
yes, Nick, I did. And? And he said you'd caught the tone quite
admirably, says Sid. He said, and I quote, "For a Mexican, that
Greek sure has an ear for today's Native Indian colloquialisms and
cadences of speech." He said that, really? says Nick, and Sid says,
Actually, no. Truth be told, it's a fairly shitty script. "Too Good
Will Hunting," Hum said, whatever that means. Too ironical, I'm
guessing. Which is ironic in itself as everybody knows Matt and
Ben never really wrote anything. No, turns out studio hacks did
everything, Sid says, shaking his head at the utter irony of
Hollywood. Anyway, boys, don't be glum. The gay Grexican-
Indian artistic community rarely receives the major studio sup-
port it undoubtedly deserves. Fuck you, Billy Henry mumbles,
moping low over his mug.

Tracing along the face of the recently refurbished bar the faint
penciled outline of what will presumably develop into the token
olive branch décor, Nick asks Sid what I need a boat for though.
Oh just a little modern-day bootlegging is all, he's told. All quite
illegal though, eh citizen? Pardon? says Billy Henry. Oh come
now, Henry, enough with the interrogation, says Sid. Besides,
you're not really a cop, you're a reservation cop for crying out
loud. You've no jurisdiction here. Yes, says Billy Henry, but if
someone's conspiring to commit a crime, well then it's my duty
to inform—

Who? says Sid. The real police? Or just the ones on bikes. By
the way, you run much with that Dairy Queen crowd, Henry? I
hear they're a real wild bunch. Enough to tell them what you're
up to anyway, Billy Henry says, and Sid says, What? That Chris
here's simply a romantic at heart? That he—and you—are fucking
sociopaths, Sid, how's that. Come on, Billy, you don't mean that.
Not solid citizens like us. Yes, a real pillar of stability you are, says
Billy Henry, moping low over his mug once more.

Hey, I resent that, Billy. I'm stable. Heck I'm the king of stability. Cut me open and you'll find me chock*full* of stability. In fact all my organs are labelled with the stuff. He pours himself another shot, muttering something to the effect of, Stable. Hell, there's no one more stable than me. Find one and I'll kill him—instantly. Heck, I'll kill him with my stability. And don't be fooled, Henry, the idea of killing someone presents no problem for me. Hey, he says, snapping his fingers, I could harvest their organs just like they do in Vegas maybe.

Together with Sid and Billy Henry, I watch Nick paint a while. You know, I say a little later, now that I think about it, I'd maybe like to land on your reservation, Billy. Yeah, right out there on the end of that wharf of yours. And hey, if you're interested in helping out, we'll be coming across late tomorrow night. Bullshit, he says, and Sid says, No, it's true. We've got it all worked out. But why? *Why*? Why the hell do you think, Henry? To change our fortunes of course. *Our* fortunes, Sid? Well mine anyway, says Sid. For the citizen here it's simply the means to a romantic end of course. Hey Chris, if this is a cry for help, I'm not listening, Nick says, to which Sid laughs uproariously, Don't worry, Nick, the World Salsa Dance Champion is about the last person he'd come to for help.

I ask to borrow the phone, and Nick points me in behind the bar. Eventually a voice says hello, and I say, Hey Hum, been out to see the whale yet? Fuck you, Sleeman, it's late, Hum says, his voice little more than a groan on the other end of the line. Listen, I tell him, I need a—

Dances with Wolves! interrupts Sid from behind.

—favour, I say. Shut up, Sid. So what do you think, I ask into the phone. Come on, Sleeman, it's really late, Hum groans. So what, I tell him. I said I need a favour. What then for Christ's sake? he says, so I say, Well, the reason I'm calling—

Dances with Wolves, Sid cries out again, can you not see me? Can you not see that I am your friend? and so I turn around to glare at him. Has he signed his organ donor card, citizen? he whispers. Has he? Tell him it's really important he sign his organ donor card. Shut it, Sid. Tell him, citizen. Shut it, I repeat, and Billy

Henry glances up from his mug. Shut it—I like that, he says with
a grin.

What then for Christ's sake, says Hum wearily, and I say, Your
boat. Or more specifically, you *and* your boat. I need you to pick
me up tomorrow night at three o'clock in the morning *with* your
boat. You're joking, he says, so I say, Never with an artist like you,
Hum. That's right, citizen, tell him, Sid chimes in. Tell Dances
with Wolves to sign his organ donor card or else it'll be straight
down in the ratings for him. For Christ's sake, I say, shut up! and
Sid does shut up, as does Hum on the other end of the line.

So are you going to help me out or not, Hum? I need to know.
Well no, I'm told. Not unless I know what for. I have to bring
something across the border, I say, and he says, Something illegal?
No, it's legal, I tell him. It's just that it's illegal to bring it across the
border. But what is it? It's liquor, Hum. A *lot* of liquor. What,
you're smuggling *booze*? he says. Like a *boot*legger? What the hell
for? he wants to know, and I tell him I'll tell him tomorrow. But
listen, Sid and I, we've got it all worked out. Tell me *now*, he insists
as Sid cries out, Dances with Wolves! once more, nearly spilling
across the bar what little is left in the Ouzo bottle. Please, citizen,
go on and interrupt me to all ends of the earth, but for the love
of God tell him to *sign*! How about you guys though? he asks the
others. If I had shirts made up would you wear one? Would you
though? That's it then, he says, lowering the bottle onto the bar
like a gavel, I'm coming right back here with a silk-screen tomorrow.

Hum asks if Sid's finished. I think so, I say. For the moment anyway. All right then, tell me, he says, so I say I can't because there's
this big Indian cop listening in. As in Billy Hank? he says, and I
say, That's right. Tell him to get lost then, Sleeman, he says. Tell that
big fucking chug to go smoke a peace pipe in his goddamned
sweat lodge—

Will do, but later, I say. First I need to know that you'll meet me
at your condo tomorrow night, at three o'clock in the morning,
with your boat. Not a chance, he says. Not until I know what for.
Fine, I say, have it your way. Tell him, citizen, Sid puts in. Tell
Dances with Wolves to sign his goddamned organ donor card and

the *shirts*! Tell him about the shirts! Tell him it's my God-given mission. Hum asks what the hell Sid's on about, and I tell him organ donation. Organ donation, huh, he chuckles. Well, if nothing else, a little philanthropy's nice to see from a Jew these days.

Friday, 2:56 am

Leaving Nick to his painting and Billy Henry to Sid, I step out into the snow even now turning to rain and walk east along Marine, eventually stumbling upon Krishna sitting alone on the Trap & Gill patio huddled up against the cold, a freshly lit cigarette in hand. I ask what she's doing here, and in answer she leans forward into the light, revealing an eye swollen shut from her husband's fist a couple of hours earlier in the night.

I didn't know where else to go, she says.

Standing pensively at the edge of the patio, suspending in my nostrils the cold crisp ocean air filtered clean by snow, I look not at Krishna but back down the silent snow-covered street to where the neon lights of the Ocean Beach Hotel spray hazy pink reflections out towards the beach. The wind is in my eyes, and tears begin to rise, as all at once the overhead wires begin to moan.

How about a friend's, I suggest. Oh because he's *passionate*, she says, having retreated once more to the shadows. My friends, they're all telling me it's because he's *passionate*. That he can't fucking help it, the prick. And with that she throws back her head and laughs. She laughs and laughs until tears run down her swollen cheeks and the cigarette falls from her grasp. Seeing this, I bend down to retrieve it from the pile of slushy snow at her feet, then set the wet but still burning cigarette on the edge of the table while Krishna tries valiantly to reassemble herself. Finally she takes up the cigarette, attempts a drag, then butts it out, employing as ashtray the nearest potted plant, much to my disappointment.

She continues butting out her cigarette, stabbing it down into the soil. Scooter's still there though, she says, and I say, Scooter? Who the hell's Scooter? My cat, she says, extracting from her coat pocket a fresh cigarette, lighting it, and exhaling a great train of smoke in little boxcar-ed increments. Yeah Scooter's going to need to get out of there, she says, so I say, What about Joe? What *about* Joe? she echoes and so, in Krishna's stale smoke-smelling Jeep, with Krishna behind the wheel and my fingers shoved down the open front of her jeans, we drive east along Marine, up past the bus stop cross atop the bluff and down towards the Semiahmoo reserve's silent snow-covered streets. Most of the houses on the reserve are dark at this hour, but in the occasional kitchen window a single bare bulb still burns. Krishna brings the Jeep to a sudden halt down near the water's edge and extinguishes the headlights, leaving the engine and the wipers running for now, the latter spawning a thin skin of ice over the lower portion of the windshield, old and ineffective as they obviously are. She pauses a moment as I align my fingers' rhythm with the rhythm of the wipers, gathering forces mechanical and otherwise for the imminent climax and later I sit quietly, glancing about at nothing, coaxing her silently through a liquid paralysis. A long way out over the flat naked bay I note the regular flash of a remote island lighthouse, while far above the lighthouse the full moon pushes its way through the intervening clouds, so far unsuccessful in its journey. I look off to the left, to the shimmering lights of houses on the other side of the border that always seem so eerie and isolated. And I look off to the right, to a long line of trees standing bronchial, white and silent against the night, alongside which the naked black windows of Joe Brand's house stare vacantly back.

Afterwards, having successfully sucked her scent from my fingers, Krishna stares directly ahead into the air blurred by small flecks of snow falling out of a deep black sky. Suddenly she shivers, releases my hand, and shoves her own hands up into her armpits for warmth. I ask if she wants to get out of here and she says no, no, she'll be all right. And eventually, once she's good and ready, I follow her across the snow-white lawn and up the short set of stairs to the front door. Just as we reach it, however, the door opens abruptly from within, revealing her husband standing threateningly in loose grey underwear, staring directly and altogether portentously at me. I bull my neck and thrust my fists deeper into my pockets, raising my chin a little. Joe Brand stares leadenly back. Stares, yes, but in the end steps reluctantly aside as

Krishna, lighting yet another cigarette, shoves on past, down the hall and out of sight. And together with Joe I watch her go, until she's far enough removed from the equation that he can sucker punch me square in the side of *Annie. Annie goes on ignoring me. Then she goes down along the line of bushes to where across the street a man is raking—she calls out to the man but he does not hear. Meanwhile I go on whispering and watching the boys whipping as one goes in behind him there, tightening his coat sleeves around the backstop pole, while another takes up the willow and has a go at him a while. They go towards him one after another, first the one boy whipping and then the next boy whipping. Then the girls go forward and whip him as well. They go on this way as Annie goes down along the line of bushes. Finally she emerges from behind the last bush and he sees her crying, and crying out himself he tells her to go. But she won't go, and the one girl goes forward and whips her as well. I sit there at the bush and watch the girl whipping, while across the street the man is raking still. He rakes and I sit, and the next time I look between the bare branches and through their belated flower absences I see the girl drop the willow at Annie's feet* again, and again my head hits the floor. Silent except for his breathing, he eases me up to my knees, then to my feet, only to hit me square in the side of the face once more, dropping me bodily to the floor. And again he helps me up to my feet before dropping me hard to the floor. Finally, getting a little tired, or else bored, he takes up a position alongside me in the hallway, both of us breathing hard now and fairly sore.

Staggering back against the wall, I try to staunch the blood now flowing from my nose. I'm here for the cat, Joe. I'm here for Scooter, I say as he mops the sweat from his brow. Squinting, he looks at me almost as if seeing me for the first time. There, he says. Where? There. In the chair. And sure enough, there he is, Scooter, lodged deep in the seat of the living room Lazy Boy. I glance at Joe a moment to see whether or not I might pass unmolested here. Cat food's in the kitchen, he tells me. Kitchen closet beside the stove.

And so, liberating Scooter from his Lazy Boy, I head through to the kitchen and then, cat and cat food in hand, stumble back past a squinting Joe Brand and out to the Jeep to await Krishna's eventual return. Finally she appears, unlike me no worse for wear, and piling some of her belongings into the rear of the Jeep, hops in beside me here. Joe said you got the cat? she says, and I say, Yeah I've got him right here. And tossing a pillow into the back Krishna informs me that Scooter's a girl.

Apparently Krishna has already put in a call to Katie, and has thus secured a couch to crash on for the night. And so we drive in silence, each of us taking turns scratching Scooter behind the ears while trying to light a cigarette with the onboard lighter, failing miserably with each consecutive effort. Finally, though, I emerge triumphant, lit cigarette in hand, and pass it proudly only to look on sadly as she butts it out without so much as a single puff or second glance.

Katie's new house is up near the top of the hill on Buena Vista, aligned almost perfectly with the pier. In anticipation of our arrival she's up and around of course, appearing on the landing in a long white sweatshirt and glasses, sipping intermittently at a bottle of homebrewed beer. Krishna takes Scooter and heads inside. Bleeding, I remain behind. Meanwhile, the snow turns to rain, slashing down at the ground at seemingly arbitrary angles, bringing with it the smell of the beach and the staunch blackness of the bay beyond. If I listen carefully I can hear the waves breaking out along the breakwater, first one and then another. And somewhere below that breaking I swear I can hear someone crying, way down deep and nearly out of range altogether.

Eventually, once the path is clear, I venture out in search of a washroom in order to tidy up my face a little. And some time later, with the wind whistling through the trees and the power lines outside, Katie finds me perched in amongst the moving boxes on the edge of the bathtub, bleeding down into her toilet bowl.

Gonna throw up, Katie? Toilet's right here.

She stands there rigid and wide-eyed behind her glasses, silently watching me.

Keep it down, I tell her. I don't want Krishna to read anything into all this sympathy you're offering me. She demands to know who did this though, so I tell her Krishna's husband, Joe. What, and Krishna doesn't *know*? she says, and I say that it was dark, so no. *Ah*, she nods knowingly, so you tried to kill yourself again did you. Well swing for the fences, kid. Strike two though.

Katie takes a washcloth and dampens it under the tap, then proceeds to wipe my face with it. After a particularly punishing swipe I ask her, as politely as possible and if it wouldn't be too much trouble, if she might tread just a little more lightly here. She has to get the blood off though, she tells me, arresting her stroke a moment, but only a moment, before pounding away at my cheek once more.

Well this certainly explains the mystery of the blood on the cat, she says at length, studying me over the frames of her glasses. I tell her I can't see out my right eye anymore. What do you mean? she says, and I say I can't *see* anymore. It's like a curtain came down on half the room or—

Shut up, she tells me, holding my chin fixedly, tilting my head back to facilitate a more detailed inspection of the damage. Where's all this new blood coming from though? she says, and I say my forehead. Check my forehead—yeah, there. It hurts like hell up there. Ah, there it is, she says, forcing the hair back around the hairline. Oh wow, this one's a gusher too.

She holds the bloodstained washcloth firmly to my forehead until the bleeding has slowed sufficiently to warrant an uncertain abandonment. That it then, Katie? There's your lip, she tells me, averting my thumb from the vicinity of her forehead. What's wrong with my lip, I say, and she says, Nothing. Other than this large angry chunk hanging down out of it. I attempt to test my lip with a finger, but again she smacks my hand away. Quit it, she says. You're only going to make it worse.

We grapple briefly, and finally I take her by the hips and shift her bodily back and out of the way. Then, locating the chunk of displaced lip with my fingers and pressing it firmly between my teeth, I try my best to sever it as cleanly as possible—unfortunately it proves just a little too thick. And so, having exhausted the one and only option I can think of, I go about stuffing the chunk back up into position. And finally, when I'm good and ready, I take a good long look in the mirror.

Good God—

Don't move! she says. I'm trying to take a visual imprint of the moment. Hey, I could've taken him, Katie. I could've though. You know, if I'd wanted to. Thing is, you have to really *feel* like taking someone. Well, she says, evidently Joe felt it pretty good.

I ask about her glasses. What, she says, you didn't know I wore glasses? Yeah, when I was a kid I got stabbed in the eye with a fork. I could have sworn I told you about that. *Stabbed in the eye with a fork*, I say. No, Katie, you never told me about that. Who the hell did that, I ask, some kid? My brother actually, she answers. I don't think he meant it though. I mean afterwards he was clearly upset. Well no kidding, I say. Jesus Christ. They're only for reading though, she says.

We move into the bedroom where so far only the bed has managed reassembly, and where slowly and painstakingly Katie helps me undress. Eventually, in the dark, I feel her make her way down—so far down in fact that I'm forced into an early retreat—and so I roll her over onto her back and kiss a long meandering path down to her feet. But then the kissing hurts my ruptured lip too much, and so I try to find my way with my fingers and later, as her stomach muscles flutter and her pelvis rises, she covers her face with a pillow and releases. She shudders a while, long and satisfied, and when she's finished shuddering, expects to return the favour.

I push her away. Stiffening, she rotates slowly to the wall in protest, and after a while asks me why I come here exactly. What are you talking about, Katie. I've never even *been* to this house before. I mean why do you come see me like this, she says, allowing me to roll her back to a slightly more convenient conversational arrangement. Why do you always insist on *servicing* me like this. I'm afraid I still don't understand what you mean, I say. I was simply coming to the aid of my friend Krishna and—

I'm serious, she says. All right then, Katie. Fine. I see tonight's your turn to suppress all forms of amusement. Because I'm missing something in my life right now—how's that. What are you missing, she says. Besides the obvious. I don't know, I say, a certain vitality. A certain . . . intimacy. Romance. I really just need to make someone happy right now, all right?

She directs a long and complex sigh at the top of my head. You know I can't compete with this—this angel of yours, she says, and I tell her I'm not asking her to. And don't worry, it won't be much longer now anyway. Much longer till what? Till I'm not around anymore, I say, feeling her body brace suddenly beneath me. So you're still intent on—on leaving, she says hesitantly, speaking euphemistically, and I say that actually I'm more intent than ever. Yeah how come exactly? she says, and I say, Well, to be honest, for my own peace of mind. So then you'll be at peace by resting in peace, she muses. Actually, that's kind of funny.

I lie quietly a moment listening to her inner workings, while outside the plastic-insulated window rain angles down through the streetlamp's pale amber glow. You're really going to leave? she says, and I say yes, I'm going to leave. Why, because you feel guilty? she says, and I say that's part of it, sure. But what *for* exactly? she says, so I say that sometimes I see myself through my wife's eyes, and I don't like what I see anymore.

I move up the bed to kiss her, forcing my tongue against her clamped front teeth. Though of course one shouldn't leave without first saying goodbye, I say, and she squirms excitedly. Clearly that would be wrong, she says. Rude even. Extremely rude, no question, I say, running a thumb lightly along her lips before parting them gently, feeling the regular bump bump bump of the teeth and then the moist muscular softness of the awakening tongue beneath.

She pulls me down to kiss my eyebrows, my eyelids, my cheeks, and then abruptly stops kissing me altogether. It's not fair is it, she says, drawing her own face up and away, and I say, No, it's not. It's not fair. But then that's the way it goes. But I don't want you to leave, she says. Hey, it's not some big necessary thing we've got going here, Katie. It's more just, what, a little bit of monkey business, I say, at which point she surprisingly starts to cry. And trying my best to console her, which I've been told really isn't very consoling at all, I remain quiet, even a little cold and distant, allowing her to cry alone a while.

Fuck, she sniffles. Fuck, I promised myself I wouldn't do this. I promised myself I wouldn't care this much. Why? *Why*? Well because I like you, she says, but I'm not allowed to love you, that's *why*.

Rolling over onto my back, I begin to explore, with my tongue, the provisional patchwork of my lip. The nerves seem to have retreated somewhat, leaving behind a thick solid knot of not precisely dead, but certainly comatose flesh. And after a thorough investigation has been completed, in which a new stream of blood has been opened up and tasted, I tell her it's a simple matter of clarity. I'm just not sure I can remain clear anymore. What do you mean, she says. If it goes any further—any further than it already has, I mean—I'm just not sure I can remain clear in the fact that I was once, not so long ago, a rather broke but otherwise happily married man, I say. And would that be so terrible? she asks. I believe so, yes, I answer. As I said, it's like sometimes I see myself through my wife's eyes, and I don't like what I see anymore. So you still love her then, she says, and I say, Of course I still love her—I'm her *husband*. She's my *wife*. We were married on a *beach* for crying out—

But isn't it more the *idea* of her? she interrupts. Oh *please*, Katie. Shop your soap opera psychoanalysis someplace else. Well isn't it? she says, drilling me in the thigh with a tight, hard, surprisingly effective fist. Maybe, I shrug. Okay, I'll give you that. Well how does that work then? she asks. How does what work? Well how can you expect to stay married to the idea of someone when they're—

Correction then: no idea. Never an idea. No, clearly I'm married to you, I tell her. You know what I mean, she says. Well does loving the idea of someone necessarily prohibit you from falling in love with someone else, Katie? Not necessarily, she says. Well there you have it then: I'm in love with both of you, I say.

I fiddle with my forehead and its freshly forming scab, while somewhere beyond the wall the old furnace kicks on in the night.

Tell me something though, she says a little later. When did you know, you know, that you were *really* in love with her. Hmm, I say, I suppose when she told me she loved me. And when did she know that she loved you, Katie says, and I say, Oh that's easy. When she found out I liked to collect golf balls. Golf balls? Yeah, golf balls, Katie. When I was a kid I liked to collect golf balls. You know, from the field alongside the course. What? What is it, I say, feeling her smiling in the dark. She likes me, she tells me. Yes, I get that feeling, I say. No, she means she likes spending her time with me. But I'm leaving her. I'm determined to leave her. And she still doesn't understand why that has to be.

She withdraws her hand from mine, and together we lie quietly a while. Soon, though, under the stimulus of my inquisitive fingers, she begins to thaw a little. Fascinating piece of kit you got here, Katie. Absolutely fascinating, I say as she continues to moisten, breathing steadily and heavily.

I ask how come she got beat up so much as a kid. Well, she sighs, because she was Indian—or half Indian—and blonde, and that annoyed the hell out of the other kids on the reserve apparently. Did she fight back? Well of course she fought back—all the time. After a while, though, she didn't bother. How come, I say, and she hesitates.

Well because it was all just a lot of monkey business, she says at last.

Friday, 5:34 am

An hour or so later, having awakened abruptly with the early morning light, I shuffle out to the bathroom to re-examine the damage, finding things pretty much as I left them—that is, deteriorating at a fairly rapid rate throughout the night. Both sty and canker sore, however related, continue to cultivate at a feverish pace. And the skin encircling the gash on my cheek remains purplish and swollen, while the cut on my forehead, in dire need of stitches, seems intent on an indefinite weeping. But the worst part, by far, has got to be the lip. Or more precisely, where I stuffed this one thick chunk back up in. The edges have turned black and crusty with dried blood, while the surrounding tissue has returned to being swollen and ornery to the slightest touch. I search through the boxes in the bathroom until eventually happening upon some scissors, at which point, avoiding as much as

possible the recently reinvigorated nerves, I very carefully prune
away the dried black crustiness in an effort to somehow improve
that element of my appearance. It doesn't go so well. Each snip
serves only to produce an ever-increasing obligation, until my
entire face appears about due for repair. And so, again very carefully, I splash water across my face in what amounts to a fairly
futile attempt at remedying that patch of blood-caked hair currently matted against my pimple-encrusted forehead, the impression of the latter having diminished substantially since Joe Brand's
impromptu facial. And finally I jump in the shower, wary of
course of too much water pressure.

What's going on? asks a voice, and turning I find Katie squinting in from the edge of the curtain. I'm showering, I tell her.
Well I can see that, she says as I turn off the taps, grab a towel
from the rack, and start in gingerly on my head and hair. And
dabbing nimbly at my face, remembering to steer clear of my
fore*head we hear the pounding of the waves on the beach, one after
another after another. And later, as we lie together naked on the sand,
we watch as a young boy materializes from the late night darkness
offering us a stack of clean, new, freshly folded towels. When I ask how
much, he says, Five dollars, por favor. You got five dollars, Annie? I've
only got a ten, I tell her as the boy places his stack of towels carefully
on the sand, his short brisk movements silhouetted against the bright
lights of distant Plata Del Carmen. I pay him his five dollars, and later
half-jokingly remark that only in Mexico can you go skinny-dipping
and expect to have some local sell you towels for the occasi*on, I have
this plan, Katie. Later on today, around two, say, I thought maybe
I'd go shopping across the border. Wow, shopping, that *is* quite
a plan, she says. So let me get this straight: you're going to go
shopping. In the States. And bring it back here. Well if nothing
else, you're certainly an ambitious bastard. Shoot for the stars,
kid. No, but listen, I say. I'm shopping for liquor. Liquor? Yeah,
I'm shopping for liquor for the restaurant, I say, and then smuggling it back across the border. Why, though? she wants to know.
Well because Rick wants me to, I tell her. And if you don't? she
says, so I say, Well then I suppose he'll find another manager
who will. And besides, I kind of have to. Why do I have to?

Because I owe both Rick and his brother a whole lot of money, I say.

She looks up at me, blinks once emphatically, then shakes her head and sighs disappointedly.

Anyway, I say, it's all of what, a few hundred feet from that marina on the American side over to Indian land where, I might add, a coalition of the willing will be eagerly awaiting our arrival. Who'll be waiting, she says. My brother? *My* brother? But you know he's fundamentally against that sort of thing. Oh I think he's coming around, I tell her.

I toss the towel in the hamper and begin to get dressed. Where do you think you're going? she says, and I say, To work. Oh bullshit, she says. Clearly you're going down to your bench to pine over her right now. I've seen you talking, you know. Clearly you're mistaken then, I say. I only talk to Stephan and Mr Soon now.

She risks a step from the relative warmth of the carpet onto the cool bathroom tile, wrapping her arms up around my neck and nuzzling in a while.

I can't kiss you, Katie. Can't or won't, she says, rising to her toes, drawing her eyes up opposite mine. Home-wrecker, I say. Adulterous bastard, she says. Home-wrecker, I say. Oh fuck off, she says, pulling quickly away. You'd never have let me. Oh I don't know, I say. No, you wouldn't, she says. It was obvious. But clearly you ought to come back to bed and let me wreck you right now. Clearly, I say. But you won't, she says, and I say no, I won't. All this sneaking around, it's getting to me. Who's sneaking? she says, and I say well I am, for one. That's your choice, she smiles, reaching up to kiss my cheek—the unbroken one—before moving onto my chest and down.

I prayed for you, you know, she says, and I say, You did? God help me, that was decent of you though. No, she says, I mean I prayed to *have* you. To get you. Or at least someone like you. Don't worry, it was all a very long time ago.

Somewhere outside a seagull cries. Katie sneezes and rubs her shining eyes. Anyway, she says, I prayed to whatever it is that's out there that I'd get someone like you someday. Clearly, though, it was you who came to me, I say. In fact I remember like it was yesterday. You dropped off your résumé—hey, quit it! Were you put on this earth to annoy me? she says, threatening to bite me again. Is that it? Is that your entire purpose for being? Not entirely, no, I say. Well you know what I mean, she says. I prayed for you and I got you. You're like this, what, this mentor to me. Well God help us both then, I say.

Again, outside, the seagull cries, and Katie pushes my protective hands to the side. Tell me about Australia again, she says, and I say I'd rather tell her about Ireland. Artists live tax free in Ireland. She wants to hear about Australia though, she says. Well, I sigh, it's hot. And the bugs are big. I mean really big. And all the aborigines hang around this place called King's Cross and get pissed on VB and . . . Tell me, doesn't it make you angry, Katie? Doesn't what make her angry? I don't know, the universal plight of the indigenous, say. Should it? she says, and so I take hold of her forearm and rub it feverishly between my hands until she pulls it away.

What are you doing? she says. Giving you an Indian burn, I say. Well quit it—*quit* it! she says, managing to break free. All right, I say, how about an Indian leg-wrestle then? wrapping my leg around hers in what amounts to a fairly fruitless attempt at the technique in question. All right, all right, she says, shoving me away. You think too much, that's all. Probably, yes, I say. Well you have no idea what's it's like, all right? she says. Growing up blonde on a reserve. And believe me, Katie, that bothers me immensely. What time is it, I say, and she clutches me close, telling me that her internal Indian clock is telling her that it's getting close to six o'clock in the morning.

Yeah, well, I can't help it, I say. Thinking too much, I mean. The pigeonholing, see, it just gets to me. Yeah, well, the only thing that bothers me is being called a slut or a whore, Katie says. And that happens quite regularly, I say, and she looks up at me a moment, and then turns abruptly away and says, More often than you'd think anyway.

I press her back against the counter. People call you that really, Katie? She pivots to the mirror and adjusts her hair, then says not really, no, not anymore. Her brother used to though. Billy did?

Really? Yeah, after she got raped and all. I guess he really didn't deal with it so well, she says, and I say I guess not, no.

He never calls her that anymore though. Not since she broke his nose. I ask what for, and she says because he pissed her off, that's what for. No, I mean how come he called her that. Brothers, she shrugs, who knows. Seriously though, Katie. Well when it first happened, she tells me, when she first started going to counselling and all that, she was still sleeping around a lot and stuff. Well what else is a girl to do, really, I say, whereupon she looks at me, and in turn I hold up my hands for clemency. I apologize, Katie. Go ahead. And she supposes she was still pretty messed up. And later on, since she was still kind of a flirt, her brother always thought she was sort of slipping back into the lifestyle that got her into trouble in the first place, and so he started calling her a slut and a whore and stuff. And so she hit him. Hard. And he didn't call her those things anymore after that.

You're still a flirt though, I say, and she shrugs, It's a tool. Tool nothing, you bait them, Katie. Sure I bait them, she says. It's just a way of gaining control. And getting them back, I say, and she says, Sure, and that. Dangerous occupation, woman. In the immortal words of Pat Benatar, stop using sex as a weapon. Sex as a what? A little before your time maybe, I say, and she says, Clearly you *are* old after all. Not so old I can't take a round out of you still, I say, wrapping my arms snugly around her waist and pressing my pelvis into hers repeatedly.

My, what big arms you have, she says, and I say, All the better to pin your ankles back behind your ears, my dear. Oh please, she says, I hardly need help with that. You're a real slut, you know that, I say, and she laughs menacingly. Oh you *know* you're the only who could get away with that, she says.

She starts to look away, but instead looks up at me more intently and says, I have to tell you, though, I have a real aversion to you coming over so late and then leaving again so early. An aversion do you, I say, holding my nose and blowing gently. Yes, she says, I think that maybe you should just stay all night. Come on now, Katie, all this sneaking around's what keeps it interesting, you know that. But I thought you weren't comfortable with that aspect of it, she says, and I say I'm not. Well clearly you're consistent then, she says, pulling away to adjust the position of a hairbrush relative to the soap dispenser.

What, I say. Nothing, she says. What is it, Katie. Tell me. Zack says you're not taking my feelings into consideration, that's all, she tells me. Well clearly Zack's raised a considerable point, I say. But remind me again, who is Zack exactly? You know—Zack, she says. My roommate's boyfriend. *Angela's* boyfriend. Uh yes, and where is Angela by the way? Zack's. They like it better at Zack's. How come, I say. Well Angela gets pretty loud, and Zack gets embarrassed. Well how considerate of him, I say.

Finishing buttoning my shirt, I say, So Zack thinks I should take your feelings more into consideration, does he. Absolutely, she says. And how about your roommate, Katie? What does she think? Angela? she says. Angela thinks I need the experience. Angela's all about new experiences. Sort of like Sid, I say.

Katie looks at me, hiding her top teeth with her bottom lip, as though trying to stave off the impulse to bite me again. Then, standing on her toes, she reaches up to suck my chin. Say, what time did you say you need the Robert Blake tomorrow? she asks upon disengaging, and I say, Around two—today. Pick me up at the restaurant at two *today*. But I thought you'd be going to see your wife today, she says, and I say I would be, normally, but now I spend all my time coming up with new and inventive ways to keep from seeing Stephanie. Now may I use your toothbrush, Katie? Or do you have an aversion to that sort of thing too.

Friday, 5:58 am

Outside it's misty, cool and grey, but not raining, and almost all the snow is gone. The road is muddy, the ditches alongside run high with water, and beyond the close crowded trees that line the road the lawns of the individual yards appear too soggy to cut through effectively and so, fists thrust deep in pockets, I move out along Buena Vista heading east, gathering speed, eventually accelerating to a fairly decent clip, despite my mounting list of injuries making fairly decent time, breathing hard now through pursed and swollen lips. Eventually I arrive at a set of stairs cutting down between two brand new beach houses a half block up the street from my own sad place, around the backside of which, to no one's surprise, least of all mine, I find what must have been a full bag of Idaho Spuds lying scattered across the asphalt. I know it to be the work of Jeff of course, but Jeff of course is nowhere to be found. I wander in amongst the discarded potatoes, and stooping to acquire one, turn it over thoughtfully before depositing it promptly and all too violently to the ground. I pick up another potato and discharge that too to the asphalt, watching as pieces of spud shatter across my shoes and over the driveway, repeating the operation until each and every potato is gone. Before long a whole fleet of seagulls appear, together with the requisite escort of obnoxious crows, and so I bound up the stairs and into the house to see what else might be found. Unfortunately there isn't all that much around. I do manage to find some of Jeff's medication, though, strewn here and there over the kitchen counter in capsule form, and tossing each of these off the deck and onto the ground, watch the gulls circle off in rapid confusion. Eventually Cojimar comes rolling along, and once she's had her fill of vainly chasing birds, I take up the broom and offer her coat a thorough sweeping before returning, reluctantly, indoors. Along the way to the bedroom I trip over a box in the hall. I wonder why it is there. I push the box to the side of the hall and underneath the table, but still it manages to bother me there. So then I place the box back in the middle of the hall, albeit a little further along towards the door. In this way, then, there's no need for me to go into the bedroom. I don't even want to go there. There will be plenty of time to go into the bedroom when things get back to normal in there.

About to shut the front door behind me, I notice the television is gone. On top of that the computer is missing. As well as the DVD player. Checking the door for damage, and realizing it hasn't been forced, I still can't help but feel the victim of some sort of crime in progress. First thing to do, then, is check the bedroom. Trouble is, that box is still there. Right square in the middle of the hall no less. So then I try peering in around the nearly closed door—but it's no use, it's dark, and I can't make anything out in there. For this reason, then, I decide to count the black hairs I've saved. They all seem to be in place, each individual strand present and accounted for. Some do seem to be broken in places however, so I should probably do something with it, possibly even something significant, and in the end, together with all the two-by-three inch cards of notes, I place the hair in that box in the hall and move on out the door.

Change of clothes in hand, I bounce back down the creaking wooden steps and out onto the driveway out back. Hey, says a voice from above, and I look up to find Jeff sitting on his deck, his presence somehow amplified by the raw salt air rising up the bluff. Hey Jeff, I say, what's going on? Oh not much, he says, just playing a little guitar. And truth be told, it is a fairly small guitar he's strumming on.

What happened to your face? he says, and I say I got beat up. By Joe Brand. Any pigeons? Just these two trying to build a nest in the base of the barbeque here, he answers, as though reluctantly resigned to their presence. Did it hurt? Did what hurt, Capt'n? Don't call me that, he says. You know I don't like when you call me that. All right, did what hurt, Jeff, I say, unsure whether to look sad or simply produce a smile instead. Your face, he says, and I say, Yeah it did actually. Now put your chin in. You know, he says, I've been wondering—

Put your chin in, Jeff. It is in, he says. No, it's not, Jeff. Now put your chin in—that's it, I say as immediately and mechanically, but not without a certain degree of don't-tell-me-what-to-do-with-my-chin obstinacy, he retracts his chin from its default forward-thrust position. Now what is it you've been wondering about, Jeff? Well did you really love stiffen knee? he says.

I pause a moment as, hanging from the eaves just above his head, a set of coloured metallic wind chimes clink and jingle in the breeze. I ask him if he's taken his medication today, and he says not yet. Now did you? Why not, Jeff. Why haven't you taken your medication today, I say, and he says he will. Soon. Now did I or didn't I? Did I or didn't I *what*, Jeff? Did you, or did you not, ever really love Stephanie, he says, and I say of course I loved her. Why? Well if you didn't, it would really be a huge disappointment to this embarrassment of a family of yours, he says, and I pause. My family doesn't em*bar*rass me, Jeff. Well then it would really be a disappointment to this embarrassment of a brother of yours, he says, chuckling smugly under his breath, taking a moment to flex his fingers individually before returning them collectively to his guitar once again.

Turning my battered face to the bulging ocean air, I ask Jeff if he's happened to see anyone suspicious hanging around here the last day or so. His chin shelved forward, he doesn't respond, but continues to strum away at his ridiculously small guitar for now. Jeff, did you happen to see—

Your cat there was in a fight the other night, he says, for the moment overriding me. Actually, I've noticed Jeff overriding me a great deal in recent weeks, and it suddenly occurs to me that, as with this new and occasional aversion to his rank, the timing of these flare-ups seems to mirror that of his occasionally neglected meds of late.

Abandoning that train of thought for the moment, I glance down at a Cojimar seemingly no worse for wear. I give her tail one good long exceptionally gratifying tug, lifting her back legs briefly into the air. A fight, huh, I say. How'd she do? Better than you evidently, he tells me. Wouldn't let go though. Would not. Wooden knot. A *knot* of *wood*, he says, catching himself. Had to throw a rock at her just to get her to stop. Well you shouldn't throw rocks at cats, I say, and he says, Why not? Really, wine ought? he says, holding the tip of his chin between thumb and forefinger, projecting his lower lip in an elaborate thinker's pucker. Well because it tends to hurt them, I suggest. And besides, animals tend to work these things out themselves. Penelope was around, he says. She was was she, I say. Well that explains the boxes in the hall. So what'd ol' Penelope have to say? Only that they're moving me back home, he says, strumming his little guitar once, softly, before hammering down on it several times in succession.

A small item of information she evidently felt the need to pass on to you, I say as, growing frustrated, his mental dilemma resolving itself in bitter silence, his jaw slides forward involuntarily to jut out over his guitar once again. I was going to tell you, I say as he strums what appears from here to be an F chord. I was, Jeff. I was going to tell you before I left—quit that. I said quit it, I say as he studies my face, moving his lips with mine, forever antici-pating the next word, changing expressions at just the right time. Christ, though, she didn't have to go and take the goddamned DVD already, I say.

I watch him play, watching his fingers work themselves in amongst the necessary frets of his remarkably small guitar. From the F chord he slides into an A, then over to G, switching repeat-edly, strumming significantly, until the insult of the sequence more or less hits home for me.

Yeah, so anyway, I've been wondering a lot about that lately, he says. What's that, I ask as he plays FAG once, twice more before taking a moment to prudently tune a string. You mean did I love Stephanie, I say, and he says yes. Did you. Lovestiff. Annie, he says, placing the guitar aside and standing up to lean casually against the deck's railing, contorting his face into a strained translation of a smile obviously intended to convey complete sanity on his part, and further, to dissolve any sort of concern of mine. Instead it just ends up an insane leer. And so, frowning to hide any and all rem-nants of this awful grin, and to atone for something neither one of us can explain, he picks up his guitar and strums it steadily into submission once again. Then, as if to show fastidiousness in front of me, he starts to whistle along with the chords rather touching-ly, almost tender-heartedly, just as a great gust of wind rises up from the bay. And so he starts to sing instead, graduating rapidly to a forlorn and discordant wail—but to no avail, the wind is just too powerful, and so he stops singing and playing altogether, stag-gering around instead in a haphazard way. And finally, taking up his guitar and chucking it over the railing and onto the narrow stretch of grass below, he stands there assuming the look of some-one who has really just accomplished a great deal in life.

I look at the guitar, lying there small, mute and lonely on the lawn, and finally, with nothing more to say, and nothing left to see, I leave him staring doggedly after me as I cut diagonally across the driveway, down the stone steps and along the lanes in between, finally emerging again on Marine, across from the bus stop with the little wooden cross, before making my way down to the pier and Annie only to find Po booking off early, it seems.

Finishing up a little early today aren't we, Po?

He doesn't answer, but takes one look at my butchered face and grunts enigmatically.

Where's Stephan, I say, but he doesn't answer. Po, where's Stephan, I repeat, feeling myself smile. It hurts to smile. He went to see his sister, he tells me quietly, almost kind-heartedly, while still managing to maintain that special brand of detachment he seems to keep on reserve for me.

The nearby trees are naked and wind-battered, little defence against this cold hard wind now ripping in across the water. By the way, I say, what exactly do you think of this bench, Po? I mean do you even think it's nice?

Po disjoints another rod and shoves the components deep into the bed of the pickup.

Well I think it's nice anyway, I say, exploring the planks with the flats of my palms. It's the pressure treatment that makes it though, hey. No, you can never have too much pressure treatment, they say.

I rub a splatter of pigeon shit from the bench.

To be honest, though, I do have some issues with you, Po. That is, beyond your general unwillingness to engage either your son or me in any sort of genuine conversation. Your being a fisher-man, for one. Me, I've never been fishing. I'd like to go though. Sure I would. In fact if it weren't for the fact that Stephanie was against the very *idea* of fishing, I would like to go fishing very much right now.

Disjointing the last of his rods, Po shoves the whole mess into the flatbed.

Catch anything, I ask as he shoves the tackle box over against the wheel hub and slams the tailgate shut. Catch anything today, Po? Not today, no, I'm told. Fish don't bite on full moon. They don't? No, they don't. Why not? Who knows, he shrugs, stepping around to the driver's door. So then why go fishing if you know you're not going to catch anything, I say, and he shrugs again, offering nothing. *Really*, Po. I didn't know that. Perhaps you could teach me some more sometime. But then that's not really why I'm here, to be honest. No, to be honest—oh let's do it, Po, let's *be* honest—I really don't know why I'm here anymore.

Po grinds to a reluctant halt outside the open driver's door.

Now the detective said that you get used to this, and that this particular sensation fades, but then who ever asked for his prognosis anyway. Besides, you just try and get along and act as though nothing has happened. That's how it's done in the best circles anyway. And somehow circling around it is always the best way—for the others. Well fuck the others. Practical though, they say. No need to draw anyone else into it. Christ, though, of all the ways. Of all the ways that has to be the worst. No, you know what's worse? When two months after the fact you still have to unclog the fucking drains.

Po places one butt cheek on the seat and turns his attention to the radio. Meanwhile I hold my nose and blow sharply, feeling the pressure gradually let go.

I remember when it first got started. In fact I remember the very day. She managed to hold onto it for some time, so long in fact that we actually thought she might keep it, but then it really got started and we started to find it all over—on her clothes, in the bathroom, on the hairbrush, and all over the bed that day. That was the worst. The bed. There was no getting used to that. That strange sensation of waking in the night to see her bald head on the pillow and not quite knowing whose it was. Then watching her get up to use the toilet and finding her almost unreal in the moonlight, alien even, as I lie here in bed in a pool of sweat that's not even my own. And then the next morning, everything pleasant and warm out on the deck together, she with her John Deere baseball cap on, me with coffee on, and other times all niceness gone and glad to be out on the beach alone somewhere. But then always returning to find new clumps on the pillow—always on the pillow, mind you—and grabbing it all to place under my own, thinking how I might save it to have made into a wig one day so that it'll somehow seem more her own. Well how pathetic. How utterly fucking pathetic that all seems *fair, she says, and I say, What hardly seems*

*fair? This separate set of rules you get to play by here, she says. I hard-
ly play by a separate set of rules, Annie. You most certainly do, she tells
me. Any time there's something you think is even remotely worth doing,
you just go ahead and do it without any consideration for me.*

*Outside, on the street, a large golden retriever pins its ears back, prepar-
ing to defecate against the curb. Fuck off, I tell the dog's owner through the
open patio window, and with a shrug he casually moves off, dragging his
reluctant, still hunkered-down animal behind.*

*Jesus, Annie, look at the price of this stuff. What stuff? This Coenzyme
Q-Ten stuff, I say, extracting the bottle from the bag. Fifty bucks? What
in God's name for? For my heart, she says. Your heart? What the hell's
wrong with your heart? Well nothing, now, she tells me. But the chemo's
supposed to be pretty hard on it appar*ently we were all going to do
it together. That was in the beginning. It was always beginning.
It's always the beginning of something somewhere, they say.
Anyway, we were all going to do it together at that Iranian barber's that day. That barber, he had a funny name if only I could
remember it correctly. I never can remember it correctly. Still, I
wonder what became of them. That was before the attacks in
New York, if you remember, and then someone shot a bullet
through his glass. Bigots like that are always shooting bullets
through windows, Po. Before bullets through windows bigots
never did anything like that. Not together at least. No, you never
do anything together, it seems. And you certainly never get
around to doing all those things you say you will as there always
seems to be time for it later.

With one foot on the brake, and the other set firmly on the
pavement outside the door, Po continues to tune in the radio
while tuning me out just so.

You do that though, hey. To be left alone. You figure out exactly what they want you to say and then you say it, with as much
conviction as possible, and then, if your performance is convinc-
ing enough, they leave you alone that day. It's all just a way of
dealing with the cards that you're dealt—like a system. Or a strategy. Or a phantom appendage in some way. What's that called
though, that sensation? Christ, who knows. I bet Darcy knows. It's
certainly effective anyway. Like not taking the law into your own

hands in any way. No, never take the law into your own hands, Po. Absolutely never. Let the authorities handle it, hey. After all, vengeance is a no-no, Dinallo says. Still, I'd maybe like to remember that Iranian barber's name. "Fucking immigrants," he said to me that one day, "why can't they just speak English." Funny, that. That was about the last funny thing, I'd say. I should have written it down. I never do write them down. No big deal though. Just another box in the hall anyway.

Po wipes his forehead with his sleeve, slowly replaces his John Deere cap, and then stares solemnly at his gauges for a time. Finally he turns the key. And holding my nose and blowing sharply, I listen for it, hearing it, way down deep and nearly out of range altogether, a steadily rising crying drowned out suddenly by the terrible screeching of the engine's somewhat troubled ignition.

It's the dedication, he says. Pardon, I say, and he regards me evenly. Pardon, Po? It's the dedication that makes it, he says. Otherwise it's just a bench.

Friday, 7:09 am

A little later, with the wind gathering the smell of seaweed off the bay, I walk out the length of the pier, all five hundred and seven steps, to watch the seagulls circle about the breakwater a while before walking the same five hundred and seven steps back to Annie, only this time accomplishing the feat in just four hundred and ninety-three. Some good citizen is busy repainting the white rock white, I see, concealing the previous day's ugly black swastika graffiti.

Thomas comes bounding down the promenade. Jesus, he says, what happened to you? Got in a little punch-up, I tell him, no big deal.

He leans over, hands on knees, breathing hard before me. Your boss? he says, and I say no, not my boss. Really? He figured it was my boss. Well it wasn't, I assure him. Are you sure? he says, and I say absolutely, why? Just ran into the Grexican, he grins, gesturing back up the promenade. Fuck this town, really, I say. You realize you look like shit, he tells me. No pun intended. Listen, Thomas, could you please fuck off? I've got some very pressing guilt to attend to here.

Yanking off his toque and dragging a long slow forearm across his forehead, he turns to study, stretching out behind him, the pier lying wide, heavy and grey upon the bay. Hate to see the other guy, I bet, he says, and I say, Not really. *Ah*, he nods, got the better of you, huh. You could say that, I say. Anyone I know? he asks, and I say, Krishna Brand's husband. *Joe*? he says. Really? What the hell happened? Caught you two humping or something? I should be so lucky, I say. Maybe he didn't like the fact you're smuggling on his turf then, he says, and I say, All right, who told you. He shrugs and grins, Just the word on the street, my man. I mean it though, Thomas. Fuck this town. Fuck it all. Oh come on, Chris, don't be that way. Everyone's just excited, that's all.

He stretches his legs by squatting briefly and repeatedly to the ground. Eventually this routine transforms itself into jogging on the spot before me. There's a pool going by the way, he says, and I say, Fuck off, there is not. Yeah, on whether or not you make it across unscathed, he says. Really, Thomas? So what's it up to then? About four dollars, he says, give or take. So interest has peaked somewhat then, I say, and he says, No, not at all. Though I did have to front that first four dollars, hey.

He stops jogging long enough to launch into some deep hamstring stretches. And so, breathing in the salt air, I squint well out beyond the pier, beyond even the clouds currently tilting down dangerously over the islands and the mountains there. So which way are you betting, I say, and he says, In Hum's boat? I'm betting you make it. In fact I'm counting on it. Jesus, I'm not Federal Express, I say as he continues stretching out, flexing a heel up towards his rear-end.

All right, what the fuck are you grinning about, I say, and he says, Nothing. What is it, Thomas. Been there, man, he shrugs. At the Beasleys'. With Reena. I've been there. Fuck off, I say, and he says, No, it's true. Bunk beds? I've climbed that ladder. Course we never used to film it, he grins, and together we stare out over the water a while.

At length he says, That Reena, though, she's a real freak. Not really, I say. Yeah, maybe not, he says. Todd, though, he's a real prize. Oh, I say, he's a rare one all right. *Rare* one, he says, fucking *ass*hole's what he is. He does lack a certain dignity, Thomas, you're right.

Out around the breakwater, the seagulls slide down against the wall of wind one after another, their distant cries slicing the air.

I do feel bad for Reena though, he goes on. I mean I can't help but think that a sweet woman like her, well . . . thing is, she's confused. Or rather, they are. How so, I say. Well for one—and this was months ago, mind you—there they were in the OB this one night, having a drink, and I happened to pass by while they were having this rather intimate conversation, he says. Anyway, apparently she thinks—or rather *they* think—that there's a fundamental difference between the clitoral orgasm and the vaginal orgasm. Like the vaginal one's that much better, hey. And she's never had one? And she's never had one. Not that she knows of anyway. And certainly not without some sort of finger-assisted stimulation at any rate.

Hands on hips, Thomas spreads his legs wide and leans forward and down, bobbing slightly at the waist.

So Reena thinks she's missing out then, I say, and he says, Exactly. And Todd thinks he's doing something wrong. Or rather, that *she* is. Or that she's not put together quite right somehow. You see, Todd's convinced he's given women purely vaginal orgasms before. Well of course he has, I say. Heck, we all have. Exactly, Thomas says, leaning around and back, directing his nose at the overcast sky, affording me, in the process, a widescreen view of his nasal passages.

So they're after the elusive, non-digit-assisted G-spot orgasm are they, I say, and he says, Yup, in search of the Holy Grail they are.

Far out over the breakwater, the seagulls continue to slide down against the wall of wind one after another. First the one slides and then the next one slides. Then the rest of them slide together.

Bobbing forward from the waist, Thomas says my bruises make my eyes look very blue. Interesting, I say, and he says, No, I mean more blue than grey. Usually your eyes look very grey. Why, are you hitting on me, Thomas? I'm flattered, really. Don't bet on it, he tells me. Bet on what? asks a voice, and turning we find Darcy directing a few strands of hair to the corner of her mouth.

When you said first thing in the morning, Darcy, I didn't think you meant *this* first thing. I was up, she tells me. Hey, what happened to your face? Well what the hell's it look like, Thomas says. One of your goons beat him up.

Darcy smiles wryly. Looks sore, she winces. It is sore, I say. Ask him who did it, Thomas says. Who did it? Doesn't matter, Darcy. Okay, what was it about then? she says, and I say, Again, it doesn't matter. Wow, profound, she says. Anyway, bet on what? Capone here's got himself a cross-border booze run tonight, Thomas says. *Rea*lly, Darcy says, eyes narrowing slightly as she turns to study me. Yeah, big booze run, he says. Huge. Bringing it across on a boat tonight, am I right? Doesn't look fit to cross the road right now, Darcy says, looking at me and frowning. Jesus, I hate this town, I say. I really do. Come on, you don't mean that, Thomas tells me, having launched again into his now familiar, and familiarly annoying, jog-on-the-spot routine. I do, I say. I really do. I hate everything about it, Thomas—including you.

Darcy takes a seat on the bench beside me as Thomas bounds off down the promenade. Good luck tonight, he calls back over his shoulder. I'll get my order to you by noon, all right?

And suddenly, but not surprisingly, it begins to rain. I look at Darcy sitting there beside me on the bench, and at the prosthetic hand speckled with rain.

We better not sit here, I say, and she says, Why not? I don't mind the rain. We just shouldn't sit here, I say, and by the hand—the real one—I lead her across the street to the Trap & Gill patio where I take two chairs from the stack and arrange them around a table.

I nod towards the window where Pat can be seen hard at work as usual. Want some coffee, Darcy? Tea? Pornography? No, nothing, she tells me, rummaging through her bag in search of cigarettes until finally emerging with a brand new pack. Have you got a light, Chris? Sorry, stupid question, she says, offering the bag one last desperate search only to come up dry.

Anyway, here's your money, she says, flipping an envelope out onto the table. I stare solemnly at the thick white envelope before me. I feel so . . . so *dirty*, I say. And so you should, she says, tapping a cigarette free of the pack and inserting it between her lips. You're a criminal. Or at least you're going to be. Only thing I can't understand is why. Well you seem to have done fairly well for yourself, I say, and she says, So what? That doesn't mean—

Look, it doesn't matter, Darcy. It doesn't matter why I'm doing it, only that I do, okay? All right, fine, she says. But why not use the owners' money? What do you think I've been living off this past month, I say, turning to consider the wind-battered trees out along the promenade, their still naked limbs dripping in the rain. It's cold and the drops hang stiffly in the branches. Who knows, I might even open up the patio tomorrow, I say. Why not today? she asks, legs and arms crossed, unlit cigarette dangling limply from her lips, and I say no, not today. Today'll be too slow.

She places the cigarette on the edge of the table. Hey, are you all right? she says, and I say, You mean besides the obvious? Yeah, she says, besides that. I'm fine, why? Well you're not as, you know, funny as you usually are, she tells me. Well maybe because I'm exhausted, Darcy. Or maybe because I don't feel particularly funny right now. Christ, I did get the snot beat out of me just a couple of hours ago. Who did it? she says, reinserting the unlit cigarette, and I say, Friend of a friend. Get her back? she asks, and I say no, but I got him pretty tired though, no question. You want I should talk to someone? she asks me. *Talk* to someone, Darcy? Hey, you got your face pushed in, Chris. I'm concerned. It's not *that* bad, I say, and she says, Speak for yourself. You're not the one who has to sit here looking at it. And besides, I know these body mechanics that'll fix whoever did it real good. *Body* mechanics, Darcy? You know, Angels, she says, and I say, No thanks. All right, but they got a menu, she says. Legs, arms, jaws, hands, all the way up to knocking the son of a bitch off. Oh, like the manager at the OB, I say. No thanks. All it takes is a phone call, she says. No, Darcy. No. Christ. All right then, fine, suit yourself, she snaps, pivoting in the direction of the suddenly bitter wind slashing in over the waves, offering herself in profile.

You look like a Muppet, I say. A what? she says, unlit cigarette tilting upwards to the vicinity of her nose. A Muppet, Darcy. You look like a Muppet—from that show. The Muppet Show, she says, and I say, That's the one. You look like the guitar player from the Muppet Show.

Peering out at the pale grey haze of the horizon, she gauges the weight of this insult a moment before removing her cigarette and placing it carefully on the edge of the table.

Well someone certainly got up on the wrong side of the bed this morning, she says, and in such a way that I immediately apologize. Really, though, I'm just a little stressed out, I say. Now I may need you to tend bar over lunch if that's okay. Fine, she says, but I thought I was supposed to be working the floor today. Look at my face, Darcy. Go ahead, look at it. I have been, she says, and believe me, it ain't pretty. Well then picture, if you will, this very face gazing benevolently over your salmon burger and freedom fries, I say, gazing out at the bay, and at the seagulls crowding in over the breakwater, far beyond which a tanker, grey and white above the deck and blue and red below, drifts slowly out of the haze veiling the horizon, heading westward for now. Behind this tanker drifts a second tanker, this one longer and covered in bright lights, appearing almost ghostly white at this distance, behind which drifts a third tanker I can't tell if I really see at all.

You must miss her, she says, and I say, Excuse me? You must miss her, she says. Having her around, I mean.

She returns the unlit cigarette to her mouth, and I study her in silence a moment.

Look, Darcy, could you please do something with that cigarette? Either go in and get a light off Pat, or else put the fucking thing away. Well *sorry*, she says, tossing the cigarette into her bag along with the pack. You don't have to be such an asshole about it.

A pigeon picks its way energetically down the edge of the sidewalk before promptly sailing off and out of sight, while the trio of tankers continue to drift their way almost imperceptibly along the horizon.

She's fading on me, I say. Sorry? she says, and I say, Stephanie. She's fading on me. And I don't know what to do about it. Maybe ask Katie, she says, and I look at her, wondering, then shake my head disappointedly. Look, it's no big deal, she says, and I say, You know then. Everybody knows, Chris. It's no big secret. This town again, really, I say. Hey you have to get back in the game eventually, she says, and I say no, I don't actually. I don't have to get back in the game, and it *is* a big deal to me. It's a *very* big deal to me. Christ Almighty. You don't think she knows then? she says, and I say I hope not. You know, she might even give it her blessing, Darcy says, and I say, *God*, I hope not. That would be the end of it then.

Unbeknownst to Darcy, under cover of the tabletop, I've successfully reached over to take her prosthetic hand in mine, clutching it lightly and comfortably as though we've been casually holding hands the entire time. Not surprisingly, the device feels cold and dead in my hand.

You're going to stop seeing her then? she says, and I say no, I won't stop seeing her. I can't stop seeing her. It's just that it's getting so difficult lately. Of course it's difficult, she says. It's the difficult that makes it good. The only way to fall for someone is deeply.

She changes position slightly, and I quickly let go her hand.

I just don't understand what it is I'd have to do to leave her, I say, and Darcy says, Neither do I. Neither does Katie. But then I have a pretty good idea what you'll have to do if you want her to stay.

A horn bellows in the distance, introducing the morning train. The lead engine approaches slowly, sliding up and around from the south where the rain lashes the coast, following the long gradual curve of the bay. And soon the beach is hidden behind a sliding curtain of metal on metal, rumbling along the rhythm of its rails.

I'm going to leave by train one day, I say. Yeah, I tried that, she tells me. You tried to kill yourself by stepping in front of a moving train, I say, and she says, Well not in front of it, but *onto* it, sure, absolutely. You, I say. Hopped a train. While it was moving. No, I said I *tried*, she says.

I look at her steadily, until she eventually returns the favour. Well hey, I'm impressed, I say, and she says, Well you shouldn't be. I wish

I'd never done it. It was a really stupid thing to do apparently. Why do you say that, I ask, and she looks at me blankly a moment before placing her prosthetic arm on the table before me.

Oh, right, I say.

Friday, 11:54 am

So, yeah, sometimes I think that maybe she was placed on this earth to suffer. You know, to suffer for all my sins. Now I know that sounds ridiculous and more than a little pretentious but if she was, I mean if I *knew* she was, well then I could certainly understand everything she's been put through, hey. Otherwise I have no explanation for it at all. I mean they say that good things happen to good people, and that a good man's hard to find. But then they also say that it's the good ones who always seem to suffer the most, and that only the good die young. So then where do you draw the line.

Fuck! she says. What, Darcy? What happened? Cut my thumb on some broken glass, she frowns, sticking her thumb in her mouth and nursing it a while. Go on, she says after a time.

Well all I know is that she suffered. Yes, she suffered, and she persevered, managing to get through all that cancer and chemo with such unbelievable energy and dignity that sometimes . . . What the hell are you looking for now? Band-Aids are in the back. No, it's not that, she says, down on her haunches, rummaging through a cupboard, quite vexed. It's this bar. This bar's a fucking mess. Leave it alone, Darcy. Please. And for Christ's sake, quit sucking your thumb. You're going to get it infected.

Wrinkling her nose at a jar of mouldy pickled beans, she releases her thumb long enough to toss the entire jar away.

Sometimes, though, when I lie awake at night and see Stephanie sleeping next to me, I have to wonder at the logic of it all. Not that there necessarily *is* a logic to it, see, or that there necessarily *should* be a logic to it, but that there *could* be a logic to it, and that such divine logic is *between the bare branches, through their belated flower absences, I can see them. Going towards him one after another, first the one boy whipping and then the next boy whipping. Then the rest of the boys go ahead and whip him together a while. I go on whispering at*

Annie. Annie goes on ignoring me. Then she goes down along the line of bushes to where across the street a man is raking—she calls out to the man but he does not hear. Meanwhile I go on whispering and watching the boys whipping as one thing I have to wonder, though, is how one person can be expected to suffer for someone else. And I wonder if they know at all. If they know, in advance, that it's going to be their lot in life to suffer like they will. Probably not, I've always thought. For if they did have the explanation for their suffering in advance, well then in turn they wouldn't suffer—they'd be at peace the entire time. And believe me, he definitely wasn't at peace with it. And still isn't, in my mind.

Outside the window I see the empty mud-covered patio, the scalloped grey ocean slightly out of focus beyond it, and the cars passing along the road in between. And I can't believe it was something as simple as karma either, I say, as that just strikes me as ignorant somehow. I mean to think that he could be someone deserving of such a fate is simply not to know him very well. I mean to even *conceive* that someone like my brother could have been anything less than good, honest and upright in some past life is to sell him far too short somehow. And the idea there could be some God standing idly by, refusing to lift a finger while something like that unfolds is, well, completely beyond my ability to imagine, you know? Know what, Darcy says, closing the cupboard and rising up with a groan, and I say, You know, you're awfully damned brassy for a girl who's been working here all of an hour or so. Well it's been an awfully informative hour, believe me, she says, so I say, Yes, well, it could be your last as well. Now for Christ's sake, quit sucking up, quite sucking your thumb, and learn to slack a little.

Lisa comes up to the bar asking for two glasses of water. Darcy pours the water.

She did, hey, I say, watching Lisa back away from the bar. What's that, Darcy says, examining her thumb. Stephanie, I say. She gave me her blessing. When she was really sick there for a while. When she thought she might not, you know, make it or whatever, she actually gave me her blessing to be with someone else. That's incredible, Darcy says, and I say, You're being sarcastic. No, I mean

it, Chris, that's amazing. Check this out though, she says, directing my attention to an Indian-sweatered Wendy standing astride
her ten-speed'on the patio, peering in through the window.

What do you want, I ask Wendy through the open door, galva-
nizing Eddie into action. Growling menacingly, he twists around
and back, offering his dog balls a quick and tactical shift to the left
before twisting back ready to attack. What happened to your face?
she says, and I say, Nothing. I'm renovating. Now what is it you
want. In answer, she cups her hands to her face and places the
entire assembly up against the glass, managing, in the process, to
spill backwards onto the patio her brand new blue Ocean Beach
Hotel baseball cap.

Check out the new one-armed bartender, she says. So, what,
Krishna not working today? Not today, no, I say. And you know
the patio isn't open yet. Oh I know, she says. I was just out for a
ride with Eddie here and thought I'd get some take-out though.
Why isn't Krishna working today though? she wants to know,
detaching from the window long enough to gather up her fallen
cap as across the way, huddled close in under their umbrellas
against the rain, those few souls still brave enough to face the ele-
ments continue shuffling their way along the promenade, advanc-
ing relentlessly in the direction of the whale.

Got the day off, I say. Personal reasons. *Ah*, she nods knowingly, foraging in her ear with a finger. What is it you want, I ask
impatiently. Oh I don't know, she tells me, shuttling her finger in
and out of her ear a few more times and smiling brightly at the
findings. One of those lobster clubs maybe. By the way, I heard
about your little escapade tonight. You did, did you, I say, and she
says yeah, she did. And I tell you what, my money's on you. Good
stuff, now—

So where are you going to bring it across? she asks, tilting her
head to one side, and I say, Well you see the wharf there? Over
at the reserve? Well I'm bringing it over on a boat from the
opposite peninsula, from over at the marina at that condomini-
um complex there. And that Indian cop's lending a hand, huh?
she says, and I say, Oh I don't know about that. To be honest, he
hardly seems all that enthusiastic with the idea. But he'll let you

pass, she says, and I say, Oh he'll let me pass. He is Billy Henry after all.

After a quiet lunch, with most of the customers gone, I stare blindly at the five pieces of metal arranged neatly on the bar before me, trying to will them together as one.

Darcy asks what I'm doing. Well, Darcy, if you must know, I'm trying to put this beer tap back together. Why'd you take it apart in the first place though? she wants to know, and I say, Good question, but let me assure you the answer's even better.

I pick up one piece, the housing, and turning it over tentatively, explain how, back when I first applied for this job, my résumé stated clearly, among other fictions, that I was fully qualified at cleaning beer lines, and how in light of that outright lie, up till now at least, I've been bringing in outside help to accomplish the task, or else foregoing such cleanings entirely. But now Rick, in his infinite wisdom, has seen fit to crack down on some of my expenditures—including lemons, limes and line cleanings—and in turn remind me of the outlandish claims my résumé made over a year ago. What the hell he's doing looking over my résumé, I can only guess. And what he's doing actually taking someone's résumé at face value, God only knows, at best.

Darcy laughs.

But then again, maybe he's just being spiteful. I mean that I could certainly understand. Or maybe he's simply been reviewing the particular set of circumstances that duped him into hiring such a shirker in the first place. Christ, I haven't the faintest idea.

Having failed to deploy them in any significant way, I return the beer tap components unassembled to the cloth and pick up my glass, shaking what little ice remains. I'll have another Greyhound when you're ready, Darcy. Except this time in that really short glass there with just enough juice to change the colour, okay? It's imperative to be able to see your hand through your drink, I wink, wondering immediately if that were as inappropriate as it sounded, considering her missing limb.

Placing the shot glass on the bar, Darcy picks up the vodka bottle with her good hand and balances the neck across her prosthetic forearm. Then she very carefully measures out the alcohol. Like that? she asks, adding just a splash of grapefruit juice and placing the translucent cocktail before me on the bar. Perfect, I say, taking a single lip-stinging sip before returning with fervour to the puzzle on the bar.

Been down to see the whale yet? she says, and I say, Excuse me? Have you been down to see the whale yet, she repeats, and I say, I heard what you said, and no, I haven't. Why, have you, I continue, regarding her intently. After I saw you this morning, sure, she says, and I say, You didn't, really. Yeah, sure, she says. And you should too. Come on, you really don't think so though, I say, and she says, Sure I do.

And as she steps away to empty the glass washer, I return once more to my puzzle, taking up two pieces and trying to arrange them in some—any—meaningful manner.

Look, Darcy, I have to let you go, I tell her upon her eventual return down my end of the bar. Yeah, it is pretty darned slow, she sighs, looking around the nearly empty Trap & Gill. No, I mean I have to let you go *permanently*, I say, and she says, What? Why? Well to be honest, because I think you might still be here five years from now, I say. What's that supposed to mean? she asks, a tide of pink swelling up well beyond her hairline. It means you're topping out, Darcy. You're absolutely topping out. And I have to say, the thought of that scares the hell out of me.

Justifiably pleased with this one piece sliding fluidly back and forth inside its housing, I proudly offer it up for show, only to realize that I somehow have it in backwards, if in actual fact I'm supposed to have it in there at all. Consider it a favour, I say. Some favour, she says, her forehead corrugating painfully. Naturally, I reach across the bar to massage it for her, only to have her slap my hand away.

All right, a little tough love then, I say. Look Darcy, it just seems to me like you need a little push. A little shove. You're getting stagnant and like I said, that scares the hell out of me.

A somewhat unexpected, surprisingly compliant note comes into Darcy's voice as she says quietly, So you're firing me. I'm

firing you, yes, I say. But you can't fire me, she says. You owe me
that money. And besides I quit my other job already. Yes I'm sure
that bridge has been burned sufficiently too, I say. Look, Darcy, it's
good you're getting out of here. This town, hey, it can suffocate
you. You're a real asshole, you know that? she says, regarding me
with sudden rage, at which point I point the housing at her and
fire back, Don't you go pigeonholing me.

She continues to glare at me, breathing heavily, as I say, Listen,
it's just not working out. But it's nothing personal, believe me.
What, I wasn't *good* enough? she says. Actually no, your bartend-
ing skills are just fine, I say. Impeccable, really. No, it's something—
else. What, *this*? she says, tugging off her prosthetic arm and slam-
ming it down on the bar. No, not at all, I say, frowning at this
oddly captivating, suddenly disembodied and oversized Barbie
arm before me. But to be honest, I really can't say. Not just yet
anyway. Rest assured I have only your best interests in mind
though, hey.

Darcy glares at me once more before storming off to the back
to collect her things, leaving, for the moment at least, the prosthetic appendage behind for my inspection. In her absence, Lisa
comes up to ask what the hell is going on here, and when I tell
her it's none of her damned business, she too takes a turn at
storming around a while. And as they each stomp about, cursing
repeatedly under their breath, I return to the as yet unassembled
collection of beer tap components and artificial limbs on the bar,
thinking how, if Darcy leaves it behind, I will drill a hole in the
arm's end and make it into an amusing sort of draft handle, the
very unlikely but hilarious existence of which will almost certainly pack the customers in on a nightly basis. Unfortunately, just as
my final plan is taking shape, a thoroughly red-faced Darcy leans
in over my shoulder to inform me she needs that two thousand
dollars she lent me.

Can't do it, I say, and she says, I'm not joking. I need that money
now. Listen, you're not getting that money, Darcy. Not now. Not
ever. All right?

I take up this one beer tap component, a pin of sorts, and install
it inside the housing, my first real success in this area in what feels

like hours. Listen, she says, you'd better give me that money back or else—

Or else what, I say. Retrieving her prosthesis from the bar, she rocks back on her heels a little and says, You figure it out. Oh, I'll try, Darcy. Now give me back my draft handle, I say, and she looks at me in a bewildered way. Look, I'm serious, Chris. I want that money. Listen, I say, I'm not getting you the goddamned money, okay?

Katie passes Darcy at the door. What was that all about? she asks, sliding up onto the stool beside me. Don't know, I say. Doesn't take good news all that well apparently. What's the good news, she says, and I tell her I'll tell her later. How are you though, Katie? Fine? Tell me you're fine. And that you wouldn't dare go down to see that whale. Tired, she says, concealing a yawn with a fist. I think it might be all this low cloud cover. Or else the rain. Or else my manager forever waking me up in the wee morning hours, she grins, so I grin, as toothily and stupidly as possible it seems, if her ensuing imitation is any indication.

I ask how Scooter is, and she tells me Scooter's fine. And Krishna? How's our lovely Krishna. Not too bad, she sighs, all things considered. A little bruised maybe. Told me to tell you she can't work tonight though. Figured, I say. But that only leaves Laura, so I'm going to need your help if that's okay.

With the third component of the beer tap successfully installed, I work the lever smoothly back and forth. Krishna talked to Joe, I say, and Katie says, Yeah, she called him this morning. That's good—I guess, I say, and she says, Maybe not. He's outside right now. Really, I say. Where? There. In the parking lot. Blue truck. Clearly he's waiting for Krishna to show up so he can take another round out of her, Katie says. Then again, maybe he's just waiting to take another round out of *you*. My very first stalker, I say. How lovely. Maybe I should go talk to him though. Maybe you should, she says. Clearly that'd be just the right thing to do in this situation. Hey, I'm no shirker, Katie. A slacker maybe, but certainly no shirker. And besides, I'm sure he's in a better mood now.

Katie frowns at my chaotic collection of beer tap components. What exactly is it you're trying to do here? she says, and

I say, Well what does it look like? Having disassembled and cleaned it in what was, I assure her, an incredible display of managerial initiative, determination and enthusiasm, I'm now attempting to reassemble the goddamned light beer tap. That's the spout, I'm told. Spout? Yeah, she says, the tap's what fastens onto the keg back there. Whatever, I say. Never say I'm one to shirk my responsibility though, Katie. Lord no, never a shirker. All evidence to the contrary right here. You've got that piece on upside down, she tells me. What, this? How do you know, Katie? Well look at the ones in front of you here, she says, indicating the nearest functioning draft tower. That flat part faces down. Clearly you're some kind of mechanical genius though, I say. What about this, I ask, holding another piece aloft. That one's right, she says. Except push those two washers down— that's it—now screw this piece on finger tight. Other way. Now screw this one on the same way. Finger tight, I say, and she says, That's right, finger tight. You're not as stupid as you look. Yes, and no shirker either, Katie. I'll concede, perhaps, a certain fictionalizing of my workplace skills, but a liar does not necessarily a shirker make, I say.

A few turns of the wrench later the spout is back in place. And so, having re-tapped the keg back in the cooler, I drain the line into a bucket until what looks like genuine light beer comes sputtering through. Maybe I should go talk to him though, I say, and she says, Joe? You want me to come with you? Na, I say. No need for him to know you're in on it too.

Crossing the rain-swept street, I take a seat at Annie and wait for Joe Brand to appear. The bench is wet, and smells of it, and I check over the craftsmanship once more. Meanwhile, out around the breakwater, the seagulls continue to slide down against the wall of wind and rain one after another.

I stand up from Annie as Joe puts his truck in gear and backs it out of the stall, then glides slowly towards me along the line of parked cars. Then he stops, so I sit. I go on sitting at Annie. Joe goes on watching me. Eventually, from the corner of my eye, I see the seagulls sliding. And soon an eagle comes along and joins them there.

At last Joe emerges from behind the last parked car, squinting nearsightedly through the rain-splattered windshield. I wonder if he can even see me here. And I wonder what he'll do as the eagle, pursued by the seagulls, slides towards me along the length of the pier. I sit at Annie and see them sliding, and the next time I look up I see that Joe's truck has disappeared.

Seen Krishna? he asks, standing suddenly beside me in jeans and T-shirt, squinting down against the rain, and I say, Not since this morning, no. And you know, Joe, you really ought to get those eyes checked out. Fuck you, I'm told. Where'd you see her last? Sorry, Joe, can't tell you that. I wish you would, he says.

Stuffing my fists deeper into my pockets, I gaze out over the incoming waves. The sky overhead seems entirely too low and grey, and tilted over dangerously on one edge. You hurt her pretty bad, Joe, I say. Looks like you caught a few yourself, he says. I look up, quickly, before looking back out over the bay, to see him bend a piece of gum into his mouth and toss the wrapper into the nearby shrubbery.

How's Scooter? he asks after a short dubious pause. Good, I say. Actually haven't seen all that much of him lately. Scooter's a girl, he says, and squinting, asks again where Krishna is. I have a fairly good idea though, I say. But you won't tell me, he says, and I say, I won't, no. He smiles plainly and says he's been talking to Billy Henry, hey. Billy Henry, huh, I say, looking up. It hurts to look up. And what'd our old buddy Hank have to say? Only that you're planning on bringing something across the border, Joe says, and once again I gaze out over the bay. Quite the mouth on that Billy, hey Joe? Ridiculous really. Well that's it then, no more bottles for his collection, I say.

Joe chews his gum, a single scythe of the jaws, then stops. Then he smiles again in a facetiously friendly and good-natured way. Anyway, he says, I tell you what, I see you so much as touch Indian land, and I'm gonna kill you, okay?

Friday, 2:23 pm

Nearing United States Customs, she slows the Beretta from a crawl to a dead stop, hammering down on the brakes at the last possible moment so that I slam forward bodily against my seat-belt.

Okay, what's the problem, Katie? Oh, no problem here, she says, staring spitefully ahead. You seem, I don't know—agitated, I say. You're evil, that's all, she shrugs matter-of-factly, and I'm just going to have to accept that fact, I guess. Evil? Me? Really? Totally and completely evil, she says. Say, what kind of mistress are you anyway? The kind that hooks up with an evil son of a bitch like you, that's who, she says.

Replacing the envelope in the glove compartment, I watch the Beretta's wipers move steadily back and forth against the rain, the road, the cars crawling along in line, the low flat customs build-ing ahead and, finally, that other country beyond.

Look, this has nothing to do with you, I say, and she says, No, clearly it has *ev*erything to do with me. Look, either sleep with me or don't sleep with me—I really don't fucking care—just don't twist the notion of spending time with me into something to kill yourself over. Time to come down off the cross there, pal.

She hammers down on the horn as, one car ahead, a feeble looking Ford Escort attempts to cut in line.

Well that's rather harsh, I say, and she, Yes, it is. It is rather harsh. It's harsh that people can come together in this life but can't always stay that way, okay? But then hey, that's just the way it is. It sucks. You might not like it. But then maybe you're not sup-posed to like it. At least that's the way it seems to me.

The Ford Escort successfully cuts in line, and for his efforts Katie offers the overly altruistic Honda driver directly in front of us the finger not once but twice. The driver waves back a face-tiously friendly hand.

Now you could accept that fact like I do, she says, and try to take something positive from the experience, but *no*, with you everything's got to be this great big production all the time. Everything with you's this all-important self-imposed *judgment*. It scares me you're so fucking self-critical all the time. Now I don't mean to be unduly harsh, especially, you know, considering, but for someone in your position you sure carry a fucked-up amount of guilt around.

A silence develops as we contemplate, from our respective positions, her overly harsh critique of my evidently pathetic existence. In the interim, the Honda driver ahead goes over the line.

Well that's a bit of a different tone from this morning, isn't it, I say, and she says she's just tired of being such an endeavour for me, that's all. Now tell me what to do. Just let me work it through, Katie. I meant with the border guard here, she says. Your *face*. Oh, that, I say. Right. Tell him I got in a fight with an Indian last night. Clearly he'll understand *that* much living around here.

We make it through customs without any setbacks, and continue south along the I-Five, passing through the small, slowly dying border town of Blaine and out into the flat open country beyond. Soon the forest closes in on either side of the highway, stout green cedars crowding closely together to severely narrow the focus of any potential sightseeing.

Anything else eating you, Katie? You know, besides me? Just general things, she says, like my life. I hate my life. How come, I say. Well I'm twenty-two and a waitress and everything I love leaves, she says. Just about everything that means anything to me leaves. Hold still, I tell the exposed rump of what may have once been a racoon, currently sprawled along the side of the highway here.

Ever heard of a Philly Blunt? she asks a little later, watching, via the rear-view mirror, the racoon recede behind us. We tried it last night. It's pot wrapped in cigar paper. Zack, of course, supplied it. Good old considerate Zack, I say. My, how that name does come up. So this Philly Blunt, how was it, I ask. Good, all things considered, I'm told. Though I still couldn't get my mind off my extraordinarily lousy life. Clearly I need to get a new gig. Yeah, something with benefits maybe, I say. That's always been the measuring stick for success in my parents' eyes anyway: a job with some sort of benefit package, hey.

I swing the rear-view mirror over to check my face and, reasonably satisfied, swing it back into place. Outside the windows the forest continues to slide by, a thick impenetrable cloak of olive drab. Now the navy, I say, they still pay my brother's benefits of course, but me, well, I don't have anything like that, hey. And that's why I'm still considered a failure in my parents' eyes, Katie. A shirker. That and the fact nothing's sold.

I flick the tree-shaped air-freshener back and forth as we drive in silence a while.

Yeah, I've got to get something soon, Katie continues eventually. The Trap & Gill's hardly paying the bills—especially this last month—and I can only handle so much more of the Brothers Beasley groping me like they do. I mean you let them grope you, she reflects, thinking you're somehow going to get a decent tip or at least a *drink* out of it, but then they always just settle the bill at the bar with you. Meaning me. Cheap bastards, I say, and she says clearly it's the Indian in general.

I offer the air-freshener one last resounding flick for good measure before opening the glove compartment and recounting the money, dividing it up by product and price.

Hey, she says, did you hear about the whales? and I say, Yes, I've heard all about that godforsaken whale, thank you. No, the new ones, she says, and I stop counting. New ones, Katie? What do you mean *new* ones. You mean to tell me there's *more* out there? Yeah, there's this pod of them that's been hanging out around the point there, she tells me. What kind of whales, I say. Grey? Yeah, grey, she says. I think so anyway. Same as the beached one there.

Eventually I replace the envelope in the glove compartment and slam shut the compartment door, just as a large signboard appears alongside the highway indicating a wonderful and not-to-be-missed world of discount clothing ahead. Soon another signboard appears, this one advertising gas and food. Next exit's our booze store, I remind her.

So hey, I say, what do you want to talk about now? Us, she says, and I say, Us? Really? But we always talk about us. That's because we're such an interesting subject, she says. I think it's pretty much exhausted though, isn't it, Katie? At least for this lifetime, I mean. Well have you ever been to any camps? she inquires after a thoughtful silence. Camps? Yeah, camps, she says. You know, as a kid. Billy and I went to this camp once and it was the best time we ever had. Well yes, I say, now that you mention it, my brother and I did go to a camp once ourselves—this old western horse camp, it was—and we each had this horse we had to take care of for the week. Mine was Eight Ball. And believe me, Eight Ball was a heck of a horse. Black with this little tuft of white hair on his ass that looked just like the number eight of course. Now he did step on my foot one day, but boy, what a great horse either way. How about your brother's horse, she says. That'd be Misty, I say. Now Misty was a mean old nag. How come? she asks. Dunno, I shrug. Maybe she had a mean disposition. Or maybe she just didn't like my brother. Or maybe because we treated them like go-karts the way we dragged them out of the stable each day and gunned them for an hour. See, Misty would never do anything but walk. And then sometimes she wouldn't even do that. As hard as he'd try, my brother could never get her to do anything but walk—not even trot—and then like right out of the blue she'd bolt off and my brother'd go flying.

Katie starts to laugh, struggles diligently trying to stifle it into something much more solemn and suitable, then starts to laugh uncontrollably once again.

So anyway, I say, on the last night of camp, we all had to get together to find out who'd been swearing during the week. I don't know why, but swearing was really frowned upon in the early eighties apparently. No, it's true, I say as she begins to snicker again. So anyway, we all get together in this old western court-house-like building, where each of us is called up to the stand, one after another, and anyone who's heard that person swearing at all during the week stands up and announces it to the masses. Well my brother, when it's his turn up, he's of course been swearing a blue streak at Misty all week, and so plenty of kids including me put up our hands and he promptly gets his name added to the list. So then it's my turn. Thing is, with everyone still carrying on about mean ol' Misty, no one but my brother's paying any attention, so I end up getting off Scot-free. Boy, was he ever angry, I say, smiling at the memory.

So what'd they do with the ones who got caught? she says, and I say, Washed their mouths out with soap apparently. I'm not kidding, Katie. Couldn't get away with that sort of thing now of course, but back then, well, back then it wasn't such a big deal, hey. They didn't pick on him though, she says, and I say, Who, my brother? Oh no, they didn't pick on him. Not that I remember anyway. And I think I'd remember. I mean he was just so effeminate, hey.

Studying my hands, I test the places where the calluses were removed a day ago or so. The skin is pink but the sensitivity is subsiding. As they regenerate themselves, I suppose.

Well that sounds like a fun camp, she says. It was a fun camp, Katie. It really was. For instance, this one night the girls crept over from their dorm and removed all the boards from our bunks. I was in the bottom bunk, see, and my brother was on top, and when he got into bed the whole thing just totally collapsed. On you? she says, and I say, No, I was still in the bathroom at the time. See, they'd warned me ahead of time. So then I guess your brother got picked on a little, she says, and I say, Yeah, well, maybe a little. He certainly didn't catch any whippings though. Not like this one other time. That's awful, she says. Yes, it is, Katie. Kids are terrible. But then I guess you already know that. You of all people know that. That must've been awfully hard on you too, she says, and I say, Yes, it was. And your brother, he's younger than you? she says, and I say, Older. That's what made it so difficult, hey.

Friday, 5:26 pm

The telephone rings. Katie answers it. It's for you, she says, and passes it over the bar. Chris speaking, I say into the receiver. Good evening! says an entirely too cheerful voice in return. My name is Mr Richards. That's R-I-C-H-A-R-D-S. Lovely weather we've been having isn't it? Not really, I say. No, you're right there, he says. Not much of a spring, I'm afraid. But I'm sure it'll come around eventually. I'm sure it will, I say.

Anyway, Mr Richards continues on in his same overly cheerful way, I take it you know who I am then. Well no, not exactly, I say. Although I do have a fairly good idea who it is you represent. Now you terminated Darcy Beauchemin's employment this afternoon, correct? he says, and I say I did. And I believe you owe her some money? he says, and I say I do. Well we'll be taking over that debt then, he says, and I say I see. As of now you owe three thousand dollars, he explains. You owed Ms Beauchemin, I believe, roughly two thousand dollars, but with accrued interest you now owe us exactly three thousand dollars. Now that's three thousand American, understood? I think so, sure, I say. Now this sum is payable by seven o'clock tomorrow morning, he continues, that's seven AM, and each day you don't pay, an additional one thousand dollars interest will be added to the total. I see, I say. Well that certainly is a hefty penalty, isn't it. But what if, say, I never pay? I doubt you want to go there, Mr Richards chuckles good-naturedly. But I'm not, you see. I'm not paying. Not tomorrow. Not the next day. Not ever. I'm never paying actually.

There occurs a short pause in our conversation as Mr Richards digests this information. At length he says, Perhaps I haven't quite made myself quite clear . . . Oh no, you've made yourself perfectly clear, I say. Transparent, really. And I assure you I'm not paying you your money. You know, we do have ways to make you pay, Mr Richards clears his throat and says, and I say, Oh *please*, enough with the melodrama already. I know all about you, or enough anyway, and I'm sure you're all very intimidating and dangerous, just as you portray yourselves to be, but to be honest I'm not really concerned either way. I have a restaurant to run here and I really have to be on my way. But before I go, if you're interested, as I'm sure *Ms* Beauchemin's told you, some time early tomorrow morning I'll be arriving at the Semiahmoo reserve with the product I've recently purchased with her—or your—money, and if at that time you wish to discuss the matter further, well then I'll be happy to tell you no several times over at that point too. That's no, Mr Richards. N-O. Now really, I have to G-O. The place is literally crazy right now and they really need me out there on the floor.

I hang up the phone and pour myself a celebratory scotch on the rocks. And having tasted the Chivas, and consequently gagged, I place it aside and pour myself a much more manageable cranberry juice and 7–Up.

At length Rick Beasley arrives, walking in with his customary self-important stride, and noting the complete lack of a dinner crowd, following prescribed ritual, bellies up to the bar for a chat. What the hell happened to your face? he asks, signalling for a drink to make its way immediately into his grasp. Long story, I say, handing him my Chivas. Looks terrible, he says. Hardly even recognized you. And glancing around the dining room at the few patrons in attendance he says that lucky for us it's one of those rare quiet nights.

He takes the carafe of water and pours it slowly over his recycled ice and scotch. Where's Todd, I say. Don't know, he shrugs. Figured he'd be here by now. Why? No reason, I say. Must have something else going on then. Must have, he says.

Wendy comes in to take a seat at the bar, at which point Rick offers to buy her a drink. She accepts a Bacardi and Coke, takes a sip, and with the back of her hand wipes some Coke from her lip. And finally, unable to endure the spectacle of these two disparate characters together, I wander aimlessly around behind the bar, busying myself with nothing in particular.

Eventually Katie flags me down. You got a friend here, she tells me, bulging her eyes towards the door Joe Brand is about to come stumbling through. Stepping out from behind the counter, I meet him at the corner of the bar. Krishna here? he asks, his eyes blurry and misshapen with drink. Not here, big fella, I tell him. And I think you'd better be getting along too.

He ponders me blinkingly down the bridge of his nose, then drags a long slow hand through his hair. I was looking for *Krish*na, he says, regarding me in a pleasant puzzled way, as though suddenly reconciled to the fact that he will forever be misunderstood in some fundamental way. Yeah but like I said, she's not here, I say.

He pauses, blinks slowly, then shrugs laboriously and says, Fuck, I really figured she would be too. Well come on then, get me a beer, he goes on, staggering past me to the bar. Actually, I think you've had enough already, I say, circling around to front him once more. There's coffee though. Get me a beer, he says, rummaging through his pockets, and I say, Can't do it, big fella. Come on, Chris. Nope, not gonna do it, Joe. Now go on and get the hell out of here. Get out before I have to Indian leg-wrestle you.

Regarding me with another one of those pleasant puzzled expressions of his, he gropes out in the direction of the bar, sighing tremendously at the utter injustice of it all. You won't serve me a fucking *beer*? he says, and I say, Not tonight, no. How about an Indian burn though? They're always on special here. But I heard you give the staff free booze, he says, squinting down at me, breathing heavily, and I say, Occasionally, yes, but may I remind you, Joe, you haven't worked here in almost a year. And whose fault is that? he asks, imploring me with his hands. Mine, I suppose. Exactly, he says. Yours. So give me a beer. No way, I say. No Brand gets anything for free from me. Other than your wife of course.

Joe squints at me, blinkingly, clenching and releasing his fists, rolling forward and backwards on the balls of his feet. Come on, he says, and I say, Nope. Just one, he says, and I say, Forget it. He shakes his head with drunken albeit dignified disappointment. You're serious, he says. Yeah I'm serious, Joe. Now go on and get the hell out of here. Get out before I scalp you, I say, grabbing him by the arm and shoving him along towards the door. We don't serve no Injuns here.

And surprisingly, despite all best efforts to the contrary, he does leave too.

What was that all about, Rick says, pushing his empty scotch glass back across the bar, and I say, Don't know. Misses his wife maybe. Krishna not working tonight? he asks, and I say, Not tonight, no. Switched with Laura. Why, hoping to grope her were you? How was lunch? he asks, shaking his head, more amused than annoyed. Once we get the patio open I'm sure it'll pick up, I answer. Once the weather changes, he says, and I say, You'd think it would have to eventually, wouldn't you? Well I heard it was going to stay like this for a while, interjects a third, and together we turn to include a vibrantly smiling Wendy in our conversation of the climatic workings of the world.

Friday, 10:29 pm

And suddenly the Trap & Gill explodes. People, mostly friends and family of the owners, have been arriving in ever-increasing numbers throughout the night, but for the most part, prior to ten-thirty that is, they keep away from the bar and off by themselves. They gather in the far rear corner of the Trap & Gill at a few of the tables pulled closely together, so closely in fact that it becomes almost impossible for either Katie or Laura to get in amongst them in order to properly serve the customers there. So then eventually many of the thirstier ones end up coming up to the bar. A few take the opportunity to complain about the lack of table service, but for the most part I manage to tune them out without much trouble.

Judging by their expressions, some of the later arrivals, having only recently arrived and therefore enduring a relative sobriety, are having difficulty in paying some of the posted prices for alcohol. They heard it was on sale today. Well it's not on sale, I say, not today anyway, going on to say, to those who make it up to the bar anyway, that it's necessary that they make their shift in values gradually. It's a long slow process, I explain. And while it may be difficult to pay these sorts of prices now, later on it won't much matter either way. Later on it won't matter what they pay or even what they buy, I tell them, as all that will matter is that they were here. But as for now, having not yet achieved this elusive shift in values, they should order doubles and tip me appropriately. For if it's seen that they tip me appropriately, I say, their doubles will be triples and they'll feel that much better about the deal. You usually get your money's worth in doubles, I explain, even when the bartender is being legitimate with his pours. On the other hand, having left behind long ago any and all legitimacy this place might ever have had, Trap & Gill management now offers an even better trade on their morals. And indicating one of the sober, young, leather jacket-clad men at one of the closely packed tables in the back, I say how, for that fellow, money still has a definite value in berries picked and stolen car radios sold. He doesn't yet want to spend his hard-earned money as it still has a genuine value of its own. But later on, I say, after a little more liquor perhaps, he may just choose to buy a drink for a friend. Hell, he may even buy him two, expecting really nothing in return. But then liquor being the silent killer it is, and this particular fellow, after a few more drinks at least, being the obvious murderous bastard that *he* is, might just combine to crash a car into a woman standing alone at a bus stop for no reason at all, it seems. And these leather-clad customers crowded in around the bar, they laugh at that and throw money down into my jar, and so there's no need to explain how prices will be dropping off by as much as half tomorrow as, now that they're drunk, they really don't seem to care one way or the other.

And now, nearing eleven, they seem to be arriving in droves. And from the closely packed tables in the rear of the Trap & Gill they eventually spill forward and out toward the patio. Inevitably one young man comes up to ask whether I might consider opening up one of the windows. For reasons of my own, though, I remain somewhat hesitant to do so, but then he goads me so much that eventually I find it easier to simply give in. Due to a lack of usage lately, the window proves difficult to open. Finally, though, it swings open on rusted, painted-over hinges, and the next time I look over two windows are open, one of which the young man has stepped out through. Out on the patio now, he sets up a table and chair and, lighting a cigarette, proceeds to smoke, all the while shouting in through the window at his friends, the fact that he's still allowed to smoke indoors at the Trap & Gill obviously completely lost on him.

I ask what Katie what she and Laura are drinking. She's drinking draft and I'm having the usual, Katie tells me. Here then, have another, I say. And for Christ's sake, Laura, get off the beer.

Laura eagerly accepts a vodka-soda just as Sid sashays his way up to the bar in the grips of some young girl sporting far too much eyeliner and not nearly enough clothing. Hey, citizen, can we get a beer? he says, and I say, Well I don't know, Sid, where else have you been drinking? Down at the OB with Thomas, he admits, leaning in close. Methinks you should tell the boss you're sick and come out with us though. What illness should I contract then, I say, and he says, Why, herpes of course. Anyone without some sort of sexually transmitted disease these days is a goddamned hypocrite in my books. Better yet, make it scurvy. You never hear enough about scurvy these days. Yes, scurvy, Sid muses. The last great romantic affliction, I'd say.

I draw off a trio of pints for some customers of Laura's that to this point she's managed to outright ignore. Meanwhile, Sid glances casually around the Trap & Gill, taking in the clientele. Bit of a brown tide tonight wouldn't you say, citizen? he says idly, before long. So where's the liquor at? Across the border, I tell him. At Hum's. We left it there in the Robert Blake this afternoon. Still bringing it over by boat tonight? he says, and I say, Of course. Good man! he laughs, slapping the bar. Though I see the rumours are true. What rumours? That Joe Brand carved his initials in you. Looks worse than it feels, Sid, believe me. Uh yes, citizen, I understand completely. Sometimes you need to speak to the savages in a language you know the bastards comprehend.

The front door opens, and another group of young men and women comes funnelling through. How's the OB tonight, I ask Sid as the last of them make their way past the bar. Not bad, I'm told. Brown though. And the manager felt the need to kick us out unfortunately. Getting a little too riled up were you, I say, and he says, Yes, seems Lonnie here felt the pressing need to put on a little show for the locals. Citizen, I want you to meet Lonnie, a lovely enterprising girl with many admirable qualities. And Lonnie, this here's the citizen I've been wanting you to meet. The citizen here can do anything he wants to: become prime minister, bust out as the greatest prose writer since F. Scott, or even marry one of the cast of *Friends*. But instead he keeps running out to get beat up by large menacing Indians, he sighs, squeezing Lonnie half-heartedly. Yes, very hung up on that sort of thing, he is.

Lonnie laughs, and I move my head slightly to the right, in this way aligning her head momentarily with the photograph of the girl aboard the barge who died.

Yes, much quality aren't you, Lonnie. Yes, much quality indeed. . . . Speaking of which, citizen, Lonnie here's found us a recipe for real genuine quality absinthe on the Internet. And not that watered-down liquor store crap either, I might add. And get this, he says, she knows where to find all the necessary ingredients too. Tell him, Lonnie. Tell the citizen here where you found all the necessary secret ingredients for real genuine quality absinthe. At the health-food store, she grins. You hear that, citizen? At the health-food store. You can get oil of wormwood at the goddamned *health*-food store. My God, what a wonderful country we live in, he says.

I offer grinning Lonnie a drink, but Sid intervenes. That's another thing about that bloody Ocean Beach though, citizen: they won't serve minors in there. I'm eighteen, Lonnie says, chin up and jutting forward. I'll be nineteen in a month. Close enough, I say, so what'll it be. I want it all, she grins again, although in truth her eyes don't want for much of anything. Here then, have a beer, I say. On me.

She downs the beer in one eager tilt. Easy honey, it's not a sprint, I say, pouring her another beer which she promptly drains off by half. And then, trying to belch, she leans up against the bar, asking if I can do that bottle flipping thing. Well sure I can, I tell her. That is, if she doesn't mind seeing them smash all over the floor back here. She frowns and leans away, clearly disappointed, as behind her Sid winces at me apologetically. Rebounding quickly, however, Lonnie mashes herself up against the bar. Who's that? she asks, gesturing at the waitress, and I say, Why, that's Laura, dear. She looks so, you know, exotic, she says, and I say, That's because she's Indian. A real genuine *qual*ity Indian. Go ahead, Lonnie, ask Laura her secret Indian name. Maybe that's not such a good idea, citizen, Sid puts in. Oh, can I meet her, Sid? Please? Oh I really do want to meet her, Lonnie says, refusing to take her eyes off Laura for the time being. I've never actually spoken to a real Native Indian. I really don't think you're ready for Laura, dear, he says, and she says, Why not? Well I really can't say, he says. Not for certain anyway. Though I'm quite certain she's not ready for you.

Sid looks to me for a price on the beers. Well how much would you like to pay, I say, and he says, What, it's up to me? It's up to you, I say. Well then I think I'd like to pay five dollars, he says, rummaging through his pockets until a wrinkled ten-dollar bill appears. Yes, five dollars seems like plenty to pay, especially for a poor struggling Jewish survivor of scurvy like me.

I shove the ten-dollar bill down into my jar. Sid roars tri-
umphantly and, drinks in hand, whisks Lonnie away across the
floor. *He's back*, Wendy calls out from over near the door. And
sure enough, there he is, Joe Brand, having joined forces with the
quintet of smokers currently holding court on the patio. He
seems genuinely happy to see me though. In fact, upon my
arrival at the window, his first order of business is to inform
everyone within earshot that he was the one who rearranged my
face in this manner. Suddenly, though, what sounds like a gun,
but turns out to be, in reality, a backfiring engine, erupts from
the parking lot across the way. Immediately it erupts again, followed by a grey ball of smoke ballooning up from the tailpipe,
shifting in the wind before dissipating completely. Another car
lurches up into position: the engine roars, the tires squeal, and
the ensuing smoke rises up to engulf the audience gathering in
around the vehicle. Meanwhile, back inside the Trap & Gill,
there are now so many patrons that Katie and Laura, trays thrust
straight up over their heads, are forced to literally bulldoze their
way to their tables. Customers accost them from every side,
while across the street, around the cars, the young men and
women gather closer still. I watch the smoke, watching as it rises
up in clouds from the squealing tires to engulf the spectators,
many of whom have begun to dance, all of them moving together to a deep bass rhythm. Some of the groups seem to be com-
posed entirely of females, while in others only the heads and
shoulders of males appear. I look over near the base of the pier
where one young man, bent over at the waist, purges himself
onto the promenade bricks. A crowd of friends stands around
chanting and pulling at his shirt, until finally the young man
comes around and, nearly naked, takes a swing at his nearest agitator. They go down in a tumble, both he and his agitator, down
onto the promenade bricks. And by the time their friends manage to pull them apart, each is covered in the blood of the other.
Finally the sick one gets hold of his shirt and marches off down
the length of the pier, his slick brown face shining brightly
under the soft amber glow of the lamps thrust up from the rail-
ings at regular intervals. His friends follow along closely,

shouting and pushing and nipping at his heels, and all this time more people are coming into the Trap & Gill and pouring out onto the patio. Someone hands Joe Brand a beer. I take the beer from Joe. Katie yells out from the bar that she really needs some drinks while Rick inquires whether there are any spare chairs available. His lawyer, having just called apparently, will be arriving shortly, and they would like a table, he says, preferably one with a view of the pier.

Suddenly Laura appears alongside me, directing my attention down the far end of the lot where another large contingent has recently made its way down the hill. And now the lot is literally solid with people and cars converging around the base of the pier. Inside the restaurant the music cranks up, way up, and through the mass of bodies in between I see Rick with a full drink in one hand, a less than enthusiastic Katie in the other, hard at work himself on the stereo in between. Squeezing my way through the crowd, I offer him a quick lesson in volume control. Then I attempt to mix some drinks. The orders are spitting up out of the printer fast and furious, adding to an already impressive length snaking down onto the floor.

What's wrong, Rick says as I scour the bar and the crowd before it. Nothing, Rick. Nothing at all. Come on, what's the matter? he asks, so I tell him that someone just stole my tip jar, that's all. Wow, that's too bad, he says, and I look at him. He looks at me. Hey, can we get our drinks? inquires Katie hesitantly, having noted the already dour expression on my face. Rick tries to bring her in for a groping hug, but she manages to fend him off with some success.

Just a sec, Katie. Hey Sid, I say, but unable to hear me over the crowd and the music, Sid continues his own search, eagerly exploring Lonnie's cleavage with his nose. Hey Sid, I repeat until eventually he glances over. What's up? he asks, approaching the bar unexpectedly serious and altogether sober. What'd I do? Nothing, I tell him. Just need you to help pour drinks, that's all. And hey, just so you know, Rick just stole my tip jar.

He nods solemnly, as though, in his world, tips jars went missing by the hour. Bastards, he says. What unforgiving bastards those

Beasleys are. No matter though, citizen, we can skim it all back. Just like the old days at KFC, no? Speaking of chicken, how's that avian flu coming along? Wonderfully, I hope? Not very well, I'm sorry to report. Indeed, he says, stepping around behind the bar. Should've stuck with scurvy or herpes then. Stick to your guns, that's what Stephanie'd say anyway. Yep, "Nothing like a good gun-sticker," she'd say. And never go looking a gift horse in the mouth either, eh citizen? Nope, "Don't be a gift-horser," she'd say. What, citizen? What'd I say? Are you quite finished, I say, and he says, Why yes, I am. By the way, what is it exactly you want me to do here? Stand here and do what I tell you, I say.

And so, with Sid's help, things proceed relatively quickly and smoothly, and soon the list of drinks to be made has been worked back to a much more manageable amount.

Want me to stick around then, citizen? he says. You look awful by the way. Believe me, I feel worse, I say. Cursed rabies, he says, shaking his head. Thing is, I can't figure out why you'd let him back in here. Why I'd let who back in? Joe Brand, he says, and I say, *That's* what I was supposed to do! And I lunge out from behind the bar and over towards the open patio windows only to be met by Rick halfway.

How about that table then, Chris? Look, Rick, I'm a little busy right now, I say, failing to force my way past his considerable girth. But we've been waiting like twenty minutes already, he tells me. Okay, uh, how about that one there, I say, indicating a small table in the corner with only a single remaining chair. That's *it*? he says. Take a look around, Rick. That's the best I can do right now. But I asked you like a half hour ago, he says, and I say, Look, I've got a few more things on my mind right now than dealing with you and your goddamned lawyer. Some manager, he grumbles under his breath. Pardon, I say, and he regards me evenly. Pardon, Rick? All right then, fine, he says. We'll take the table. But see if you can't at least get us another goddamned chair, okay?

Saturday, 1:55 am

The night really gets going after that, and somewhat surprisingly keeps up for some time. The music keeps up, and the dancing keeps up, and with the rain holding off the noise from the young men and women dancing amongst the cars in the parking lot seems to go on and on. The things that happen could really only happen in a bar. Everything accelerates to a point of departure where it seems as though there can't possibly be any consequences at all. Besides, it seems forever out of place to think that anything of consequence could ever really happen in a bar. All during the night there's this feeling, even in those rare moments when it's relatively quiet, that you have to shout anything you truly wish to be heard. It's the same with any action, and seemingly with everyone else as well. The Trap & Gill may only be licensed as a restaurant, but at its rare best runs like a well-oiled brothel.

Once it's slow enough to manage comfortably with only one girl on the floor, I tell Laura she can cash-out and go home. By two the place is nearly empty, and in addition to Sid and Lonnie, the only others remaining aside from Katie and myself are Rick and his skinny, grey-haired, silver-suited lawyer. Even Joe Brand has long since disappeared. And now, having executed every other task commensurate to closing, it's time for the patio to be shut down too.

Printing Rick's bill, I make my way out onto the patio where, with Sid currently off watching Lonnie vomit somewhere, there happens to be a chair available between Rick and his lawyer. I sit here a moment to explain the bill.

But who ordered these drinks here? asks Rick at one point, placing his cigar clumsily on the rim of the ashtray to facilitate the fumbling retrieval of his glasses from his pocket. You did, Rick. For those—

You can't sit here.

—for those kids in the corner there, I say. Just a sec, I tell the little silver-suited lawyer on my right, currently puffing theatrically on his own enormous cigar. But Lonnie's sitting here, he tells me, taking yet another long drag off his enormous cigar and settling back comfortably in his chair. And hey, I say, once I'm through explaining the bill here, rest assured the chair's all hers.

I continue explaining the bill to Rick, all the while gazing out across the street to the promenade, the line of benches before it, the twin rails of train track beyond it, and further out there in the darkness, the beach and the ocean somewhere.

You can't sit here, repeats the lawyer through a thick cloud of cigar smoke. Lonnie's sitting here. Excuse me, I say as Rick asks, How about these beers then? He takes up his cigar and revolves it slowly between his fingers. Then, frowning at the burning end, he licks his thumb and forefinger and proceeds to rearrange the embers to somehow better suit him. I didn't order any of these beers, he says, and I say, No, Rick—

I did, his lawyer puts in. That's right, this charming friend of yours here did, I say as, delicately extricating his cigar from his lips, the lawyer studies me in a calculating way, sizing up my various injuries. Okay, that's fine, Rick says, perusing the bill. Wow, though, did I really drink all this? I couldn't possibly have drunk all this. No, you didn't, I tell him. Not all of it. Your little lawyer friend here helped immensely. I just can't believe we ordered this much Chivas, he says, so I say, Well you did. Now would you like me to promo it or—

You can't sit here, says the lawyer, grabbing me by the arm. I want Lonnie to sit here. I look down to where his thin pink fingers have fastened themselves securely around my forearm. Look, I'd rather you not touch me, I tell him. Get out of this chair then, he says. This is Lonnie's chair. Better yet, I say, how about letting go of my arm before I push your teeth in, okay?

Refusing to let go, though, he lifts his chin and narrows his eyes, squinting hard against the cloud of smoke drifting up from the ashtray on his right. Boys, come now, says Rick half-heartedly, appearing altogether too tired and too drunk to feign the role of impartial mediator just now. I'm not kidding, Rick, I say, staring straight at his lawyer. I'm really not in the mood for this right now.

A long moment passes. At length Rick taps me on the shoulder and says he still doesn't remember ordering all these drinks. Maybe something's wrong with the computer, he theorizes. Or maybe someone else's bill somehow got combined with ours. I say, Whose bill, Rick? Mine? and yank my arm loose, offering the lawyer one last long antagonistic glare for good measure. Look, no bills got *combined*, and nothing's *wrong* with the computer. This here's what the two of you ordered and that's *it*, okay? Are you sure? he says, and I say, Yes, *I'm sure*. And hey, if it's going to be this much of a hassle, well then maybe we shouldn't run you tabs anymore.

Taking up his cigar, Rick challenges me to a long staring contest of his own before eventually shoving the bill rather pluckily across the table at his lawyer. Well then you pay for it, Getty. You don't want me to promo it then, I say, and he says, No, Getty here's going to get it. Aren't you, Getty. Aren't I what? says Getty, and Rick says, Paying the bill. Getty takes up the bill and, with an air of shrewd sophistication, judiciously inspects it. Then he takes up his cigar. He gets as far as placing the latter between his lips before the extraordinary hilarity of the moment makes any sort of actual inhaling unfeasible. Finally, discarding both cigar and bill, he states flatly and for the record that he didn't order any of these drinks. Guffawing raucously, Rick slaps me on the shoulder and says, Too bad someone stole your tip jar, Chris, or else we'd get you to pay for it!

I return inside, where eventually Sid comes wandering up to the bar to join me, leaving the recently returned, freshly emptied, entirely too-intoxicated Lonnie to fend for herself outside. I continue wiping down the counter, all the while watching the action on the patio from the corner of my eye.

What's the matter, citizen? SARS got you down? Forget it, Sid, I say. I'm really not in the mood right now. Come now, do tell, he says. The symptoms of airborne respiratory disease have always been meant for sharing somehow. Ah, it's just these bastards I work for, I tell him. What about them? he says, and I say, Well the only thing they seem to enjoy more than running up a tab in their own bar is disputing what it is they've put on it afterwards. Looks like he's trying to get his little friend to pay, Sid says, looking out at the patio, and I say, Well of course he is. And that's another one of the Beasleys' favourite games by the way: goading one of their henchmen into picking up the tab in the presence of women and then paying them back in secret the next day.

I pour myself a glass of water. Looks like your Lonnie there's taken a real shine to them anyway, I say, and Sid sighs. Youth shall be serviced, he says. Yes, well, it certainly appears that way, I say. Ah citizen, good hunting to him. Good hunting and good riddance. Good riddance to all women under forty, he says. I'm through with them. I'm absolutely through with them. Say, can I get a really *big* one of those by the way?

I pour a glass of water for Sid and another for myself and then, since nothing yet seems to be happening with the bill, eventually make my way back out onto the patio and into the fray.

So what's happening with the bill then, Rick? And hey, do me a favour will you, big fella? Saying this, I remove Getty's hand from Lonnie's puke-splattered thigh. I somehow doubt your wife would appreciate it, I add.

Getty looks up at me smilingly, vindictively, taking a long deep drag off his cigar. So what's it going to be then, Rick, I say. Are we promo-ing the bill? Or is Hands here going to be floating some plastic. Getty's got it, Rick says, sagging back into his chair. Don't you, Getty. All right then, Getty, Rick here says you're covering the bill, I say. Now do you have a card you'd like me to put it on? Or no. Wait. I bet you probably carry that kind of cash on you.

Getty glances from the bill to me and back to the bill, and then decides he really doesn't want to pay for anything. Clapping his hands together, Rick laughs uproariously. Fine then, I guess I'll just promo the whole fucking thing, I say, snatching up the bill and stomping back inside to the bar with Rick, it turns out, in tow.

Now just a second, he says, poking at my chest with a remarkably stubby finger. You work for me. *You work for me.* You just try and remember that, okay? And if my brother or I want to stay here and drink with one of our people, well then—

Well then *what*, Rick? I should have to stay here and baby-sit the two of you all night? Get over it. Get over your*self*.

I look past him, to the photograph of the girl aboard the barge, just as he takes one measured step back, removing her from view for now. Go on ahead then—leave, he says. Getty and I'll lock up. Right, Rick, and then give me shit at the end of the month for my scotch costs being so out of whack. Look, I say, either you run this place like a business, or else you run it like your own back-yard—personally I don't give a damn either way. But whatever you decide, whichever way you think will work best, just try to let me know in advance so that I might make the proper inventory adjustments, okay? Hey, you don't like it, you can leave any time, he tells me. Oh that's nice, Rick. That's real nice. That's a great way to handle it. And here I thought you were a good guy, he says, shaking his head in disappointment. A good guy, Rick? A *good guy*? What the hell's that supposed to mean, a *good guy*? Listen, you want to stay here and get pissed with your little lawyer buddy there, so be it, that's not for me to comment on either way. *But allow me to do my job.* And in allowing me to do my job, I say, poking *him* in the chest, you will *not* question whether or not I've rung in extra drinks on your fucking tab. Christ. Good guy my ass. My God, you piss me off.

He grabs me by the wrist and starts to squeeze, if his expression is any indication, as hard as he can. I push him hard in the chest and up against the bar, smacking him flatly across the face with an open palm. What are you doing, Rick?

He continues to squeeze my wrist, his face contorting grotesquely in the light.

What are you doing, I repeat, hitting him again, and again his face changes in the light. His black, smoothly groomed moustache suddenly thickens with red and his little hard brown eyes slip unnaturally upwards and to the right. I lose track, but there must be even more contact after that, as all at once I'm down on my backside. I try to get up, but for whatever reason I can't. Still, I try to get up in order to hit him. I do hit him. Someone helps me up from behind. With his arm around my waist, Sid eases me back into a chair just as Rick comes at me from across the room. I try to put him down. He doesn't want to go down. And suddenly Sid is pulling me off Todd as well.

Saturday, 2:24 am

Moments later, guiding me along the sidewalk outside, Sid says, Well that was fun. Glad I could amuse you, Sid. What the hell's on the back of my head though, I ask, attempting to reach around and grab whatever is there. That's Katie, citizen. She's got a cloth on your cut. How bad is it, Sid? Not too bad, he tells me, but bad. Good God, that was fun though.

I eject a wad of bloody saliva into a nearby puddle. Aw Christ, I say, I don't want to go to the hospital. You have to though, I'm told. No, Katie—where is she—no Katie, I don't, I tell her, managing to rotate my head sufficiently in order to find her following along grim and duty-bound behind me. I don't have to go. There's no need for me to go, is there, Sid. Well I don't know, says Sid, maintaining a fairly decent clip for my sudden-ly weak and disjointed legs. Citizen, he chuckles to himself, the People's Champion. Joe Brand? Beaten. The Brothers Beasley? Routed. Yessir, ladies and gentlemen, I give you the latest and greatest Great White Hope: Citizen Chris, the human punch-ing bag.

Hey, I say, where are you guys taking me? Ands where the fuck is Lonnie? Lonnie's fine, Sid tells me. That lawyer prick's taking her home. Now come on, hurry up. This West Nile's much worse than I ever could've hoped for. We have to go back though, I say, struggling unsuccessfully to free myself. Easy, citizen, they're already long gone. And besides, the Beasleys already called the cops on you. They didn't, I say, and he says, They did. Bastards, I say. What fucking *bastards* they are. Now would you please slow it down a little? Christ, the cops don't respond that fast in this town. We have to get you to a hospital though, Katie insists. No, Katie. No. Now listen: I'm not going to any goddamned hospital. Besides, I'm not a bleeder. You're bleeding now, she tells me. Well sure, I might *weep* a little, but even if I wanted to I wouldn't bleed to death, I tell her.

And together, despite my many objections, they convey me down past Monk's and out towards Sid's vehicle. Nice of Todd to finally show up, says Katie at one point, and Sid says, Certainly made his impression on our Indian-fighter here anyway. Yes, well, let's please not talk about it, I say. Why not? I don't know, Katie, it just makes me feel sick to talk about it, okay? Now can we please get me across the border? I have some smuggling to attend to here.

Sid unlocks the Explorer, allowing Katie to climb up into the back. And as I lift myself up onto the passenger seat, she saddles up behind me, continuing to cradle my head just so. You're not still going to do that, she says. Why yes, Katie, I am. Oh that's ridiculous, Chris. *You're* ridiculous. I mean look at you: your face is a mess and you're bleeding all over. I'm not bleeding, I'm weeping, I tell her, and she tells me, No, what you are is a fucking train wreck.

I swing the rear-view mirror over to inspect my face as we drive past the juice bar, the Ocean Beach Hotel, the other juice bar, the Dairy Queen then the Trap & Gill not bothering to look inside, up past Annie and the long lighted pier now empty, the bus stop unoccupied, out past the Semiahmoo reserve and onto the entrance ramp leading to the highway and the enormous white Peace Arch presently aglow in lights. Fortunately there isn't all that much of a line-up at the border this time of night.

A face only a mother could love, eh citizen? says Sid as I swing the mirror back into place. Speaking of which, how *is* your lovely mother these days? Fine, I say. Worried though. But you stay away from her, Sid. I mean it. Penelope's absolutely off limits. Say, are you even *close* to sober by the way? Sober? he says. What's sober? Another one of these romantic ideals of yours, I take it? Well are you at least sober enough to get us across the border, Sid? Please say yes. Yes, he says, adding, almost as an afterthought, If the left side of the road's still mine, that is. We'll crash into anyone who contests it, I say. Good on us, citizen. Now on with this gallantry. You two are pathetic, Katie groans.

We drive in silence a moment. Then Katie says, Oh this is ridiculous, Sid. We have to get him to a hospital. Nonsense, I say. I can feel the scab forming even now. Christ, I do feel liberated though. You mean unemployed, she says. You're *fired*, if you didn't know. Yes, I suppose you're wondering what it is I'm up to here, I say, and she says no, she knows exactly what I'm up to here, what she doesn't understand is *why*. It's just something I feel the need to do, Katie, that's all. Oh, like a calling, she says, and I say, That's it, a calling. That's a good way of putting it, sure. I just need to see myself from another angle. A new perspective. It's all about perspective. And awareness. Well that's stupid, I'm told. I mean it makes no sense. How is smuggling *booze* across the *border* enabling you to see yourself with a new awareness? "And the Lord spoke to the fish, and it vomited out Jonah upon the dry land," I quote. That's from the Bible, you know. You're insane, she says, and I say, No, my brother's insane and believe me, there's a fundamental difference here.

Saturday, 3:06 am

Finally, in the darkness, a single figure approaches the Explorer. Hey Hum, I say. Hey Sleeman, Hum says, leaning in on his elbows, peering in at Sid who says, Spoken like a true artist though, eh citizen? Shut up, Sid, Hum says. So who gave you the facelift? he asks, tracing a single finger down my cheek. No one you'd know, I answer, smacking his hand away. How about you, Hum? Y'ever catch the rustler who stole your calves? Fuck you, he says. Your face, though, who did it? It's scurvy, you insensitive jerk, Sid puts in. Happened at work, I say, shoving Sid back to his own seat. Nervous, Hum? Nervous as hell, he tells me. Already, citizen, I detect in our handsome male lead a most unbecoming decline in male lead-like character, says Sid eventually.

Hum stares blankly at Sid a moment before directing his attention squarely at me. So where's the liquor at? he asks. In the Robert Blake, I say, indicating Katie's Beretta parked not three stalls away, and Sid says, You remember the Robert Blake though, Hum. So how's Jeff, Hum asks, ignoring Sid completely. All right, I guess, I say. Has his good days anyway. And work? Slow. They do seem reasonably happy with me though, I add, at which point Sid laughs harshly. Shut up, Sid. I mean it. How's my head though, Katie? Still weeping? Seems to have stopped, she tells me, albeit grudgingly. Told you, I say. I may be a shirker, but I'm certainly no bleeder. What's going on, Sleeman, Hum asks, and I turn my attention to my fingernails and say, Nothing. Just the Brothers Beasley and I, we had ourselves a little misunderstanding. I see, he says. Actually no, you don't, I say, forcing back one cuticle, then another, painfully. And how's the other stuff coming along? he asks, and I say, Not very well actually. No time, see.

I propel the cuticle of my right thumbnail so far back that it begins to bleed. No *time*, he says. What, you didn't use that month off at all? Not very productively, no, I say. So, what, you've been moping around Stephanie's bench this whole time, is that it? he says, and Sid says, Hum! That's all right, Sid, I say. No, not really, Hum. No, that wasn't the problem at all. Aw, it'll come back, Chris, he smiles sympathetically. It always comes back. I know, but it's hard, Hum. You can't understand how hard it is. Well hey, he says, if it weren't, you probably would've quit already.

Inspecting the other cuticles, I propel them back one after another as somewhere overhead a seagull shrieks, drifting off in the direction of the as yet unseen marina.

Thanks for the vote of confidence though, Hum. One artist to another, I mean. Look, he says, I never said it was an *art* for Christ's sake. And besides, it was just a fucking interview. People say a lot of things in interviews. You're not supposed to take them seriously. That's the problem with your *craft*, Sid says, people don't understand what a joke it really is. Look, I never said it was a craft either, Hum says, and Sid says, Fuck you, you did too. All right, enough, I tell them both, and with that a silence creeps its way into the vehicle. I hold my nose and blow gently, feeling the pressure gradually let go.

Okay, are we going to do this thing or not, Hum says, and I say, Sure. That is, if you think you're ready. Oh I'm ready all right, he says. Ready to get this monkey off my back, that is. Call it a favour, Hum. Apparently it's what friends do for one another. Oh we're friends again are we, Sleeman? Figure of speech, I tell him. Now Sid, you and Katie stay here while Calves and I head down and inspect the situation.

I climb free of the Explorer and follow Hum down to the marina. He's dressed in a burgundy sweatshirt and long khaki shorts and I notice that he's recently shaved his goatee. Your whole problem, it seems to me, Hum, is that you *look* like an actor. Yes, it's because you resemble the token actor in almost every conceivable way that it becomes impossible not to want to pigeonhole you, I say. Whatever, he says. I see you've tinted your hair too, I go on. Yeah, my publicist thought it'd be a good idea, he shrugs in response. You know, for the opening and all. It'll grow out though, he assures me, unlocking a gate and stepping through to a ramp descending to a maze of watercraft nodding lazily in their stalls below. The smell of dead fish and engine oil hits me immediately. The smell of a marina, I suppose.

This is rather steep, I say, indicating the ramp. Tide's out, he says. When it's in it rises quite a bit. Well that's a relief, Hum. I mean I'd hate to know you had to walk something this steep all the time, especially on those pins. No offence, but you look like you're riding a chicken, I say, but he doesn't seem to have heard me.

At the base of the ramp we turn down the long floating dock to the right, each step sending a slight reverberating shockwave out along the walkway forward and back. It seems like there's a lot more boats here now, I say. You know, compared to the last time I was here. Yeah, there's more arriving all the time, I'm informed. That's good, Hum. I mean it's good to know this development is a success. I mean I'd hate to know it wasn't a success. Then again, everything you get involved in is an enormous success. Speaking of which, how's Kevin Costner? Fuck you, he says. No really, Hum, how is he. He's good, thanks. You mean he's *well*. Figure of speech, he says. It is *not* a figure of speech, I say, and he says, All right, colloquialism then. You entire career's a colloquialism, Hum, that's your—

Look, would you please lay off? he says, indicating this four-wheeled trolley he found to help load the liquor down. And so, with our trolley, we continue along the floating dock, silent except for the sound of our footfalls.

I see you brought the car thief along, he says after a time. Problem with that, Hum? Just a little uncomfortable, he says, that's all. You'll get over it, Hum. Heck, you always get over it. An actor of your calibre never gets too immersed in his role. I take that to be an insult then, he sighs. No, not really, I say. It's just that you make a better entertainer than an actor, hey.

We come up alongside the boat, one of those miniature racing jobs slung deep in the still black water. So we'll just load it all in here, he says, patting the hull affectionately. That is, if you think it'll fit. Oh it'll fit all right, I tell him. Now what's *that* supposed to mean, he says, and I say, Just that yes, the hold of your boat here will, I believe, contain my entire supply of liquor. Why, Hum? You're an insolent bugger, you know that? he says just as Sid and Katie come wandering down the dock. I thought I told you two to stay in the truck, I say, and Sid says, We got curious, citizen. Miss Henry here and I are creatures of great curiosity. Not to mention the fact we really can't stand each other's company.

Hum regards Katie evenly a moment, then says to me, So once we're loaded, we'll just head on over to the reserve. That's the plan, I say, and he says, What do you mean, the *plan*. Again, just that yes, that's exactly what we're intending, I say. My, you're skittish this evening though. Well you make it sound suspiciously uncertain, he says. No, not uncertain, Hum. It's anything but uncertain. Fairly risky though, no question, I say.

He looks at me, his face entirely devoid of expression. And then I'll tie up and unload, he continues eventually. Correction: *we'll* tie up and unload, I say, and he says, That's implied. Christ, Sleeman, must you always be so literal about everything? Literal, Hum? What would a theatrical bastard like you know about anything *literal*, I say, adding injury to insult by offering the crimson hull of his boat a half-hearted kick. Would you please quit it? he says. All this chatter's getting on my nerves. Yes, that's the impression I'm getting, I tell him, and he looks at me leadenly and says that's not the only impression I'll be getting if I'm not careful. Would you two please shut up, Katie interjects. My God, it's like listening to an old married couple. No Katie, I'm not. I'm not married. You must be thinking of someone else, I say, plunging everyone into a long awkward silence. Katie looks at me.

Right, citizen. Okay. Never mention that, Sid says quickly, uncomfortable with silence at the best of times, let alone those times when he's arguably been complicit in its creation. That's the sort of thing that should never be mentioned. Ever. It's like an unfathomable depth of character, he adds. Sort of like Miss Henry here's quasi-aboriginal heritage.

Another pause as Katie looks at me. Hum clears his throat nervously. Yes, and I'm certainly not old, he puts in quickly. Quite the contrary actually. Mother Hum always accuses me of behaving like a perfect child. Perfect bastard maybe, Sid corrects him. Too bad the numbers don't add up. Oh Sid. Really. Totally uncalled for.

Katie looks at me.

You know, Hum, Sid continues smoothly, seeing you in this light I can see why all great men are given to such immorality. Why's that, Sidney? Well it's hard to put into words, but I think it might have something to do with your suspect constitution, Sid tells him. Constitution nothing, Hum says, I've fallen in with thieves and liars, that's my problem.

Katie turns and looks at me anew. She turns and looks at me in precisely the same way that, at one time or another, in one place or another, Stephanie always looked at me. And then, almost imperceptibly, she smiles too.

I turn to the others. Have you two eaten then? I know Katie here has; I fed her at work. I bet you did, citizen. Come now, Sidney, be civil, Hum says, turning to me. The condemned prisoner ate a hearty lunch, sir. Sid laughs, For an actor he's pretty funny though, eh citizen? Don't hoard it though, Hum. Never hoard it. No, you should take all that funniness to the people. I think it's called humour, Sid. Well I prefer funniness, Sid says. Or wittiness. Or drollness. Or—

Enough, Katie interrupts, gazing at me in wonder. My God, I'll miss you, she says. Well we'll miss you too, Katie, Sid says, jerking a thumb in Hum's direction. Though I imagine you'll be seeing a lot more of him.

Hum throws up his hands in mock surrender.

Sid says, You know he's hung too, hey Katie. Well yes, I guess you do then. Enough, Sid, I put in. You're right, citizen. I'm sorry, Katie. Still, we really didn't think you'd be so into him. Oh I knew I was going home with the wrong guy, she tells him. But you did it anyway, Sid says. My, what perseverance. What dogged determination you've displayed herein. Look, is it absolutely necessary that we get into this right now, Katie says, and Sid says, You can think of a better time then? I'd rather not get into it at all, she says, and he says, Ha! If only that'd been her attitude *that* night, eh citizen? That's enough, Sid, I warn him. Look, says

Katie, bracing herself, I'm not a slut, if that's what you're implying. No one said you were, Sid says. Though what's bred in the
bone . . . What's *that* supposed to mean? she says, eyeing him
steadily. Nothing, Sid supposes, without the rest of it. Of course
it was originally in Latin. What's the rest of it then? Sid would
rather not say. Nothing more pretentious than going on in Latin
ad infinitum, he'd say. Sid, I say, that's enough. That's it, citizen.
That's the way to do battle for your lady love, he says.

And with that he storms off down the dock, leaving Katie and
I to return to the Beretta where Hum eventually rejoins us, dragging his trolley along behind. And together we load the boxes of
liquor out of the trunk and onto the trolley and then wheel them
down the ramp to the boat, taking three trips all told, managing
to cram most of the boxes into the forward hold, the remainder
stacked on the seats in the back. Eventually Sid comes moping
along and, for his part, seeing that the grunt work is finished, vol-
unteers to return the trolley to the base of the ramp.

Together with Hum I climb down into the boat. What about
Sid and me, Katie asks, standing pensively on the edge of the
dock. Well there's not really enough room, I say just as Sid slowly makes his way back. Content to give us all the silent treatment
for now, to his credit he does shrug apologetically at Katie after a
while.

So that's it then, Hum says, having untied the boat both forward
and aft, and I say, That's it, my thespian friend. Christ, I'm nervous, he says, and I say he should be. I mean just imagine what a
smuggling charge could do for his burgeoning career. You know,
you're not making this any easier, he says, cranking up the bilge
pump, and I tell him I wasn't trying to. Though I am legitimate-
ly concerned for your career of course. Don't be, he says. Why just
last week I made more money than you will in a year. And there
we have it, ladies and gentlemen, I say to the others, the true
measure of an artist. Let's not start all that again, citizen, Sid puts
in. You're right, Sid. You're absolutely right. Well this is more than
I could have hoped for, I say, having turned to find Katie crying
on the dock. What's all this about then, I ask, leaping free of the
boat to take her face in my hands. I'm just sad, that's all, she says.

Well you shouldn't be, I say. I mean really, what's so sad about
crossing the border? Well you could get caught, she says, for one.
But I won't, I tell her. Oh I think you're hoping to, Chris. I think
you're hoping to get caught going across—or worse. Well I won't
give in, or up, she can be assured of that. Though I might give out
before it's all said and done.

Back in the boat, having run the bilge pump sufficiently, Hum
starts up both inboard engines. And despite all visual evidence to
the contrary, they actually run rather smoothly and quietly as I
too breathe deeply, allowing the fresh sea air to flood the inner-
most regions of my lungs. And suddenly I can hear them, somewhere within the confines of the bay, first the one crying and then
the next one crying, then the rest of them crying together.

Saturday, 4:49 am

So he knows we're coming then, Sleeman? Who's that, I say.
Katie's brother, he says. Absolutely, Hum. And he's willing to help?
he asks. Oh he's ecstatic at the idea, no question, I tell him.

It's so very calm out here. Out here on the water where there's
little or no wind and the boat, minus its running lights, slides
almost imperceptibly across the rather comically short and utterly anticlimactic distance separating these two very different coun-
tries here. Ahead, some fifty meters or so, beckons the green light
from the end of the Semiahmoo reserve wharf. And off to the
west the shivering amber lights of the pier. At the end of the pier,
past the double line of lamps, squats the dark smudge of breakwater, while at the base of the pier that perpetual smear of storefront
neon floats somehow out of context and, from this vantage point
at least, all but immaterially too. The pier itself seems particularly
small from this distance, even petty, and I wonder without caring
whether or not there might actually be someone out there somewhere. From this distance it remains impossible to be sure. The
only thing I can see for sure is that double line of lamps, their
banded amber light shivering and splashing over the water
towards me here.

I feel like Gatsby, Hum. What's that, Hum asks, hardly listening, intent as he is on the gurgle of his engines and their not

attracting us too much attention. Gatsby, I say. I feel like Jay Gatsby. You know, staring out at that green-lighted pier.

He throttles down slightly, and small black waves slap lightly against the hull.

You probably never even read Gatsby, hey Hum. No, I read it, he says. It was on that list of one hundred best books of the century. Oh yeah, I say. How'd it do? Fairly well actually, I'm told. Hum thinks maybe even number two. What was number one then, I say. Ulysses? Really? Christ I hate James Joyce. I know I'm not supposed to, but I do.

He doesn't pursue the subject, and I'm secretly glad for that as, despite my general feeling of confidence, my stomach is beginning to pitch over. Again I wonder without caring who, if anyone, would be out on the pier at this time. And I wonder where the actual border is here. It must line up with the Peace Arch at yonder crossing, I decide, but where the other point might be, out on those distant islands maybe, remains of course impossible to tell from here. Together with the roll of the boat the smell of unburned fuel has my empty stomach churning, and there's this feeling that I might need to lean overboard soon. I do lean overboard soon. Fortunately, though, there's only bile remaining, and for the most part the heaves subside after only a minute or two. And now, despite our lack of running lights, we're clearly within sight of our goal. But as the wharf expands in our approach, a pair of headlights suddenly flares up from out near the end, drowning out the single green light that has, till now, been our only guide landward here.

Who the fuck is that? asks Hum. Billy Henry, I say, not at all certain actually. It's only Billy Henry. Good Christ, says Hum, he nearly gave me a fucking heart attack. Don't worry, I tell him, it's just our welcoming committee. Still, he should know we'd be scared as hell out here, he says, piloting the boat up alongside the old wooden wharf, easing in between two old rusted fishing skiffs that appear as though they haven't seen any legitimate action in years. Then, slowing the engines to a rough popping idle so that I might more easily grasp hold of the dock, he touches the throttles ever so slightly into reverse to neutralize any sort of forward momentum just as Billy Henry himself appears atop the dock. He approaches from behind the burn of bright truck headlights, a shotgun clutched snugly across his thick red-mackinawed chest.

Wow, Hank, I say, expecting some sort of trouble? Yeah, what the fuck's with the heavy artillery, Billy? adds Hum as, cognizant of the fact or not, Billy Henry stands dramatically above and alongside the boat, feet spread almost comically wide apart. You guys can't dock here, he says. Not without a permit. What are you talking about? says Hum. Sleeman, what the hell's he talking about? Calm down, I tell him. Now Hank, what seems to be the problem here? No problem at all once you two get the hell out of here, I'm told. *What?* says Hum. What the hell's he talking about? And what the fuck are you *grinning* for, Chris? I mean you guys can't dock here, says Billy Henry, all the time looking directly at me.

So, what, I should pull further along then, Billy? I mean is that what you want? says Hum, running a quick nervous hand through his hair. Christ, this is nuts. I knew this'd be fucking nuts. I *never* should have let you drag me into your shit, Needham. No, I mean you can't dock here *period*, Billy Henry tells him, adjusting his grip on the stock of his shotgun. You're illegally transporting contraband, and if you land here I'll be forced to arrest you. But you're not even a real cop, Hank, you told us that yourself, I remind him. Maybe out there I'm not, he says. But up here I am. On Semiahmoo land I am. And besides, you know what? he adds, standing casually, if still too dramatically, atop the dock, as if hoping this ridiculous stance alone might somehow bring an abrupt end to our argument. Joe's up there just itching to take another crack at you. Joe? says Hum. Who the fuck is *Joe*. And what the hell's he doing taking a *crack* at you? Calm down, I say. Joe Brand. You know, Krishna Brand's husband. The one I have to thank for my facelift here. And that's why I got this puppy here, says Billy Henry, waving his shotgun at Hum as a single seagull slides out at us from the darkness of the ocean. Soon another seagull comes sliding along, looking to join in with the first one there.

Oh Jesus Christ. Sweet Jesus Christ, says Hum, heaving a premium sigh. Then, dragging the palms of his hands slowly down

his face, he turns to me. You know, nothing's ever simple with you.
No, everything's got to be this great big enormous adventure all
the time. Everything's got to be some sort of fairytale-come-true.
Relax, Hum. R*elax*? he says. Fuck relaxing. I'm about to ruin my
goddamned life here. And hey, I say, what a stellar artist's life it is
too. Now Billy, where's Joe, I go on, ignoring Hum as he rather
maniacally, yet apparently impulsively, tugs with both hands at his
hair. Up there in his pickup, Billy Henry answers, jerking the bar-
rel of his shotgun back up the wharf. And despite shielding my
eyes against the ongoing glare of headlights, it remains virtually
impossible to tell whether this is actually true.

Wants another shot at the title does he, I say. Well I don't
know, says Billy Henry, by the looks of you the belt's securely
around his waist already. Maybe I should talk to him though,
Billy. That is, if you don't mind. I do and you won't, he says, taking one firm step forward. Maybe just a quick word, I suggest,
preparing to hoist myself up. You're not stepping foot on this
dock, Chris. Death wish or not. And if I do, I say, readying
myself for the short leap across. Then I'll be forced to take you
out, he says. And blow a hole in this goddamned boat too, you
can be assured of that, he adds for Hum's benefit, taking aim at
the bow to further enunciate his point. You better not, says
Hum. Sleeman, he better not. I will, says Billy Henry. Don't bet
against me 'cause I will.

An unwelcome, entirely uncomfortable silence seeps in at this
point.

Look, continues Billy Henry after a time, I'm trying to save you
both a lot of trouble here. Take it back. Whatever you got there,
take it back. Take it all back. Or hey, dump it right over the side
here for all I care. Honestly, I really don't care. Either way, it's not
worth getting a record over. Or worse, says Hum. Right, or worse,
echoes Billy Henry, at which point I regard them both with disgust. Oh you guys have no fucking clue, I say. This here's a booze
run and booze runs *run booze*. Now clear out of the way, Hank,
I'm coming through, I say, hoisting a foot up onto the dock only
to have it promptly kicked off. I'm serious, Chris, you're not coming up, he says, sending me stumbling back into the box-filled

stern of the boat. Fine, Billy. No more bottles for your collection, I say, gathering myself up.

What are we going to do then? says Hum, having taken to flipping various indistinguishable switches on the dashboard for seemingly no reason nor tangible result. No, I mean it. What the fuck are we going to do? Why don't you just take it over to the pier? suggests Billy Henry, shifting his shotgun to the opposite arm. What, and just *walk* it up? says Hum, flipping one more insignificant looking switch for good measure. Sure, says Billy Henry. I mean hey, why not? No one's going to be out there at this time of night and besides, best time to commit a crime's right now. Is that so, I say, and he says, Oh yeah, absolutely. Between o-four and o-six hundred hours one shift's just finishing up while the other's not even started. Not even out of bed more likely, he chuckles. Actually, I got this friend who works downtown and he—

Yeah, that's fascinating, Hum interrupts. Fuck you, Billy Henry grunts. I glance up at Billy Henry a moment, then over my shoulder to the pier, then back up to Billy Henry a moment more before taking final stock here.

So we just dock at the pier, unload the liquor, and walk it right on up to the front door, I say, and he says, And just walk it right on up to the front door. And no one'll suspect a thing? And no one'll suspect a thing. And hey, he adds, even if someone does happen to see you, it's not like they'll think any big thing. Just a couple of guys unloading some gear, no big deal. And he won't say anything? And he won't say anything, and so we turn to Hum for some sort of final approval.

What, he says. Listen, I'm not taking a boat full of liquor—*my* boat full of *your* liquor—and running it up the goddamned *pier*. Come on, it'll be fun, I say, and he says, Fun? This is *fun* for you? Fuck you, Sleeman. Really. I'm not having my boat confiscated over this bizarre need you have to punish yourself here.

We all fall silent a moment as a crow calls out from a nearby tree.

This is quite the nice tub you got here, says Billy Henry after a time, tapping the bow of the boat with the butt of his shotgun. Excuse me? says Hum. I said this is a nice tub you got here, Hum.

What's she called? Oh yeah, I know, Billy. I know she's nice, says Hum, glancing about impatiently at nothing in particular. What's she called, Billy Henry wonders, and Hum gazes up at him without comprehension. Pardon me? Your boat here, Hum, what's she called? Oh, uh . . . Role Caster, says Hum. Yeah, Role Caster. It's a, you know, a play on words. Clever, Billy Henry says, adding somewhat doubtfully, But isn't that a fly-fishing thing? What, roll casting, I ask, holding my nose and blowing sharply, and he says yeah, he's pretty sure that's a fly-fishing thing. Hum? Christ, Billy, I have no idea, Hum tells him. I honestly just bought the fucking thing. Well Billy Henry's pretty sure that's a fly-fishing thing. In fact he's positive.

Hum hesitates, then throws up his hands and says, So what? So the fuck what? What the hell does that have to do with anything? Well you don't fly-fish on the ocean, I tell him. *So?* So what I think Hank here's trying to say is that the name Role Caster, however inventive and artistically inspired, is really a freshwater name, and thus belongs on a lake, I explain. Or a river, Billy Henry puts in. Or a river, I say, kicking here and there at the boat's interior. Not that this tub would be any good for hauling fish in. Yes, it does seem rather limited that way, agrees Billy Henry. Wouldn't want to have to do *any* fishing of course, eh Billy? *Oh* no, don't you think you can get me going on *that*, Billy Henry says, leading us into a short dubious pause in which we both inspect the boat meticulously in order to further infuriate its owner.

Are you two for *real*? exclaims Hum, head on a swivel between us. I smile at Billy Henry in a congratulatory way as Hum squints painfully in the direction of the pier. Well I guess we'd better be off then, Hank, I say, and Billy Henry says, Yeah, guess so. Say, Hum, y'ever show anyone that screenplay of ours? Why yes, Billy, I did. And? And they hated it. Everybody hated it, says Hum, much to Billy Henry's chagrin.

Now listen, says Hum, I'm not taking us over to the pier. Fuck that. Sure you are, I tell him. I mean where else are you going to take it. How about back to the marina? he suggests, raising his hands in animated appeal. You'd actually risk going *back* across the border, I say. Wow, gutsy. Hey Hank? We've got ourselves a real glutton for punishment here, Billy Henry nods appreciatively. Yup, a real mule, that's for sure.

Hum shakes his head miserably. Fuck you, Sleeman. Really. We're not unloading *illegal* liquor and walking it up the god-damned *pier*. I see no other option, I say, and Billy Henry says he sees no other option either. Unless . . . Yes? Unless of course you dump it, he suggests. Yes, I say, unless of course we dump it. But then that's hardly an option either. Why not? asks Hum. Why isn't it an option? I say we dump it right here. Well I suppose we could, I say. But then again, I suspect the Angels would like to see at least *some* sort of return on their investment.

Hum looks at me, his head cocked in an attitude of mute panic and intolerable outrage. *Get lost*, he says. Sorry, I shrug, but it's true. Billy, is he lying? says Hum. Tell me he's lying. Mother of Christ, tell me it isn't true. As far as I know it is, Billy Henry says. But then again, he does tend to lie quite a bit too.

Hum glares at me with something like amazement. You mean to tell me this—this liquor here belongs to the *Hell's* Angels? he says, and I say, Technically, yes. But I wouldn't let that bother you. Oh *no*, he says, why would that bother me. My God, what would your wife say if she knew.

I look at Hum while Billy Henry looks at me, all three of us standing silently, wondering where it is we've gotten to here. For his part, Hum tries to backtrack some, but it doesn't come off too effectively.

Up on the reserve the first morning birds begin to chirp, and the first hint of dawn drifts its way down the hill. Soon there's just enough light to make monsters of the nearest shadows, and in the few seconds it takes these monsters to resolve themselves into sil-houettes of trees and houses, the birdsong has grown that much more complicated and intense, a dozen different voices crowding in one upon the other in the damp predawn air.

Cheeseburger birds, I say. What's that? asks Billy Henry. Cheeseburger birds, I say. That's what Stephanie used to call them anyway. Cheeseburger birds. Listen, it sounds like "*cheese*burger" they're saying.

Together we listen closely for a time.

So it does, says Billy Henry as somewhere out there in the darkness a truck engine roars, drowning out the voices of the birds for now.

Want to know what I think? he says. Knowing Stephanie, knowing what kind of person she was, I think maybe she'd even want you to do this. You think so, Billy? Really? Yeah I do, he says. Absolutely. But you gotta leave her, man. Excuse me, Billy? You gotta leave her, he repeats. You gotta let her go. I truly believe that. Yeah me too, I say as off to the east, amid the peaks of snow-capped mountains, the sky drifts further along towards dawn, bleeding grey liquid light into the otherwise black empty night.

Be light soon, he says, pulling up the collar of his mackinaw. Yeah it will, Billy. And hey, feels like spring too, I say, searching up the wharf for any sign of my adversary. Well would you look at that. There's old Joe right there. Yup, done out in full battle regalia too, says Billy Henry as I wave Joe a friendly hand. Maybe he's sleeping, I say, having received nothing in return. He's not sleeping, he says, you can be sure of that. How do you know, Hank? Your innate native wisdom? No, because he said he wants to kill you, Chris, how's that. I say, He did? and Billy Henry says, Yeah, he did. And you know what? I truly believe he will, given the chance.

This is all very fucked up, says Hum quietly, squinting off into the darkness. All of it is. Fucked. I had no idea what I was getting into here. Welcome to the shady world of bootlegging, says Billy Henry, tapping the bow of the boat with the butt of his shotgun. Trust no one. Especially one with a catcher's mitt for a face like Mr Needham here.

Hum turns away. He turns away from both Billy Henry and me and in the ensuing silence, from way down deep and nearly out of range altogether, I hear the Role Caster's bilge pump kick up into gear.

Saturday, 5:51 am

Ahead, a handful of early morning strollers are already sprinkled out along the length of the pier, the tall thin lamps thrust up at regular intervals still lighting their way, as out along the breakwater the seagulls have long since settled into their own routine, sliding down, out and away somewhere.

A thin fragile mist has formed across the water here and there. Hunched forward uneasily, Hum pilots the boat through these clouds in the direction of the pier, the twin engines presently held in check, yet eager to be let loose once more.

I wonder what they do with it, Hum says, and I say I can't imagine. Maybe they sink it, he says, and I say maybe. Or burn it, he says. Fuck I hope not, I say, holding my nose and blowing rigorously, feeling the waves, by way of the hull, beat their cold dark heartbeat against me. Oh yeah, he says, they used to burn them all the time. Though I doubt you could get away with that these days, he adds, dropping the engines to a near idle and relaxing back into his chair. Wouldn't wash with the animal rights activists now.

Now, at this distance, the pilings of the pier stand black and enormous against a pale grey horizon. Upon closer inspection, each column rises clear of the still morning water in a thick barnacled armour, but only for the first meter or so before progressing black and naked thereafter.

Sleeman, there's someone out there, whispers Hum excitedly. Oh, that's just Stephan and Mr Soon, I say. You sure? he says, and I say, Yeah, I'd know them anywhere. Now go ahead and bring us in by the landing there, and we'll tie up alongside and be done.

Hum cuts the engines, allowing the Role Caster to wash up alongside the landing on the breakwater side, opposite the two huddled figures and their rods. I grab hold of the dock until he's ready to take over, then hop out and begin tying up. And once the boat is secure, with the three protective fenders in place, I begin the somewhat tedious process of unloading the boxes.

Nice ride, says Stephan from over my shoulder, having since wandered over, and with his help the task is quickly completed. Every now and then I sneak a peek over my shoulder at Po who seems intent on taking no notice of me here, until finally, having finished unloading, I walk over and take a seat alongside.

Hello there, Po.

Po glances up a moment, but only a moment, before returning his attention to his fishing line.

Brought you some booze, I say, but still he says nothing.

What kind of booze you like again, Po, I ask, and he looks at me steadily, pivots gradually to take in the boxes piled high on the landing behind me, and then to the boat his son now inspects so admiringly, before turning back to the listless business of his line. What, you some sort of smuggler now? he says, and I say, Something like that, yeah. He examines the boxes again, then shrugs and says he doesn't use booze much these days. Don't use booze much at all, he says. Come on, there must be something you partake of once in a while, I say. At the wedding for instance? Schnapps, he says. Too much Schnapps. That's right, it was Schnapps, I say. Well it just so happens I've got a bottle of Peppermint Schnapps right here. Or maybe you want something a little bit harder, Po. Like a little whiskey for your morning coffee perhaps.

He pivots to his coffee mug with as little exertion as possible, and then back to the languid state of his line. A little whiskey might be nice, he says, and I say, All right then, whiskey it is. Anything else, I ask, and he thinks a moment, then shrugs, Peppermint Schnapps, I guess.

I move back across the landing to the pile of boxes.

So what do you think, Sleeman? What do I think about what, I ask. Well, I mean, it's just that it's getting pretty late, Hum says, having reluctantly moved aside so that Stephan can better access the seemingly innocuous switches clustered in and around the steering wheel.

Happen to see which box had the Schnapps, I ask, and he says, Uh, maybe that one at the bottom there. No, that other one—got it? Yeah, got it, I say, removing one box from the other and placing it gently alongside.

So listen, Sleeman, it's getting pretty late, he says, and I say, Sure, I understand. And hey, thanks for the lift. Not a problem, Chris. Thanks for everything, I say, and he says, Again, not a problem. And hey, sorry about what I said.

I close the top of one box before turning the same meticulous attention upon another, in this way managing to avoid eye contact completely. No, I mean it, he says. I'm sorry for throwing it in your face like that. Not a problem, Hum. And besides, it really doesn't matter anyway.

Stephan climbs free of the boat as the bilge pump quietly kicks in. I pause, allowing a silence to develop, a silence Hum will fill with his next question apparently.

You sure you're all right? I'm fine, I tell him. Why? Sorry I can't help you any further, he says, and I say, Hey, you've already done far more for me than I ever would've done for you. I don't believe that, he says, and I say, Well you should, because it's true.

After their initial roaring bursts, the engines settle quickly into their now familiar popping idle as I untie the lines, toss in the fenders and with Stephan's help, and a good heave, push the Role Caster free and clear. Hum drifts in neutral a moment before shifting gently into reverse and piloting slowly out and away from the pier.

You sure you're all right? he calls back over the steadily increasing distance. I'm fine, I tell him. Really. Now go on, get the hell out of here.

And once he's far enough removed from the breakwater to negotiate a quick turn to port, he leans on the throttle and releases the engines, roaring back to the marina on the other side of the border.

I take a seat next to Po on the opposite side of Stephan, feeling the dampness of the morning dew creep up through my jeans. Here's your Schnapps, I say. And a little Irish whiskey for good measure.

With a free hand, Po weighs each bottle carefully before releasing it into the care of his son who, for whatever reason, seems oddly reserved this morning.

You be careful with that whiskey though, Po. That stuff packs an awfully big kick.

We sit side by side by side, all three of us watching the rod flex ever so slightly with the pulse of the tide. Eventually Po retrieves the bottle of Peppermint Schnapps and thoroughly peruses the label. You aren't talking much this morning, he says to Stephan. Not much, no, Stephan tells him. Usually you run off at the mouth with your brother-in-law around, Po says. Yeah, well, look at his face, Dad. And anyway, I miss my sister this morning.

Po returns the Schnapps to Stephan, who in turn places it atop the tackle box, at which point I return our collective attention to the all too-corrugated line stretching out before us. Eventually my focus shifts to the enormous white rock on the beach directly opposite. Where it was white yesterday, and covered in crude black graffiti the day before that, today it features a series of concentric red circles around a bold red center, somewhat in the manner of a bull's-eye.

You guys really like fishing, huh, I say. I suppose, Stephan says. In a way. You too huh, Po, I say, and he says sure, nothing else to do at his age. Not without busting a hip at any rate.

I sit quietly, looking to the bench at the base of the pier, then to the bus stop atop the bluff, and finally to the west end of the beach as far as possible, as far west as even the whale perhaps. You know, I say, I just don't see . . . What's that, Stephan asks. Well I just don't see what the attraction is, I say. You know, with watching something die like that. Hard to say, he shrugs. Element of the unknown maybe. And? And what? At that moment it takes the hook, until the moment it dies, you somehow feel a part of something larger than yourself. And that's it? And that's it. That and the joy of torturing to death another living creature of course.

Just then, what initially appears to be a seagull, but turns out to be a white plastic bag, tumbles its way down the length of the pier before hopping the railing and dropping, finally, out of sight *between the bare branches, through their belated flower absences, I can see them. Going towards him one after another, first the one boy whipping and then the next boy whipping. Then the rest of the boys go ahead and whip him together a while. I go on whispering at Annie. Annie goes on ignoring me. Then she goes down along the line of bushes to where across the street a man is raking—she calls out to the man but he does not hear. Meanwhile I go on whispering and watching the boys whipping as one* after another flickers to life along the house-crowded hillside. First the one flickers and then the next one flickers. Then several windows flicker to life together, he finds.

Out over the breakwater he can see them sliding one after another. First the one slides and then the next one slides. Then the rest
of them slide together.

So? she says, and he says, So what? So what's your next move
going to be? she says, and in answer he goes on sitting at Annie.
Po goes on ignoring Stephan. Well I don't know, Katie, he says
eventually. What does our good friend Zack think my next move
ought to be? Well, she says, considering how the police are out
looking for you. . . . Billy, he says. God-dammit. Actually it was Joe
Brand who called them in, she says, shuffling up closer on the
bench. Meanwhile, down the far end of the pier, Stephan continues hunting through the pile of boxes abandoned on the landing
there.

So anyway, she says, considering the cops are out looking for
you, and that not more than fifty feet away there are three Hells
Angels waiting to take a piece out of you, I might consider getting the hell out of here before they wise up to the fact you're sitting right here. Clearly that's the logical progression for avoiding
a beating here. That is, if avoiding a beating is the clear intention
of our little restaurant manager here. Former restaurant manager,
he says, and she says, Former restaurant manager, yes, that's true.

She sits, so he sits, and the next time he looks between the bare
branches and through their belated flower absences he sees them,
all three of them, standing in goatees, jeans and black leather vests
on the patio, one caught up in conversation with Wendy, one
seeking Eddie's ever-elusive approval, and the third wearily
watching porn through the window for lack of anything better to
do. He goes on sitting at Annie. Katie goes on watching him.

We'll ignore them, Katie, that's what we'll do. Ignore them? she
says, and he says, Ignore them. Shirk them. Yessir, two shirkers you
and me.

She brushes her fingers over the bench's embossed engraving,
beginning with the birth and death dates, followed by the first and
last names, and finally the five uppercase letters of the nickname.

No, really, what's the plan, she says. You want I should walk up
there and introduce you? That should get things rolling fairly

quickly, I'd think. Should get you fairly dead in about a minute too. Listen, Katie. What? she says, and he tells her to just listen. There, does she hear it? Way down deep and nearly out of range, smooth and steady at this distance, sliding up around the southeastern reaches of the bay. First the one car slides and then the next car slides. Then the rest of them slide together. Katie, there's something I need to ask you. What, she says. Well I was wondering if you'd come with me, he says. Come with you where? she says, so he says he doesn't know exactly, but out there in front of that train initially. What do you mean? she says, so he says he's going to, you know, leave, by train, and he really wants to know if she'll come with him. We'll leave together, he tells her, and she studies him silently a moment. You're serious? she says, and he says, Absolutely. Look, Katie, I need to know. I need to know *right now*.

The lead engine slides up past the bluff and the bus stop atop it, bringing with it the remainder of the train. Katie looks at him, then looks away, and finally shrugs and says, Yeah, well, what the hell, it's as good a time as any.

Annie

Surprising how quiet it is up here. And peaceful. Not truly quiet or peaceful by any stretch of the imagination, but perhaps slightly more quiet and peaceful than he'd been led to expect down there. And yet you still have a tendency to shout at one another despite being huddled so closely together.

He watches it slide by all grey and still and smooth. And gazing out across that still morning greyness in the direction of the islands and the mountains, and then back again towards the pier, he sees the people walking along the promenade, and some of them see him too. A few of the children point. Some of them laugh. One old fellow waves a friendly hand. For a moment he considers waving back, but then something about the situation compels him not to.

By the time they finally settle in comfortably atop the railcar, they're nearing far western reaches of the bay, where only a few days ago a tired, sick, entirely too young grey whale washed ashore for reasons unexplained. He looks for the carcass along the boulder- and log-strewn beach, expecting to find it all dry and barnacled and bloated somewhere.

Hey, isn't this where that whale's supposed to be? he says, and Katie says, Yeah, over there. On that sandy part there. Apparently they came and got it last night. Who came and got it? The Coast Guard came and got it. How come? he says, and she says, To tow it away, I guess. Where'd they tow it to then? he says, and she says, No idea. Out there somewhere, I guess.

He follows the line of her finger to the outermost reaches of the bay. I wonder where they take them then, he says, and she says, They have a place for them apparently. What, like a grave-yard or something? Yeah, like a burial ground or something. Supposedly this sort of thing is starting to happen quite regularly around here. There's the other ones though, she goes on, pointing in a slightly different direction. You see them? You can see them cresting.

And sure enough, there they are, maybe six of them, maybe more, their long dark backs sliding up through the surface of the bay all smooth and slick and graceful. They go along one after another, first the one whale sliding and then the next whale sliding, then the rest of them sliding together way down deep and nearly out of range altogether *between the bare branches, through their belated flower absences, I can see them. Going towards him one after another, first the one boy whipping and then the next boy whipping. Then the rest of the boys go ahead and whip him together a while. I go on whispering at Annie. Annie goes on ignoring me. Then she goes down along the line of bushes to where across the street a man is raking—she calls out to the man but he does not hear. Meanwhile I go on whispering and watching the boys whipping as one goes in behind him there, tightening his coat sleeves around the backstop pole, while another takes up the willow and has a go at him a while. They go towards him one after another, first the one boy whipping and then the next boy whipping. Then the girls go forward and whip him as well. They go on this way as Annie goes down along the line of bushes. Finally she emerges from behind the last bush and he sees her crying, and crying out himself he tells her to go. But she won't go, and the one girl goes forward and whips her as well. I sit there at the bush and watch the girl whipping, while across the street the man is raking still. He rakes and I sit, and the next time I look between the bare branches and through their belated flower absences I see the girl drop the willow at Annie's feet.*

Down below the field, past the gravel field, the bell is ringing. They all go down towards the school. I hold to the bush and watch them go as Annie goes over to the backstop post where he stands choking and crying still. Somehow they've managed to tie his wrists with his coat, and I watch, silent, as she unties his shirtsleeves from around his throat.

Leave me alone, Jeffrey chokes. Just leave me alone, Stephanie. Please.

But she won't leave him alone, and as I turn to watch the man raking his leaves a breeze comes up and I smell the slough. Eventually I turn back to find Annie smoothing and folding my brother's coat before returning it to him, while down at the school the last of his tormentors disappear. And still I hear his tortured crying in my ear that, Katie? Do you hear them? Listen, it sounds like they're crying from here.

She listens, then says, Actually, it sounds more like they're sighing. So do you think they're dying? she asks a little later. You know, like their friend that was here?

And as the train slides into its long, prolonged turn around the point, for one brief moment it's possible to catch a glimpse of the long unbroken body of the train. There are a lot of boxcars on this train, Annie. A *lot* of boxes.

No, I think they're managing, I say.

Acknowledgements

Heartfelt thanks to my parents, my brother and his family for all the obvious reasons, and to the enigmatic Sidney Shapiro and his astute editing abilities for making me appear a much better writer than I actually am. I would also like to thank the good people of Cultus Lake, BC (those few of you out there, you know who you are) for taking me in as one of their own, however briefly and grudgingly. Your kindness and inebriation will not be forgotten.